CRUEL DOMINION

KINGS & CONSORTS

POPPY ST. JOHN

Cover by Opulent Swag and Designs

Edited by Bookends Editing

AUTHOR'S NOTE

This book contains content that may be triggering to some readers. For a full list of TWs, please visit the author's website before proceeding.

♥

PROLOGUE

CARTER

Six Years Ago

Worthless.
A waste of skin.
Just like your pathetic ma.

The words of the man whose seed infected my mother eighteen years ago played on a vicious loop in my head. I inhaled the salt air sharply, grunting when the movement sent a shuddering column of pain down my ribcage. Nothing was broken, but it'd come close this time.

Better me than her, I reminded myself, spitting blood onto the sand, tempted to wash my mouth out with ocean water to rid myself of the bitter, metallic taste.

The moon hung low over the dark sea, tipping the black waves in silver as they lapped toward the shore and crashed, spreading white foam over my bare feet. The chill of it brought me back to the present. Propelling me away from the shithole I called home and the drunk asshole probably passed out on the couch by now.

I squinted to see down the dark strip of sand, far into the distance, catching the faint sound of something on the wind.

The last thing I needed was to be picked up by the cops right now. The ones from the rough side of town where I came from wouldn't blink at the bruise on my jaw or the hunched way I was no doubt walking, but I was nearing the nicer side, where the rich and powerful liked to look down over the water from their glass faced mansions.

The cops over here would probably lock me up for marring the perfect fucking view, even in the middle of the night.

With a snort, I kicked the sand.

"What did that sand ever do to you?"

I jerked my gaze back to the moonlit beach, and the girl walking toward me from its other end. My lips parted, reopening the small cut that'd already crusted over at the corner of my lips. *Fuck,* the salt air stung, and I wiped the back of my palm over the dribble of blood, trying to erase it before she could see.

The girl stopped, her throat bobbing uneasily as she got a better look at me.

"You look like you've had a rough night," she said, her gaze flitting over the beach behind me and away, like she was gauging whether she could outrun me. Her shoulders sagged a moment later though, as if she couldn't be bothered to care if she'd just walked right into the path of a serial killer.

I wanted to know why. The question bartered for exit from my mouth, but I held my lips shut.

Girls who looked like her didn't wander on beaches in

the middle of the night. With her soft brown hair bouncing in the breeze coming off the water. In clothes that I couldn't have afforded with an entire month's pay at the two jobs I worked to keep a roof over my and Ma's heads.

Being out here alone looking like that was asking for trouble.

"And you look like someone who shouldn't be out here this late," I told her instead of asking all the questions I wanted to, my voice coming out rougher than I intended. "You should go home."

She sniffed, turning her head to the horizon line and the moon pinned to the black canvas sky. Her emerald eyes, fringed in thick lashes, glimmered with the reflection of the sea. She looked like a ghost. So pale. So fragile. With her arms tucked around her slender body.

She swallowed hard and I saw what she was trying to hide. The red tint to the skin around her eyes. The way her chin quivered.

This girl didn't want to go home any more than I did.

"I can't," she said, her words almost completely swallowed up by the wind.

"Can't or won't?" I pressed, trying to imagine what sort of inane troubles she could have that were worth the risk of being out here, toeing the invisible line that separated luxury from fucking squalor.

She didn't answer, sitting down in the sand to pull her knees into her chest.

I looked back the way I'd come, but couldn't seem to force myself to take a single step back to the hell waiting for me at home. Besides, I couldn't just leave her here. She could get mugged. Or worse.

I was no angel, but there were worse devils out there in the dark. The kind who would want more than quiet company. And this girl didn't look more than a couple years younger than me.

Sighing, I sat down in the sand a few feet away from her, wincing at the ache in my side as I adjusted my position to put the least amount of strain on it.

"What are you doing?" she asked quietly.

"I can't go home, either. Might as well be miserable together."

Her jaw clenched, holding back what I thought might be the smallest of grins.

It should've felt awkward. Sitting alone with a sad stranger on the beach in the middle of the night. But somehow, it didn't. The darkness provided a sort of anonymity that sunlight couldn't. Non-judgmental.

"Tell me something," she said after a few beats of silence, her watching the sea, me watching her. Considering whether she was real or if the shot to the face I'd taken from my pops earlier had dislodged something in my brain.

"What?"

She shrugged, propping her chin onto her crossed forearms. "Just tell me something," she repeated. "Something real. Why are you on the beach at two in the morning?"

"Why are you?" I countered.

"I'll tell you if you tell me. A secret for a secret."

I worked my jaw, thinking.

"Whatever you tell me, it won't leave this beach. And you'll never have to see me again."

It dawned on me that she had something she wanted to

tell someone. Something she needed to say aloud that could also never leave this beach.

"What's your name?" I asked on a whim.

She pursed her lips.

"Tell me and I'll play your game. Whatever you say will never leave this beach, either."

"Anna," she said decisively after a minute, pulling her bottom lip between her teeth in a way that made my cock thicken in my jeans. "Anna Vaughn."

"I'm Carter," I told her, inhaling deeply before I continued. "And my dad beats the shit out of me when he's drunk. That's why I'm out here. If I stayed to let him hit me one more time I might've..."

A shaky breath passed my lips.

I couldn't finish the sentence, but Anna didn't push me. Her gaze dropped and she said nothing. No words of pity. No apology. Just a small nod to show that she heard me and a slight tightening around her jaw.

"Your turn."

"My father has been siphoning money from the charity he built. I found out and confronted him about it...it didn't go well."

"*Dads...*" I said, snorting.

Her lips tightened, face puckering in a failed attempt to hold in a laugh. It burst from her, the sound mingling with the wind and the waves to make the perfect song.

"*Dads,*" she echoed, still laughing, wiping a tear from her cheek with her knuckle.

"Fuck 'em," I said with a shrug, a wide grin on my own face now, too.

She had an amazing laugh.

"Yeah," she agreed, psyching herself up before she repeated my crude words, her cheeks pink. *"Fuck 'em."*

I knew right then. If Anna Vaughn was nothing more than a figment of my imagination, I'd gleefully accept my insanity and commit myself to the institution of her for the rest of my miserable fucking life.

1

ANNA

The driver, a tall, imposing man with an earpiece and sunglasses, waited to collect me when I stepped off the bus in town.

Anna Vaughn, his sign said. A name I hadn't gone by in over six years.

It wasn't too late. I could just turn around, get back on the bus. Keep traveling up the coast.

"Miss Vaughn," the driver said, catching sight of me amid the other travelers. He must have been briefed well on my appearance to recognize me. I looked nothing like the Anna who left home. Full of life and spite. Lacquered and plucked and outfitted in Chanel.

I was a hollowed-out shell of that girl now. In worn Converse sneakers and a Lana Del Rey t-shirt. Sporting bruises like a necklace around my throat and cheetah spots down my arms.

I nodded once and the driver tucked his sign under his arm and indicated the exit, where I could see a sleek silver sedan parked outside, idling in the street to keep the interior temperature just right in the hot Cali sun.

"Do you require medical assistance?" the driver asked as he opened the door for me.

"No, thank you."

He frowned at the single rolling duffle bag I dragged along with me.

"It's all I have," I answered his unasked question. Escaping in the middle of the night as I did hadn't exactly left me time to pack up all my belongings. In truth, I didn't have all that much to begin with and most of it was thrifted or bought at dollar stores.

He took the duffel, placing it into the trunk as I breathed in the smell of the ocean.

Carter. The beach. The heavy moon over the water.

It all came back like a sucker punch to the gut, and my nose wrinkled as I got into the sedan and slammed the door behind me, eager to get the briny scent out of my nose.

It wasn't long before the familiar facade of the house came into view through the wrought iron bars as we made our way up the winding drive. Home sweet home. The driver tapped a key card against the intercom panel and the gate slid open. My stomach dropped.

Fuck.

I clasped my hands in my lap, hesitating when the sedan stopped outside the grandiose entrance, bracketed by tall white pillars and gilt-edged doors.

You have no place left to go, I reminded myself.

Josh took almost everything from me. Including most of my money to gamble away or spend on booze. It was a small miracle I was able to squirrel away the few hundred dollars I did to be able to leave him when it got really bad.

At least the others didn't take money from me. I met all my exes serving drinks at the Butterfly Room, a high-end members-only bar, patronized by some of the richest people in St. Louis.

So, all my exes were wealthy in business, music, and other industries with the occasional trust fund brat. It was no surprise they were pushy and controlling with me. It didn't help that I had a taste for a certain *type*. The brooding ones. The ones who liked it a little rough. The dark spirits who fucked like there were t-minus ten minutes to the apocalypse.

With a weakness for walking red-flags, it was no surprise that I was a magnet for troubled men. More accurately: for *assholes*. Had been since I was sixteen and met my first one on the beach.

That was why Josh, sweet, blue-eyed Josh who had a normal job and drove an older model car felt so safe. I couldn't have been more wrong about him.

"Miss Vaughn, good afternoon," a man with a headset on said, sweeping the tall front doors open before I could even knock.

I nodded, giving him a strained smile. It was a mask I'd have to get used to wearing if I expected to stay here.

Rosie, our housekeeper, was the only person I'd called to give a heads-up I was coming. Hers was the only private number I still knew by heart. Aside from Rosie, staff turnover tended to be high at the Vaughn Estate. I didn't want to be at the gate, trying to convince the security staff that I was Anna Vaughn.

The one who was supposed to be away on a charity mission in Malawi building sustainable housing for the less fortunate. *That* Anna Vaughn. It was my dad's cover story for my disappearance and it was a good one. I wished I *had* spent the last six years making a difference in people's lives rather than wearing low-cut tops for tips.

"Thank you, David," the man at the door said, taking my duffel from the driver with a raised brow.

I felt fairly safe in assuming my father wouldn't be home this early on a Wednesday, but as the man shut the door behind me, I heard the unmistakable sound of Testoni shoes on parquet flooring approaching from the east hall.

Hudson Vaughn appeared in the entryway. He looked the same as I remembered, with just a bit more silver in his mahogany hair. Tall and regal, with a cut marble face and ice in his blue eyes.

The look he gave me would've been enough to paralyze me once upon a time, and that same sinking feeling tried to open a hollow pit in the bottom of my stomach. I lifted my chin.

"Can I come in?" I asked after an uncomfortable silence.

"Why did I have to hear from my security that you were coming home?" he asked, scanning me head to toe and seeming displeased with what he saw. "What happened to your neck?"

"*Dad*," I managed to force out the word. "I've been traveling since last night. I'm exhausted and I need a shower. Can we do this later?"

His chest rose and fell with a short, harsh breath. He was angrier than he was letting on.

"You're lucky you're my daughter," he said, giving a wave of his hand to tell me I could go. I picked my duffel up but he took one look at it and sneered. "Fredrick, dispose of that."

The man from the door collected it from me. I held onto

the handle a second longer, but let it go, knowing it wasn't worth the fight.

"That's all I have," I tried. A weak attempt at an argument.

My father looked down his nose at me. "It most definitely is not. I've had your closet restocked with an updated wardrobe, and you'll find everything a lady might need in your bathroom."

...updated wardrobe?

So, this was it. I was to be his doll. To smile when looked upon. To speak when spoken to. To look the part of the governor's daughter and act accordingly.

I knew what I was agreeing to when I decided to come home, but it still made my skin itch to be proved correct.

"You look terrible, go get cleaned up," he said, dismissing me as if it'd been days instead of years since he'd last laid eyes on me.

Burying the jab of pain down deep where I didn't have to feel it, I moved across the entryway. He didn't have to tell me twice.

I went straight to my room, hoping to see Rosie along the way, but she didn't show herself.

Inside, everything was exactly the same. The blue, white, and yellow furnishings that were my mother's idea. The queen bed with the gold-brown teddy bear leaned against the throw pillows. In the bathroom, a bottle of what used to be my favorite Dior body wash when I was a teenager rested at the edge of the soaker tub. Rosie did this. My father wouldn't know that I used to like to smell like ylang-ylang and vanilla. I plugged my phone in to charge and went straight to the bathroom to shower.

I scrubbed the long bus ride away, trying and failing to get the previous night out of my head.

Just like I thought he would, Josh got home in the morning after storming off last night. I knew because he called me nonstop. I blocked his number before he drained my battery.

Still not feeling quite clean enough but too tired to care, I crawled into bed, still coherent enough to hate how it felt safe.

It was a cage, but it was also home. Complete with a full security detail and cameras covering most of the property. Josh couldn't find me here. He wouldn't.

He was dating Annie Taylor. Not Anna Vaughn.

I reached over the nightstand for my phone. Laying my head back on the pillow, I typed another name into the search bar. Every single one of the results on the first page was highlighted purple. I had clicked them all a lot more times than I wanted to admit.

Carter Cole. I couldn't think of home without thinking of him.

He wasn't active on social media, unfortunately for me, but then neither was I. In fact, you couldn't find so much as a recent photograph of me anywhere on the internet from the last six years. I made sure of it.

I opened the first link, his company's website. He was a CEO of some big ass company now. Not bad for a guy who used to work two jobs when we were in high school. I sounded spiteful, and I was, but I was happy for him too. As happy as I could be for the boy who started my epic run of terrible luck with men.

The others I could forget. Their faces all faded with time and distance. But not his.

He was the one I could never forget. No matter how far I ran. No matter who shared my bed. When I shut my eyes at night, his was the face that infected my dreams.

Carter never struck me, never made me feel unsafe, never accused me of infidelity, and never *ever* threatened me. Josh had done all of those things within a month of being together. But none of the assholes in St. Louis could break the heart that Carter had already shattered.

The boy on the beach figured out how to get into investing, working his way from a startup he sold for an obscene amount of money. He stayed on as the company's CEO and had done well for himself ever since. The only picture of him on the site was one with the company's shareholders. There he was, second from the left, arms behind his back, with a slight smile pulling the corners of his mouth. His dark brown hair, shorter than it used to be, was slicked back, his face clean-shaven, looking every bit the young professional.

It was infuriating how good he looked in a suit. A guy shouldn't be able to look equally sexy in a tie and black slacks as he did in torn jeans and weathered band tees.

The pose, hands behind his back, I guessed was intentional, since in any press photos I happened across online showed tattooed hands and arms with even more ink peeking out from the low hung collars of the muscle-tees he seemed to like to wear while out running.

He looked like a devil in saint's clothing, and not for the first time I wondered how exactly he managed to climb so high. I knew the rumors courtesy of Tumblr, Reddit, and about a dozen other sites I encountered in my semi-regular online stalking. Supposedly Carter did some very shady shit to clamor out of the muck and into the gleaming spires of his company building.

Some anonymous accounts alluded to things like blackmail and mafia-connections, while others accused him of far worse. But if the coroner said it was an accident or natural causes, then it was an accident or natural causes, right? People could be so dramatic.

I closed the company page and opened the third link, a feature with a business magazine about his meteoric rise to success. These pictures were better. Besides a couple of pictures of him at his office, there were some more candid-style photos at his home. Photographers used stunt homes for these kinds of things all the time, but if it really was his house, we lived in the same neighborhood now.

Would I run into him? Did I want to?

I tossed my phone away, unable to look at his face anymore, feeling the lure of the beach that I could see outside the doors to the veranda off my room. How many nights had I climbed down the lattice to the patio stones below and run off down the hedge path and out to the sandy shore?

Too many.

If I were careful, I wouldn't have to see his face again. I'd stay long enough to secure my safety and figure out where to go next.

Carter wouldn't ever know I was here.

2

CARTER

"Mr. Cole. Welcome. I trust you're having a good evening."

The overeager clerk at the front desk straightened his tie as I stepped out of the elevator.

His bright eyes slid to my collar, where I knew there were at least a few crimson stains, and he blinked in surprise. Not my blood of course, but he wouldn't ask. They knew better than that now.

"Can't complain, *Chris*," I replied, using the name on his tag like a warning as he slid me the key card to the penthouse luxury suite and I passed him two fifties.

"H-have a fantastic night, sir," he said, plastering a big ass grin on his face. I wasn't paying him for giving me a key, I was paying for discretion. I had a standing reservation at the InterContinental's penthouse suite every two weeks. Last night, a woman named Katerina arrived and checked in under my name.

Katerina. No last name and obviously not her real name. Usually, I worked with agencies to book the most exclusive, professional girls they had, but Katerina was an independent. She was in the background of a group picture on another girl's profile and the agency said they didn't know who she was, but they were willing to find her for me.

She was my first Czech girl. Perfect English, professional website, and guaranteed disease and drug-free even though I never fucked without a condom.

My biweekly *sessions* at the Intercontinental were one of the only indulgences I allowed myself. My reward for slogging through paperwork and smiling for the press. To be fucking honest, I think I preferred wading through grave dirt and collecting on debts.

Tonight I got a taste of that old hustle since my connections were too busy with issues of their own. My knuckles still ached, and I relished every second of the pain.

I arranged flights and accommodation for the women. I only ever wanted them for about a weekend at a time, so they were handsomely compensated. Sometimes, if they were around and I was in a mood, they would act as my dates to work functions and events. Never the same girl twice. It drove the media and the debutantes drooling for my attention absolutely mad.

But any press was good press. And these pretty European women were likely part of the reason I was dubbed the most eligible bachelor of the year. As if I would ever marry.

I let myself into the freesia-scented suite, letting the door click shut behind me.

"My love?" an accented voice called from inside one of the bedrooms.

I froze, my upper lip curling.

A woman, naked save for a loosely tied hotel robe came

into the foyer. It was definitely Katerina. I'd jerked it to partial nudes of her for the past week. I'd know those tits anywhere.

Katerina was a leggy blonde with 250ccs of saline in each breast, a pretty face, and a petite frame. For the small price of a first-class round trip, hotel booking, and ten thousand dollars consideration, she was all mine.

She closed the distance between us and threw her arms around my neck.

"I waited so long, I thought you weren't coming," she cooed.

"I—" She silenced me with her mouth. Her lips against mine felt wrong in the worst sort of way. The *taste* of her foreign and unwelcome on my tongue. I gripped her arms, yanking her back as I broke the kiss with a sneer.

"I waited for you so we could order dinner together. What do you want to have?"

"Stop," I hissed, peeling her arms from around my neck. She smelled of expensive perfumes and body butter. The scent of ylang-ylang was offensive on her skin in a way that made my stomach roil and heat rise up my neck.

She was going to have to take a shower.

"Let me take your bag for you—" she said, reaching for my case.

"I said *stop*."

She flinched back, confused.

"Didn't they brief you?" I all but sneered. "I'm not interested in the girlfriend experience."

"You paid me ten thousand dollars and flew me across the world to do what? Stand still and open my mouth?" she snapped.

I liked her better already.

"I paid you for a *service*."

"Yes, they told me what you like."

I tilted her chin up so she looked at me. "But apparently they didn't tell you what I *don't* like."

Her throat bobbed.

"Go to the bedroom and wait for me, naked. I want you on the ground, kneeling next to the bed. Don't move, don't talk. Don't do a thing until I come inside. Understand?"

She pursed her lips but nodded. I released her, and she left, going quietly to the bedroom.

"And take a shower!" I called, my nose still clogged with the scent of *her*.

She disappeared into the bedroom, and I cursed, taking my tie off and tossing it on the couch.

I paid a premium for these girls specifically so shit like that didn't happen. No mistakes. No inconveniences. No bullshit.

She wasn't with the agency I talked to, so she probably hadn't been informed of my particular requests. This was the last time I'd risk it with an independent.

I dragged the back of my hand over my lips.

I didn't want to *kiss*; I didn't want to *chat*.

I didn't pay girls to cuddle me and let me touch their hair, play-acting like they were excited and happy to see me. I paid to get off in the cleanest, most convenient way possible.

Not many girls could handle the things I wanted to do to them.

I glanced at the room where Katerina had gone. In a matter of seconds, she'd already pissed me off. I hated how the ghost of her kiss lingered on my lips and wanted to scrub them clean. I hadn't kissed a woman since...

A roaring rushed in my ears and the edges of my vision dimmed as something hot and dark and aching rose up in my chest.

I leaned against the back of the couch and took a deep breath, trying to relax the tension in my jaw. I closed my eyes, imagining the ocean, being on the beach at night, hearing the water come up on the shore. I saw the moon full and big over the water. I felt the night breeze coming off the sea, smelled the fresh, salty air.

I didn't let myself go further than that. Not tonight.

When my muscles unwound, I sighed and wet my dry mouth.

I opened my case and took out the cuffs and a condom, then pulled off my belt, taking the items with me as I pushed through the door to the bedroom. Katerina was on the floor, kneeling, naked, still damp from the shower, just like I'd told her. She looked up when I came in then immediately averted her gaze.

"Don't touch me. Don't speak unless I talk to you first. Understand?"

"Yes, sir."

I told her to stretch her arms out in front of her. She flinched as the cold metal tightened around her wrists. They knew not to touch me during sex but mistakes happened, and she was already on notice after that bullshit in the foyer.

When I had a woman with me, I usually made a whole night of it. Long, drawn-out sessions, pushing and pulling until both of us were ready to explode. Tonight, I didn't even want to look at my plaything. Not after she'd fucking kissed me.

That was practically rule number one. I wasn't going to

dock her pay for the mistake, the fault for that oversight landed squarely on the service who'd collected her for me. Besides, I had other ways of punishing her.

I unzipped my fly and pulled my cock out, giving it a few lazy strokes that sent ripples of diluted pleasure down my legs.

"Open your mouth."

Her eyes widened as she tilted her chin up. Eager now, she took me into the warmth of her mouth, running her tongue expertly down my shaft, suckling slightly, diligently, making me hard.

I grabbed her hair and modulated her speed.

"Look at me."

Her eyes were already watering as she looked up. "You made me angry, Katerina. What are we going to do about that?"

She tried to make her appeal around my cock, the words coming out as garbled gibberish.

"I can't hear you," I said, holding her face still while I thrusted my hips, feeling the dam at the back of her throat against my tip. She tried again, gagging, coughing.

I pulled her in as deep as she could take me, feeling the give and the exquisite pressure just below the head of my cock as she swallowed me down deep enough for her nose to meet my abdomen. She gagged and her face reddened, eyes rolling back. I fucked her tight little throat until I knew she was seeing stars. Only then did I pull out.

Katerina drew in a ragged gasp, her pretty face wet with tears. She looked embarrassed at being unable to maintain her perfect exterior, trying to wipe at the wetness on her cheeks.

"Up," I ordered.

She stumbled clumsily to her feet, still trying to catch her breath. I folded her over the bed and slapped her firm, round ass, making her squeak. Making her dainty hands curl into the silken comforter.

"Does that hurt?" I asked.

"No."

I hit her again, harder, unable to help reliving the feel of her lips on mine. The wrongness of that touch.

"Now?"

"N-no."

I went again, smacking the reddening skin, harder, again and again until she said *yes*.

Only then did I stop and examine my handiwork. Her ass red and tender. The folds between her legs dripping wet with desire.

She liked it.

Good.

I pulled the condom out and slipped it on before pulling her up by her hips, making her hold herself raised atop the mattress.

"You shouldn't have touched me, Katerina." I pressed my cock between her folds and reached forward to curl my hand around her neck. She arched her back like a good girl, giving me better access.

"I'm sorry," she said with a shuddering breath. "Forgive me?"

I pressed my cock to her opening, squeezing her neck as I slid into her, giving her only a moment to adjust to my girth before I'd take exactly what I wanted.

She cried out as I thrust in to the hilt and shoved her down into the mattress.

Her core tightened around me and I threw my head

back, clenching my teeth at the sensation before I gave in to my own wicked desire.

She bucked as I wrapped my hands around her hips with a bruising grip, letting out a little whimper of pain even as she wiggled her ass into my abdomen, silently begging me to move.

Hissing, I withdrew halfway and slammed back into her. Harder than before. Hard enough for her whole body to jerk from the movement.

With each thrust, I drew her to me, making her pretty pussy take me over and over again. The *slap* of our bodies joining grew louder with every second, almost loud enough to rival her panting cries as I lost all sense of decency and ravaged her greedy cunt.

I pistoned in and out of her, hating her for kissing me. Hating that she wasn't Anna. That none of them were Anna.

That they would never fucking be Anna because she was gone.

A ghost who definitely wasn't building fucking homes for the less fortunate in Malawi. I'd checked. I'd scoured the earth for her and still came up empty-handed.

I let it take over, the monster, the creature. I dug my fingers into her ass, fucking her like I hated her. Relentless, even when she squirmed. Her muffled moans against the bed turned me on. I went faster, fucking her through her orgasm, even as her wet cunt tried to force me out. I fucked her until stars exploded against my eyelids, every muscle coiled and jerking with my release.

Sweat poured down my temples and soaked through my crisp white button-down. I never got naked with the women I had sex with. One more thing too intimate for what we did together. Too revealing. No one needed to see what hid beneath the layers of cotton and ink.

She collapsed afterward, shuddering, her breathing uneven and ragged as she drew her knees in and pressed her forehead against them in an attempt to calm her body while I straightened myself back up.

"You should use the spa while you're here. Charge everything to the room," I offered, unlocking the cuffs with slow, measured movements, the mask of the professional businessman back in place.

"You're leaving?" she asked. "Will you come back?"

I reached into my wallet and drew out its cash contents, unworried that there was close to a grand in large bills between my fingers as I pressed them into her hand.

"Have a safe flight home."

W hen someone knocked at my bedroom door the next morning, I squeezed my eyes tighter shut beneath the covers. My exhaustion-addled body had mostly recovered from the trip but my mind still craved silence and darkness. Solitude.

The door creaked as it opened, showing just how little use this room had while I'd been away. Dad wouldn't tolerate a creaking hinge in his home for long.

"Anna?"

My eyes shot open and I tossed the covers off, pushing myself up. The last time I heard her voice she was telling me I was lucky I got her nose and not my father's. Always preoccupied with meaningless things. The material. The objective.

"Mom?"

My mother stood in the doorway of my room holding a tray.

Her lips twitched up into something close to a smile as she strode into the room.

"Hello, darling," she said, setting the tray down over my knees. "You look terrible."

I laughed. Of course that would be the first thing she said to me after all this time. But my laughter morphed to tears, washing the bitter edge to our reunion away. I slipped the tray from my lap and kicked my way out of the covers, putting my arms around her.

She looked the same somehow. Still the glamorous middle-aged woman that I left behind, with maybe just a few more units of Botox and filler. Despite the unnatural tautness of her skin and the several layers of makeup, she actually looked better if that were possible. Not in the objective sense, but somehow deeper.

Her green eyes glowed bright and she looked dignified in her cream slacks and ivory blouse; the combination was her version of a casual at-home look. She looked *alive*. More or less alert.

When I'd left, I didn't say goodbye to her. She was at her worst then, with the pills and the booze. I doubted she'd have been present enough to even understand me. She would've said what she always did when I spoke. *That's nice, darling,* and sent me off with a pat on the back.

Her marriage to my father was miserable. She came from a rich, property-owning family so the natural next step was to marry into a rich political one, true love and happiness be damned. I'd always been taken care of by housekeepers and nannies, my mom only poking her head into my life whenever she surfaced from her stupor. And even then usually only to point out some flaw or tell me I should listen to my father.

Was she off the meds? I hoped so. She brushed my hair

back and pulled a couple tissues out of the box on my vanity, handing them to me.

"When did Dad tell you?" I asked, dabbing my eyes before giving my nose a quick blow.

Her lips pulled into a tight-lipped false smile and she turned from me to throw open the light-blocking curtains, making me hiss as too-bright, likely afternoon, sunlight filled my room, burning out my corneas.

"Just this morning," she replied, coming back to perch on the edge of my bed with nothing less than perfect posture.

The way she said it made it clear she was wondering how long he'd kept the information from her. But she didn't ask. She wouldn't.

"I didn't believe him at first. I wouldn't unless I saw you myself."

"And now that you have?"

Her unusually thoughtful green eyes analyzed me. She didn't say anything about the bruises yet, even though I knew she could see them, especially now in the light.

"An explanation would be nice."

It wasn't like we ever had what a normal person might call a strong relationship. But, even taking that into account, I felt I owed it to them to give them something. They were fully within their rights to turn me away, but they didn't. Mom just brought me breakfast in bed. Never in the seventeen years before I left had she done that. Not once. Not even for a birthday. Not even when I was sick.

"Okay," I answered tentatively. "What do you want to know? It's not exactly an enthralling story. I worked. I lived in a mediocre apartment. Had a couple of shitty boyfriends..."

Shitty was putting it nicely. Her gaze fell to the bruises along my collar.

I swallowed.

Don't ask.

Please don't ask.

I wasn't ready to talk about it. Just having her look at what that asshole did to me was pushing back to the verge of tears. Making my stomach feel hollow and chest hot and my fists twist into the plush blankets.

"You can talk to me about it when you're ready. I know you've been through... some trouble recently. Rest. Have some breakfast."

Some trouble?

I knew that tone. I knew those words. *We can talk about it later* was always Mom's go-to. *Later* always meant never. Back then, it hurt. Now, I was grateful for her complete inability to talk about anything even remotely upsetting.

"Thanks, Mom."

She patted my knee, gesturing to the tray again. "Eat," she commanded. "Before it gets cold."

I hadn't been hungry when she walked in, but my stomach grumbled as I pulled the tray back onto my lap. There was a plate of fresh fruit, a few strips of crisp bacon, a short stack of mini pancakes, and a selection of other pastries with orange juice and a latte.

"Am I interrupting something?"

My father lurked in the doorway like the oppressive shadow he was, giving my mother a look that might sour the milk in my latte.

Mom stood up, brushing down the front of her slacks. "Nothing at all, dear. I just came to bring our Anna some food."

My fingers twitched with the childish urge to grab hold of my mom and beg her to stay. I wasn't ready for the Hudson Vaughn experience.

He nodded to his wife as if they were business partners passing one another in a hallway, entering my room without invitation as she excused herself. Some things would never change. Like my parents' inability to be in the same room together for more than a few minutes unless it was for the purposes of publicity, putting on a front, or consuming a meal in utter silence.

Mom threw me her best impression of an encouraging smile before she vanished from view.

Hudson Vaughn held a garment bag over his shoulder which he dropped onto the bed near my feet.

"What's that?"

"It's a dress. We have a gala this weekend."

We? I was already expected to be part of 'we' again?

"I suggest we take some time to get your story straight. People are going to want to know what Malawi was like."

"Wait, if it's this weekend, why are you giving it to me now?"

His stare could've withered all the roses in the gardens. It was the same look he gave me when he found out what— or more accurately *who*—I used to do on the beach every time he found my bed empty in the middle of the night.

"So that we can get it tailored if it doesn't fit properly," he said as if it were the most obvious thing in the world. "For the past six years, everybody who knows us believes that you have been in Malawi building sustainable housing in rural settlements. Now that you're back, you need to be formally re-introduced to society. To your old friends."

They were not my friends. If anything, they were his.

Friends was a little generous of a term for the people who were at best, his colleagues, donors, and acquaintances. Or their offspring.

"The tailor will be here this afternoon to make any adjustments needed. In the meantime, you have a hair appointment at eleven."

"A what?" I asked, brushing croissant flakes off my lips, hating that it was the best thing I'd eaten in weeks.

He looked at the crumbs on the sheets like they personally offended him. I took another, messier bite, letting more crumbs fall to join their comrades on the Egyptian cotton.

He cleared his throat, but the tightness in his jaw kicked up a notch, and I knew I was already striking more than a few nerves.

"You need to look like Hudson Vaughn's daughter," he said in a tone that brokered no room for argument, speaking about himself in the third person like a total jackass. "You represent me and this family. We have a reputation to uphold."

He straightened his tie. "At least everyone thinks you were roughing it in rural Africa so your current *appearance* won't come as too much of a shock to anyone."

Wow. Thanks, Dad.

Everything in his life...engineered to perfection. As always.

He made up the charity-mission-in-Africa story because the truth would show his constituents that his perfect family-man image was faker than the porcelain veneers in his mouth.

"Aren't you at least going to give me a couple of days to settle in?" I asked, sarcastic, provoking his brows to slant sharply.

"You showed up out of the blue after six years of running away from us," he said. "We had no idea whether you were alive or dead."

"Would it have made a difference?"

"Drop the defiant teenager act. You're a grown woman now, Anna. Act like it. You're back because you finally learned that the real world isn't as forgiving as me and your mother are."

I pressed my lips together against a scathing reply. It hurt mostly because he was right.

The world outside these walls, outside this city, and without the protection a life with my family afforded, had been nothing like I imagined it would be. I'd been free in so many ways, but somehow I always found my way back into a cage.

I had to remind myself there were good things about my life away from here. I liked my job for the most part. Until Josh and I moved in together, I had a cute studio apartment filled with plants I could never keep alive and things I liked. I had a few friends, well, if you could call the barista at the local Drip and the doorman *friends*.

It wasn't perfect, but until Josh, it was something that was *mine*.

When my father realized I wasn't going to give him the confirmation or gratitude he was looking for, he continued. "That doesn't matter now. Your life since you left us until this moment doesn't matter. What matters is you're here now. And if you intend to stay a member of the Vaughn family, you have to look the part."

He took something out of his pocket and handed it to me: a glossy, metallic credit card. "Ask your mother who does her beauty treatments. You're looking a little tired.

Skinny, too. Eat that before you leave for your appointment." He pointed at the food.

Do this. Do that. Be quiet. Be perfect.

Home sweet fucking home.

A longing for my studio apartment in a city far away hit me like a brick. He was already squeezing me back into the Anna Vaughn-shaped box that he made for me, and I didn't get to have this one tailored. I was halfway through a chocolate Danish, but I lost my appetite, dropping it back onto the plate while I brushed my fingers together, scattering more bits of pastry over the bed.

"Was there something else?" I asked when he didn't move to leave, watching me make a mess with barely concealed disgust.

"Yes. Be back by three for the fitting. Saturday, I'll re-introduce my daughter, *Anna* Vaughn—" He pauses and I wondered how long he'd known I hadn't gone by that name. If he perhaps *did* know the name I went by and could've found me whenever he pleased. It would make sense. I was careful not to be found, but I always wondered why no images of me ever surfaced anywhere on the internet, not ever. And how no one ever found out I wasn't in Malawi.

Damn. He was even more cold than I realized.

"My daughter, *Anna,* who is back home and ready for the next phase in her life. Law School."

My mouth fell open. "Not this again, Dad."

"If you don't like it you're welcome to go back to wherever you came from. I don't suppose you used your time away to get any other sort of reputable degree?"

I clamped my mouth shut.

He snorted, the words *I didn't think so* practically

written all over his face. "David is waiting downstairs to take you to your appointment."

He turned to the door, stopped, and turned around again.

"Dr. Brandt will come by this evening," he added.

I took a slow, deep sip of my latte. Dr. Brandt was the go-to concierge physician for rich people with something to hide. Anyone who needed a Xanax prescription or to get their teenage daughter an abortion called him.

I didn't need either, but I knew I wasn't a picture of health and wellness.

This was as close to tenderness as my father got. He cared that something happened to me, but he cared more that we were going to be seen in public together, and he needed to make sure I looked good.

"I trust the *problem* you encountered in St. Louis won't be following you home?"

My mouth went dry.

"No."

"Good."

I watched his retreating back until he disappeared, standing up on shaking legs to pick up the garment bag and walk it to my closet, sticking it on an empty spot on one of the dress racks. I unzipped the top part to peek inside. It was a lilac, floor-length gown with long sleeves and a low back. Very elegant, but not me at all. My mom insisted the color suited me and dressed me in it often, but I always thought I looked better in warmer or richer hues.

For half a second, I wondered what would have happened if I'd stayed here. If I tried harder to be perfect. Memories of my mother's empty wine and champagne bottles every brunch and dinner came to mind. It didn't matter if I tried harder because it was impossible.

There would always be a higher tier to try to attain, just out of reach.

I wasn't staying here a second longer than I needed to once I figured out my next move. And that move was sure as shit *not* law school.

Checking my phone, there were some messages from a number I didn't recognize. I tapped the first one.

Unknown: *You blocked me? Grow up.*

I didn't read the rest, blocking that number too.

I changed into a black, long-sleeved blouse and straight-leg jeans from the Hudson Vaughn approved wardrobe, making sure my splotchy neck and arms were covered in a gauzy Burberry scarf before heading downstairs to the waiting car.

So many things had changed in a landscape once so familiar. Somehow it was a comfort to know that I wasn't the only thing that didn't remain constant here. Not everything was structured. Boring. Restricting.

There was only one thing in my life that felt real in that terrifyingly uncertain way.

...meeting Carter was more than just a breath of fresh air, it was finally *breathing*.

I picked my fingernails, annoyed at how he kept pressing his way into my thoughts. Embarrassing, really. I would bet a good chunk of change he hadn't even thought about me once since we last met. Between all those European women he was photographed with at business events and galas, how would he even find the time?

David dropped me off and said he would wait for me. I resented that being my father's daughter came with those perks, as much as I was grateful for them. I walked into the salon and went to the desk, telling the receptionist I had an appointment.

"What name is that under?"

"Vaughn. Hudson maybe. Or Annie. I mean *Anna*," I corrected quickly. *Annie Taylor* was Josh's girlfriend who lived in St. Louis. I was Anna Vaughn.

I am Anna Vaughn.

"Oh my God, Anna?"

I turned around, hearing my name. It must have come from the woman who was looking expectantly at me with a smile on her face. She was familiar, but in the way that you knew the melody of a song but none of the lyrics.

"Summer?" I tried, recognizing something in the shape of her nose and the set of her eyes. She laughed excitedly.

"Oh my God, it *is* you. When did you come back to town? How long has it been?"

I couldn't answer any of her questions before she engulfed me in a hug.

"I'm sorry. I literally got back yesterday."

"It's been way too long. Are you busy today?"

My kneejerk reaction was to tell her fuck yes I was busy from now until Forevuary, but the daughter of Hudson Vaughn wouldn't be so rude.

"Um, not this afternoon," I said, choking on the sweetness of my tone. "But if you're free for dinner, I might—"

"Perfect!"

Her animated excitement made me feel like a total asshole, especially when my sluggish mind began to fill in the antiquated memories. The *feel* of our old friendship.

Summer Rockwell. We'd gone to the same private secondary school. We were the kind of friends who were close until it was time to graduate. At first, she seemed so different but the more that I looked at her, the more I saw the girl I went to school with. Her hair was short now, freshly blown out. It suited her heart-shaped face well. She was a saint for not mentioning how bad I looked.

But then, she'd always been that way. Kind and sweet and excited about everything. Never noticing anyone's flaws. It was why I liked her so much. And also why I never really 'clicked' with her even though we spent years lunching and getting our nails done and watching the boys' rugby tournaments after school.

If I was a dark storm cloud personified, she was the sun, and I could use a little more of that right now.

We exchanged numbers and I went to my stylist's chair, feeling lighter, her effervescent energy floating me up along with her.

I reminded myself that my father and memories of Carter weren't the only things I was coming home to. There were some people in my life who weren't terrible, Rosie being one, and there was the ocean and the beach.

There was the opportunity for a fresh start. A clean state. No matter what Daddy dearest said, nothing had to be the exact same as it was before... starting with the disaster on my head.

The stylist let me sit and threw the apron over me before getting a good look at my hair.

"So what are we doing with this mop, doll?"

I almost wanted to apologize to her. My hair was dry and frizzy. When I left, I got the bright idea to dye it lighter to disguise myself which had only damaged it. And with my life imploding over the last couple months, I hadn't bothered to try to tone the soft beige strands so they were brassy

36

now, my natural color stretching an inch or two from my scalp.

"Darker, I think."

Truth be told, I didn't have enough energy to come up with anything more than that.

"Yeah?" she said, running her fingers through the hair at my crown. "Back to your natural, maybe? Looks like it could use a break from all the lightening."

I must've made a face because she amended. "How about something in between? A nice rich balayage that will grow out with grace while your hair heals?"

"Sounds perfect."

4

CARTER

"Here alone, Cole?"

I raised my brows at the man speaking to me. Nathanael Hsu, heir to his father's shipping company and a Harvard-educated douchebag. We had nothing in common, yet he was trying to talk to me like I was a peer.

Once upon a time, when I was a poor kid and he was the star at his prep school, Nathanael would have spit on me before he attempted small talk. I wanted to rub that in his smug little face. To make him choke on the fact that we were equals now, both invited to the same charity gala.

Instead, I forced myself to play the game.

"I'm flying solo tonight," I told him.

"Shame," he said, shaking his head. "Usually you've got the only pretty little thing worth looking at."

He was usually right, but tonight, I sent my original plus one on a flight back to Prague. Katerina was supposed to leave after accompanying me to the gala, but I didn't want her on my arm tonight. Truth be told, I didn't ever want to see her again. I could still feel the foul press of her mouth against mine.

Though, even if Katerina had been perfect, I wouldn't have invited her to attend with me, not after I learned Hudson Vaughn would be re-introducing his daughter to society tonight at this very same gala.

Anna.

My Anna.

The woman who had haunted me for the past six years, her memory lingering like a vengeful ghost.

The rumors had already spread. Before she even showed her face, Anna Vaughn was all any of the assholes here could talk about. They all seemed to have heard the same story: *Oh, Anna's been in Malawi, building houses for the less fortunate.* None of them were smart enough to recognize it for the obvious bullshit it was.

Certainly not Nathanael Hsu, anyway.

"You heard Anna Vaughn's showing up tonight?" he said. "She was such a hottie back at Langford Prep. I always wanted to tap that."

My grip on my whiskey tightened so hard, I could practically hear the glass cracking. This asshole didn't deserve to touch Anna. If he even got within breathing distance of her, I would take a pair of pliers and remove his fingernails, one by one. I'd consider it a fucking honor.

"Excuse me," I said, before I did something I'd regret.

I peeled off and made my way into the crowd of guests mingling with fluted glasses of overpriced champagne, listening to them prattle on as if they truly thought they were making a fucking difference in the world.

The gala was a fundraiser held by the Yates Foundation. Darren Yates was the governor before Anna's dad won his first term. Since then, he'd stepped back from politics and run the charity with his wife. They did a lot of underprivileged youth outreach causes. Get our kids off the drugs and into the classroom. That kind of stuff.

As a former underprivileged youth, I could barely stand the stench of bullshit. School wasn't going to do much for me when my dad was beating me up every night and I always fell asleep in class because I needed to work two jobs.

Education was good, but it wasn't the only way to get to the top. Once you found a foothold, it was easy to figure out that being smart alone didn't help you climb. Being ruthless and cunning did.

It's why I only came to these rich assholes' parties when I had my own agenda to fulfill. Tonight, that was finding Derek Hobbes. A task that got bumped to second place on the list of priorities the instant I knew *she* would be here. But seeing as the illustrious Hudson Vaughn hadn't shown his face yet, I figured I had time to get the second priority out of the way.

I scanned the crowd, trying to find the shorter man. He was the CEO of a small construction company in the area. Once upon a time, Hobbes Construction was a behemoth, one of the biggest companies in California. But decades of mismanagement had shrunken it to a tiny vanity project, worth only a few million. I could barely call it a competitor to my much larger construction business.

I wanted it anyway.

My people and Hobbes' had been working it out behind the scenes for months, and as long as an antitrust suit didn't pop us, the deal was all but done. Hobbes Construction would be mine, once Derek signed on the dotted line.

I came to the party tonight to make sure that happened.

Moving through the guests, I shook hands and exchanged pleasantries. I kept conversations as short as possible, looking over their shoulders to find either of the people I was really looking for. I knew for sure that Derek would be there.

Anna, on the other hand, might be little more than a rumor. The whispers said that Hudson Vaugn would be *unveiling* her like some sportscar tonight. His perfect daughter, back in town and ready to take up the Vaughn mantle again, be his precious doll.

I didn't believe it.

Couldn't seem to make myself.

She couldn't be back after all this time. Just like that. After searching and *searching*. She wouldn't just be here, in this room, so close I could smell her, touch her, see the way her hair would shine under the iridescent lighting.

I scanned the crowd for her furiously between hand-shakes, needing to put it to rest. To be certain that it was only gossip and she wasn't back. Then I could go home and open the good bourbon to wash away the memory of her face for another night.

Every roughly 5'7" woman with rich brown hair made me do a double take.

Finally, I spotted Derek Hobbes at the dessert table, loading up a plate with passionfruit tarts. I moved smoothly toward him, greeting him with a hearty slap on the shoulder. He practically jumped out of his skin at the touch.

"Derek! So good to see you here," I said, not bothering to pretend and sound warm.

He gulped. "Carter. You're...here."

"So I am." I had a good foot on him, and an excellent view of his thinning blond hair. "We haven't had a chance to meet in person about my acquisition."

"Yes, *er*, I usually send my representative for that," Hobbes says. He was obviously nervous seeing me, which could mean one of two things. Either he's as high strung as his miniature poodles around an alpha dog, or he was second-guessing my purchase of his company.

Which would royally piss me off.

"I hope you still find my offer attractive," I said. "I was told the last meeting ended well."

Hobbes' ruddy complexion went pale. "Yes, well. Certain things have come to light that I have to investigate. Legal issues, you know..."

Fuck. He was getting cold feet. Either he had a higher bidder in mind or someone was threatening an antitrust suit.

I placed a hand on his shoulder and squeezed hard enough to bruise. "I'm sure it's nothing our lawyers can't work out between them," I said smoothly. "I would hate for us to be on opposite sides."

Hobbes physically cringed. Good—he knew my reputation. That might be enough to scare him off. I wasn't opposed to a little bloodshed in the boardroom, but I hated wasting leverage on a small fish like Hobbes.

"So true," he croaked out. "Well, I should be going..."

He turned and practically ran away, the plate of tarts clutched to his chest. I would have laughed at the pathetic display if I hadn't spotted my other target. Seeing the two of them, my entire body went cold.

Hudson Vaughn was hard to miss. Tall with excellent posture, even as a man in his sixties. He moved smoothly through his second gubernatorial term and rumor had it he had his eye on the presidency afterward. We made eye contact, and I was not to scowl at the man. We met often at things like this and every time we went through the motions of pretending we were on good terms.

That man was responsible for one of the worst days of my life. If he were anyone else, I'd have killed him. But he was Anna's father, and she had the heart of a goddamned saint.

Usually, he was with his wife at these events and tonight was no different. Michelle Vaughn smiled broadly in a white evening gown at his right hand side. On his left was...

Her.

I couldn't be certain at first, but then she lifted her chin to greet a man coming to welcome her home and there was absolutely no mistaking it, even from across the room.

Anna Vaughn.

She was in a fitted lilac gown that swept the floor. Her hair was curled old Hollywood style, waving down one side of her face. The face that'd haunted my waking and sleeping hours for the last six years.

Her lips were painted soft pink and there was a delicate diamond necklace around her slender throat.

God.

I wanted to use that necklace to pull her to me, making the platinum and diamonds cut into her delicate skin. I bet she would moan. I could hear it, that sound. Like sounds she made that time on the beach when I entered her for the first time. That little whimper of pain that morphed into the most beautiful sound as she moaned my name.

Fuck.

Fuck.

I wanted to smudge that perfect lipstick with my cock. Wipe away the tears trickling down her high cheekbones while she gagged on it, submitting to me like she used to. Making foolish teenage promises to be mine forever.

Foolish or not, the promise was made, and I was going to make damn sure she kept her end because I'd made her a promise too.

That my heart was hers. That I'd never give it to anyone else.

And I hadn't.

I'd kept my promise.

Now it was time for Anna to keep hers.

I reached for a glass of champagne from a passing tray, swallowing down the dry tang of it to quench the burn in my throat and douse the fire in my stomach. I had six years' worth of things to say to her.

The crowd parted for me as I stalked toward them.

"Hudson," I said in greeting. "How good to see you."

The whole family could obviously hear the venom in my words, because Hudson's practiced smile went flat. The blood drained from Anna's already pale face. Only Michelle was able to keep her smile, probably thanks to the vodka martini in her hand. I doubted it was her first.

"Carter," she said, extending her manicured hand. "Thank you for your generous donation."

That's right—she was on the board for the Yates Foundation, perfect society wife that she was.

"I'm happy to give to a good cause," I said, bowing my head. "Hudson, you're looking well."

Unfortunately, that much was true. Whatever deal he'd

struck with the devil had given him a handsome, vibrant exterior, no matter how decayed he was on the inside.

Hudson only answered me with a polite nod. Just as well—even hearing his voice made my skin prickle with fury.

Them out of the way, I let my eyes fall to her and only her, willing her to meet my gaze as she curled her hands into the silky fabric of her gown at her sides, clenching enough to leave angry creases as her knuckles turned white.

"Anna," I said, my voice low and rough, "It's been a long time."

Her jewel-bright eyes lifted to mine, and for a moment, it was like we were right back there on the beach, her dark hair loose and textured with salt, her perfect skin wiped clear of make-up. An electric charge transferred between us without even having to touch.

Then she blinked, and we were back in the moment, with her painted-on face and hair perfectly highlighted and coiffed. I could see how time had changed her. Anna had always looked thoughtful, almost mournful. Her face was slimmer and more angular now, all her baby fat gone. The smooth lines of her jaw, cheeks, and nose were so familiar to me but I ached to trace them with my hands again. To relearn every inch of her.

Then to rip away every false piece, every stupid society air and expensive product, until she was left bared to me.

Anna's eyes widened, and I saw a flash of real fear in them.

Good. She should be scared of who I am now.

Without another word, without even *acknowledging* me, she spun on her heel and walked into the crowd. My fist clenched as I watched her flee.

"You'll excuse us, won't you, Carter?" Hudson said, not bothering to hide his smugness. "I should say hello to the hosts. Do enjoy the event."

It took everything in me not to yank him back by his hair plugs and break his jaw.

He strolled away, leaving Michelle and me standing together. I had nothing to say to the woman who stood by while her husband tried to shove Anna into a mold of perfection she would never fit into. As far as I was concerned, Michelle Vaughn was a shell of a person, content to be a pawn in someone else's game. Not worthy of my time. Yet, I couldn't walk away from her.

Mostly because I didn't trust myself to move until Hudson was further out of reach.

"You really are looking well, Carter," she said in a soft tone. "You've obviously made something of yourself since you and Anna were friends. I've never seen a business empire rise so quickly."

I could barely conceal my surprise. Based on what Anna had told me and what I'd witnessed myself at past events, Mrs. Vaughn took too many pills to notice what was going on in her life. I didn't think she had any idea I existed six years ago, much less that I knew her daughter. Maybe Michelle Vaughn was a more useful source of information than I thought.

"So, Anna's back." I took another glass of champagne from a passing tray and forced myself to sip it like a normal person.

"Ah, yes. Anna was working on housing development in Southern Africa for the past few years."

The same bullshit story. I raised a questioning brow, but Michelle didn't cave. She just smiled and said, "We're happy to have her back. I hope you two get the opportunity to catch up."

I barely stopped myself from laughing out loud. No doubt Michelle wanted me as far away as possible from her little princess, just like her husband did.

"We will," I said, the promise sounding more like a threat as I stalked into the crowd.

I wasn't letting Anna go again.

Not when I'd finally gotten close enough to taste her.

As soon as I got her alone, I'd make sure she couldn't fucking forget me.

The room had filled even more, and enough women were wearing lilac or dusty purple gowns that tracking down Anna was harder than I'd hoped. The elite wanted their women all looking the same—chaste, expensive— untouchable in pastels and ivory. Fucking prudes.

Anna would look ten times more beautiful once I'd stripped her down and ruined her. She wouldn't be getting away from me again, even if I had to break her so thoroughly that I was the only man she could fit with.

A few business acquaintances tried to stop me to chat, but I looked right through them. I was done wasting my goddamn time with them.

I finally found her, standing at a minibar, ordering a glass of red wine. I couldn't stop the wicked smile spreading across my face. I quietly stalked behind her, enjoying the view of her gorgeous backside in the silky gown. I was going to own that tight little ass.

"Boo," I murmured in her ear, and she jerked away, whirling with a gasp. "I found you, Anna."

Fuck, she still smelled the same. Like ylang-ylang and

vanilla. Her skin looked so soft, it felt like I could bruise it just by touching it. God, I wanted to mark her everywhere.

Her eyes darted to the people around us. Obviously, she was deciding whether she could ignore me in front of the bartender and all the guests standing close to us. Hudson Vaughn's perfect little princess could never be ill-mannered in public, of course.

"How long are you going to pretend that you don't see me?" I whispered, leaning in close.

She inhaled sharply before turning to face me, her wooden smile firmly in place.

"Carter Cole? How are you? It's been so long."

That overly polite, sing-song voice came from years of practice doing things like this. She had never used it with me before. This was the girl who used to cry in my arms because her maniac father didn't let her breathe without his consent. She was and yet wasn't the same person.

"Too long," I said. I stepped forward and she shifted back. The movement was natural, maybe even a reflex but she didn't want to be close to me. I took a slow breath to keep myself calm. She was lucky we had so many eyes on us.

"So," she said.

Her eyes, usually pools of emotion, were impossible to read.

"That's all you have to say to me?"

Her practiced smile didn't falter for a second.

"The last time we talked, you told me I was a spoiled brat who didn't have any real problems. That you got what you wanted from me and never wanted to see me again."

"So you do remember me," I said with a smirk.

"I do. You remember me too, which makes me wonder why you think I would have anything to say to you."

When I said I never wanted to see her again, she had actually left. I knew she would, she had to but she hadn't just left. She fucking *disappeared*. She dropped off the map completely. I knew she did, I'd looked. She wasn't in Malawi building houses. She wasn't at Yale. Photos of her didn't exist on the internet. She was gone. I even looked for an obituary just in case she was dead.

But I'd never stopped thinking about her, never stopped craving her. Even now, when I pumped my cock in the shower, it was her I pictured kneeling in front of me. My obsession with her was the only thing keeping my dark heart beating, even if the only thing powering it was memories of her.

That was about to change. She might have still been angry with me, but I'd make her fucking forgive me. Then, I'd learn every fucking thing I missed during our time apart, until I recognized every dark corner of her soul again. It wouldn't take long. Even after all the time that passed, I still knew her down to her fucking core, just like she knew me. She was the only person still alive who ever saw any real softness in me.

And if I couldn't give that to her, then she'd take the hard parts. She was strong enough to survive that.

"You're still angry," I murmured. "So be angry. Make me hurt like I hurt you, Anna. I might even like it."

Her green eyes widened with shock then came alight with fury. There she was: the fiery, rebellious girl I remembered. She opened her mouth to tell me off.

Before she could, a bright flash went off to our right, and Anna cringed away. An event photographer snapped photos of two couples near us, no doubt getting pictures for the local society papers. I prepared myself to paste on a smile and fake it. I'd been photographed at parties with dates more times than I could count, because it was good publicity for my business.

But for some reason, Anna ran, darting between guests to get away.

What the fuck?

I got the sense it wasn't that she didn't want to be photographed with me. I saw her fearful dear-in-the-head-lights look just before she bolted.

I followed her through the crowd and out a set of French doors into the cool evening garden below. A few people had abandoned their empty glasses out here, but it was too cold for anyone to linger. Anna and I were finally alone.

She stood facing away from me. Her dress had a low dip in the back, and her spine and shoulder blades showed through her skin. It was normal to lose some roundness with age, but she looked weak. Almost frail. I had watched my mother battle cancer. I knew healthy weight loss didn't look like that.

How hadn't I noticed back inside?

At the curve in her back was a partially hidden yellow-brown mark. A bruise. My vision went red as rage crashed over me. My muscles tightened, ready to fight whoever had dared to fucking touch her.

Barely thinking, I grabbed her arm, probably too tightly. She spun around, pulling it out of my grasp.

"Carter, what the hell are you—"

"What happened to your back?" I demanded.

"My what?" she asked, confused.

"Your back. Who did that to you?"

"My... *oh*." Her confusion cleared.

"Was it your father?"

I wouldn't put it above him. Hudson Vaughn was a dirty, dangerous man. It took one to know one. Both of our sperm donors were hell bent on ruining our lives when we were younger. I got away from mine but Hudson was still in Anna's life.

"My what? What are you talking about?" she said. I could see right through her; I knew a healing bruise when I saw one. I also knew when she was lying to me.

And was that more bruising under the layers of makeup on her face? Her neck?

It was hard to tell, but the more I looked the more I thought I was right.

My throat went dry as hell and my blood heated.

"You know what I'm talking about," I said through gritted teeth. "Someone hurt you."

Her face went totally blank. "It's none of your business."

I stepped in closer, backing her into a vine covered trellis but she only jutted her chin out defiantly, staring with the fire of a thousand suns into my eyes. Refusing to back down.

"Oh? Not my business?"

I jerked her chin up and to the left, trying to get a better look at the bruise Hudson's makeup artists couldn't quite erase on her cheekbone.

She pulled away from my touch and shoved me hard in the chest, her own heaving. "I'm perfectly capable of taking care of myself," she snapped. "Which is convenient for you, since you already got everything you wanted from me a long time ago."

"Anna."

She pushed past me.

"*Anna.*"

She whirled, rage in her green eyes. Rage and *pain*. "Fuck you, Carter Cole. You're not allowed to care. Not after..."

Her lips pressed tight against a quiver, face pinching trying to hold all that emotion in. All of the evidence of the truth—that she still felt something for me. That maybe, she never stopped.

It was all the proof I needed.

My stomach soured and the beating thing in my chest remembered how to ache as she tore her eyes away from me, shook her head, and stormed out of the garden and back inside.

This time, I didn't bother stopping her.

Because she was right. I pushed her away. I did this to us. To her.

I deserved the cold looks, her distance, even much worse.

When Anna and I were younger, I used to think she was ashamed of me but that wasn't true. I was ashamed of myself.

I was punching way above my weight class and it ate at me. She didn't care about the divide between us, but *I* did. I never felt like I was enough for her. Not smart enough. Not polite enough. Not wealthy enough.

Not meant for a girl like her.

But I was different now. I'd transformed myself into a man worthy of her.

Just as intimidating, powerful, and domineering as her father, and I'd let my soul be corrupted, just like he had. The only difference between us was I at least had a code I lived by. I'd never steal from the poor or the destitute.

No, I ate the rich and gave them my leftovers.

Now, I didn't care about what I deserved. I just took what I wanted.

I couldn't have her back then, but now, I intended to fucking keep her.

5

ANNA

"So, how was Africa? Where were you exactly?" Summer asked.

I chewed my burger slowly, pretending to savor it so I could buy time while I tried to remember the official story Daddy's PR woman fed me over breakfast this morning and came up blank.

"It was great. Really nice people," I said in a way I hoped conveyed my disinterest in talking about it. I felt bad lying to Summer and shitty for kowtowing to my father's perfect lie about his supposedly perfect daughter, but I couldn't tell her the truth. She wouldn't get it, and like my dad always said, trust no one with family secrets.

We were friends once upon a time but that felt like another life. I was a different person now, so that meant she probably was too. The actuality of my existence over the past six years was more than a little shameful and I wasn't ready for her judgment.

"I feel a little guilty for not donating more of my time," she said, dunking her straw in and out of her drink.

"Don't worry about it. It's a shame that charity has to exist in the first place," I said. "How was China? You mentioned that you spent a year out there."

There was a wistful smile on her face.

"It was good. Different, but good. I'm glad that I went. I wouldn't give up the life my parents gave me for anything, but it was nice to... I don't know, honor that part of me."

I was happy for her. Mr. and Mrs. Rockwell completed their happy family with an adopted baby daughter from Chongqing, China. Meeting them was the first time I realized that some people's parents kissed, on the *mouth*. Like in movies.

"Will you ever go back?"

"Oh yeah, definitely. Hey, did you ever end up going to law school?"

I laughed through my grimace, looking down at my food. "Didn't happen. Besides, it's too late for me now, right? I'd rather not be the oldest one in the classroom."

"No way. It's never too late, but you didn't want to go anyway, right?"

"Still don't," I said, sighing. That was one of the worst fights I'd ever had with my father; law school-gate. I was going to Yale to study pre-law before seamlessly moving into law school the way he had and he didn't care what I had to say about it. It was one thing for him to say I had to dress a certain way and give me a curfew. I could deal with that. In his house, I had to live with his rules.

But my future too? When did it end? I didn't want the kind of marriage he and my mother had, and knowing him, he'd be introducing me to his approved suitor list as soon as he finalized it. I shuddered to imagine the kind of man he wanted as a son-in-law. *Himself*, basically: thirty years younger with valuable family connections. Any degree I earned prior to him marrying me off would've been nothing but a framed certificate in a hallway somewhere. I shuddered.

"If not law school, then there has to be something you'd want to go back for," Summer pressed.

"Any suggestions?" I asked.

"What do you mean, do I have any suggestions?" she asked, looking confused. "*Photography*," she said when it took me too long to catch on.

"Oh." I looked down into my plate of food again. The fries were cold now and instead of looking inviting, they looked shriveled and flat. "Right. That."

"You still take pictures, right?"

I shifted in my seat. Yeah, I'd taken plenty of pictures, but they weren't the kind of photos I could just show off.

Photography had always been a way for me to deal with the world around me. Back in high school, I used it to keep my life at a distance, safe inside a frame. I spent years feeling like I was failing to fit into my father's mold, like I could never be the person I was supposed to be. Photographing the cotillions, the expensive schools, and the trips to the beauty salon made me feel like an anthropologist, capturing the weird world I'd been thrust into.

Then there were the photos I took on the midnight beach with Carter's arms around my waist from behind, his scent in my nose and his lips whispering against the nape of my neck.

Some of my best work.

After everything happened and I left home, I started working at the Butterfly Room in St. Louis and took pictures of that. The women I worked with were funny, brash, and sassy. I loved taking photos in the break room, capturing them pushing up their boobs, putting on their make-up, and trying on each other's teeny-tiny dresses. They sang along to shitty pop songs, painted each other's nails, and made goofy faces when they caught me pointing the camera at them.

Then there were the harder shots. The ones I took after a girl had three too many men touch her that night and needed to vent her frustration to the others. The ones where the others would huddle around her, making her feel safe and loved and protected.

The vengeful looks in their eyes when they went back out onto the floor, ready for revenge in whatever form the girls deemed fit for the crime.

When we were out working, all anyone saw was our bodies. We were commodities, existing only to serve the patrons who paid enough to cover cocktails at the glorified titty bar. In my photos, we were *people*, with humor, intelligence, and dignity.

Most importantly, I photographed what Josh did to me. Every time he struck me, every time he left a mark, I'd take a picture. Taking self portraits of the abuse he inflicted on me was the only thing that made me feel like my body belonged to me again. If I could photograph it, then I didn't have to shove it in the back of my mind and pretend it never happened. I had the proof, and that made me feel strong.

Of course, I could never show anyone those pictures. There would be way too much to explain.

Instead, I just shrugged. "Sure, I take photos. But it's more of a hobby than anything else."

Summer cocked her head. "Don't downplay it. Photography is a real skill. I know girls who pay thousands of dollars to get people to do their Instagram posts."

"I'm just...not interested," I said. Talking about photography with her was just...too real, somehow. It hurt.

"What about guys?" she asked, thankfully changing the subject.

"*Hm?*"

"Men. Are you seeing someone right now maybe?"

My lip curled back and I shook my head briskly. "Oh no. Single and staying that way."

Summer laughed.

"Wow, that bad?"

No, *worse*. I deleted another string of threatening text messages from Josh just this morning. He wasn't even doing it for a response. Anything he could do to distract, inconvenience and harass me was a win for him. He was a mean, petty man, both drunk and while sober.

I couldn't wait until my new phone to be delivered to the house. The stupid thing should have arrived already.

"Let's just say I'm not looking."

Unbidden, a memory of Josh punching me in the stomach after I came home late after closing the lounge swam to the top of my mind. My jaw clenched. Ugly thoughts broke through. Heat burned in my stomach and fizzled through my limbs. I clenched my fist around the sweating glass of my drink. I was never strong enough to fight back, but he made me wish I was, just so I could hurt him the same ways he hurt me.

I hated that he made me think things like that. I was never violent. I was never disillusioned and cold, but it was amazing what the wrong man at the wrong time was capable of doing to you. I vividly dreamt of smothering him with a pillow or slipping a knife into his carotid when he passed out drunk more often than I cared to admit—and always awoke with the taste of bitter guilt on my tongue.

"We all have those guys we regret," Summer said.

Regret was an understatement. I asked her whether she had had better luck. Her boyfriend, James, was in his last year of med school. He was an upstanding member of society who treated her like a princess, doting on her every chance he got while supporting her aspirations until they were ready to have kids, and filling her bank account with more money than she could ever spend.

What was that like?

And why didn't it appeal to me?

It sounded...boring.

Suffocating.

"How about if I—" Summer started, then faltered, snapping her lips closed.

"What?"

She smiled sheepishly.

"I mean, James has friends... you said you weren't looking, but neither was I when I met him," she said with a suggestive raise of her eyebrows.

I was in no shape to be anybody's girlfriend. Not even one of James's eligible colleagues. A surgeon boyfriend would impress my father, for sure, but after Josh, I wasn't interested in *any* man. With my luck, I'd garner the attention of Josh the sequel.

"I just got out of something so no. I'm not."

The expectant look didn't leave her eyes, but she nodded, giving up. My last relationship took from me a year I was never getting back. Maybe one day I'd try again, but right now, I still felt empty and anyone who tried to look inside would just be disappointed.

Summer and I departed with a hug and a promise to see each other again soon. I'd promised to get home for a dinner with a guest Dad was hosting tonight. He told me that under no circumstances was I allowed to be late.

I rested my head against the window as David drove me back home.

"David?"

"Yes, Miss Vaughn."

"You can call me Anna," I said.

He paused.

"Yes, Anna?"

"You wouldn't happen to know who is coming to the house this evening, would you?"

"I'm afraid I don't have that information."

I didn't believe him, but I didn't think it was any use pressing him. David knew all my movements outside the house. The security at the compound knew when I left and came back. There were cameras outside and inside the house so whoever watched them knew how often I checked the fridge for snacks.

I thought my freedom was worth everything that I lost when I ran away. There had to be more to life than what I was allowed to have. At the moment, I wasn't sure anymore.

Rosie let me in when I got to the house, and I found my will to smile when I saw her face, pulling her soft body to mine for a tight hug.

"Miss. Vaughn," she protested, but when it became clear I wasn't letting go just yet, she patted my back, beginning to relax.

"I missed you," I said, straightening, her familiar scent still in my nose.

"Yes, well," she said, face red as she straightened her apron. "If you hadn't left, you wouldn't have had cause to, now would you."

I only grinned wider. There was the take-no-shit attitude I'd missed so much.

"You're right," I told her with a little laugh. "Like always."

She coughed into her closed fist but couldn't entirely conceal the ghost of a smile tugging at one corner of her mouth.

I sighed, knowing this welcome would be the only warm thing I'd experience for the rest of the evening. A chill skated up my arms. Whatever, no, *whoever*, my father had in store for me was bound to be a fucking treat.

"Guess I should..." I trailed off, my limbs heavy as I crossed the entry to the grand staircase, but Rosie was having none of it. She trudged up after me, huffing as she followed.

"Anna, your father left instructions for you to get ready for dinner."

"Do you know who's coming?" I asked her over my shoulder, suppressing an eye roll.

"You know that's not my area," she chastised, but she and I both knew there wasn't much that happened in this house she didn't know about. "But...I believe it's one of his younger colleagues."

I chuckled cynically, tossing my purse on the bed. By "younger colleagues," she meant "eligible young asshole." Tonight's dinner was a setup, and I would be the main course.

Of course Dad's plan for me didn't end with lying about charity work at galas.

I'd skipped law school, so he went ahead with phase two.

I was to be a trophy wife, married off to one of his cronies. Maybe whoever married me would be Dad's vice president when he finally started the presidential run he'd been threatening for years.

This was how he saw me. A broodmare, to be sold off for gold and a head of cattle. My fists curled, nails biting down into my palms.

"I don't know how you do it, Rosie."

"Do what, dear?"

"Work for him."

She gave me a confused look, as though it wasn't a daily challenge for her not to smack him upside the head.

She and Denise, his personal assistant at work, were the only people able to maintain long-term employment with Hudson Vaughn. Denise and Rosie orchestrated the complicated ins and outs of my father's life, from flights and rallies to events to suit fittings. The two of them probably knew enough secrets to put him in federal prison for life without parole.

Sometimes, I wished one of them would.

Fuck. I knew I had it good here. I woke to breakfasts I didn't have to pay for or prepare. I never had to worry about missing a train or bus because a personal driver was hired to take me wherever I wanted at any time. Every need was taken care of.

But there was something so empty about a life that was so frustratingly predictable.

If I missed something about being in St. Louis, it was

the fact that every day felt like a challenge. When I came home hours before the sun came up, after my shift at the Butterfly Room, I felt like I had really *done* something. I would be tired with the sort of bone weary exhaustion only earned from a nine hour shift in heels with a fake smile plastered on your face.

Every day was an achievement. Here, every day was the same. Planned to within an inch of its life. *Staged.*

And no matter how long I played the part, I'd never felt like I belonged. There would always be a part of me that just didn't fit.

"I pressed your blue Chanel dress," Rosie said. "Your father wanted you to wear it tonight."

I rolled my eyes.

"Don't you think about not wearing it to prove a point," she lectured, obviously reading my mind. "I took the time to press it, and I don't want him thinking I didn't pass the message on."

"Fine," I promised. "I'll wear it and look nice, but for you, Rosie. Not for him."

"I don't care why you do it. Just do it."

She bustled off, probably to bust somebody else's balls, but paused in the door with her hand on the frame. She didn't quite look over her shoulder as she said, "It's good to have you home, little bug," and then she was gone, leaving me with the sting of tears in my eyes because she was the only one in this house who could say that and mean it.

I shut the door and leaned against it. I had to look on the bright side—whatever bullshittery my father had planned, at the very least, there would be good wine.

Flopping down on the bed, I opened my phone to search for Carter.

Sue me—my day had been exhausting and old habits died hard.

Flicking through the usual photos, I found a few on google from the gala.

There he was as I'd seen him. Tall and brooding.

I could see the difference between the photos.

One definitely taken before he'd ever seen me. With his new mask firmly in place.

And one from after, or at least I guessed so by the scowl on his lips and the way he was angrily pushing his hair away from his face.

That one was my Carter. The angsty boy on the midnight beach, only older.

My thighs squeezed and I bit my lip, trying to temper the feelings seeing him always roused in me.

God, I missed him.

And I *hated* that I missed him.

I slid my fingers under the elastic band of my panties, gathering moisture from my entrance while I studied the shape of him in his perfectly fitted suit. Imagined ripping it off him. Imagined him in his trademark dark wash jeans and loose black tee.

He was every inch the gorgeous CEO, and he probably had women lined up around the block to play his sexy secretary.

Scrolling down, I saw more pictures of him taken at events. He always had a different date on his arm. Here was a big-eyed blonde woman, so tiny that she barely came up to Carter's collarbone. Then a svelte, dark-skinned model who gave me serious Grace Jones vibes.

I quickly swiped past them, not wanting to see.

My eyes widened when I spotted a completely different

shot. It was Carter on a yacht somewhere, a glistening blue sea in the background behind him. It was taken with a long lens, obviously by some paparazzi. I couldn't look away from it.

Carter was glistening with water, the sunlight emphasizing the lines of his muscles. His sun-kissed skin was marked with extensive tattoos, which only made him look more like a devil, out to seduce virgins to join him back in hell.

I knew that if I zoomed in, I could see the scars, too. The ones I'd run my fingers over on the beach so long ago. I could still smell his warm skin, still imagine the weight of him over me.

I pressed harder on my clit, circling it until my entire body felt tight with pleasure. Memory and fantasy blended into a potent brew, making me get even more wet. I could hear the obscene sounds of my fingers moving over my folds. My eyes screwed shut while I brought myself closer and closer to the edge.

I couldn't stop the breathy moans escaping me.

Fuck him.

Fuck Carter Cole.

I almost screamed his name as I came. My back arched, and my vision went black, the cage around me vanishing, just for a moment.

6

CARTER

"Little late for a meeting, isn't it, boss?" Paulson said.

"Is it?" I asked dryly. It might be late for anyone else, but 6pm was right in the middle of Paulson's work day. PIs weren't exactly known for keeping normal business hours.

Still, Paulson looked rough. He hadn't shaved his uneven beard in a few days, and there were visible coffee stains on his cheap button-up.

"So, why wasn't this meeting an email?" he asked.

"You've failed me, Paulson," I said, picking up the platinum letter opener I kept on my desk. I twirled the handle casually in my fingers, and Paulson visibly gulped. He knew exactly what I was talking about.

"You're right," he said quickly. "I should have known Anna would be back. Hudson Vaughn kept a tight lid on things."

"For what I'm paying you, I expect you to get into all his nooks and crannies," I said coolly. "Or are you trying to say you're no longer up for the job?"

"No, no," Paulson assured me. "In fact, I've got some new information about Anna Vaughn that I think will make up for that little lapse."

I glared cooly at him, pressing the tip of the letter opener against the pad of my thumb. My instincts warred between letting him dangle a little longer, and impatiently demanding information.

"What do you have for me?" I said finally, cutting to the chase.

The man smirked and pulled out the chair opposite me. Over the years, Paulson had become a favorite of my private investigators. He scored low on professionalism, but high on results. His willingness to go the extra mile always earned him my continued patronage as well as a few thousand extra to pad his bank account. It almost made me forgive his catastrophic failure to alert me that Anna was back.

Almost.

I had competitors. I needed to stay one step ahead of them. But this time, Paulson wasn't looking into Hudson Vaughn or anyone else in this damned city worth mentioning on the six o'clock news.

"I've got a few answers about where she's been the past few years," Paulson said eagerly. "And of course, surveillance of her since she returned."

"Let me see the report," I said. He opened the bag he carried and took out the file. The printed pictures of her on the sidewalk, coming in and out of a car, and having lunch with another woman felt so intimate. A primal sense of satisfaction filled me. She was *mine*, and now, I could watch her all I liked. I could consume her every move. Her every word. Until I knew her inside out. Until I knew her better than my own reflection.

"Well, right now everything seems fine. She's out and about, usually alone. She has a driver and nothing seems out of the ordinary."

"And the injuries?"

I hated revealing Anna's bruises to Paulson. It seemed too private, too intimate to share. But I had to know whether her father had caused them. If Vaughn was hurting Anna in that house, I was ready to drop a bomb on it. I only had to get her out first. Fuck the collateral damage.

"No luck infiltrating Vaughn's security system yet, so it's hard to know for sure. I didn't see her anywhere near a hospital either," he said.

I chewed on my bottom lip. That meant Anna's injuries hadn't been severe—or, at least, that a visit from a home doctor was enough to treat them. Paulson pointed at the report impatiently.

"I found out a little something about her past. Keep looking."

I leafed through the file, past the recent pictures of Anna, to a group photo of a bunch of strangers. I squinted at the image. Two women and three men at what looked like an upscale bar or something, huddled together for the group shot, smiling at the camera. What the fuck was this? My lip curled in agitation, then I saw it.

"Where was this?"

"The picture is a year old. The one holding the pool cue? His name is Josh."

"Tell me something useful, Paulson," I spat.

"He's been to jail for resisting arrest and booked in for domestic abuse," Paulson said. I stared at him. "I found a couple more pictures of them like that. Close. Lovey-dovey even."

"She dated this man?"

My upper lip curled into a snarl, analyzing this *Josh* in a new light. No. He didn't look her type at all.

"No solid intel yet, but you wanted to know who might have hit her. This could be the guy. After I found these photos, I followed the trail and managed to dig up a few more. Looks like she worked at this place. It's an upper class bar for wealthy clientele in St. Louis. Flip to the next ones. See. The other men look to be...close to her...but Josh appears to be the most recent."

Heat raced across my back and I looked up at the image of the moon over the water, going back there, to that calm place to get the thought of her with *numerous* different men that weren't me out of my fucking head.

I wanted to castrate each and every one of them.

So much for building sustainable housing in Africa.

It wasn't as if I could judge her. Not with the way I went through women faster than you could fucking blink. But I still loathed that anyone else managed to get close to her.

She promised me.

She fucking promised me.

Anna Vaughn was *mine*.

...until the day you shattered her.

I threw off the thought. That didn't matter. I didn't mean it and if I thought for one fucking second that she would disappear before I had the chance to make it right I never would've...

It didn't matter now.

"I can't speak to Mr. Vaughn," Paulson continued. "It's still possible he could have hurt her, I just haven't found any evidence of that yet. But if *this* was her man." He tapped the image lying on the table. "He was knocking his exes around long before Anna. He probably wouldn't have spared her."

Bile rose in my throat looking at the pixelated image of the man with his arm around Anna's waist. The glazed over, too drunk look in his eyes. The way her hand on his almost seemed to be trying to peel it away from her skin.

Was there some strain in her eyes? Some fear?

I pressed my palms flat to the table and breathed deep through my nose. When I opened my eyes, Paulson looked nervous.

"There's one more thing," he said. "It's big. Just don't shoot the messenger."

I turned the page quickly, and immediately recognized a notice from a dark web bulletin. An advertisement featuring a picture of Anna, offering a quarter of a million dollars to anyone who could deliver her alive.

What the fuck was this?

My mind raced and my blood went cold and the dead thing in my chest came alive with a deep, painful beating that made my skin prickle and a thudding start in my ears.

What. The. Fuck.

I rushed to make sense of it, connecting the dots, putting things in order in my head to find where and how I could fix it.

This was her last boyfriend and she obviously left him. Whether or not these injuries were his doing, I had no doubt he hurt her before, and he obviously intended to hurt her again. Who else would've put out this bulletin?

Those photos were taken at this club for the wealthy

and powerful. He'd have the money for this ransom. The connections to make it happen.

If he wanted her alive, he probably wanted to keep her as his goddamn sex slave, or worse.

I covered a shuddering breath as it pushed from my mouth like steam from a boiling pit of hell.

That wasn't fucking happening.

Did she know?

Did she know he was looking for her? That he plastered her face—*my Anna's face*—all over the dark web for every sick, depraved criminal to...

Josh had no idea what devil he invoked. Because I would move heaven and earth to keep Anna Vaughn safe, and then I'd serve her Josh's head roasted on a fucking pike.

"Take it down," I hissed. "Destroy the ad."

"Already done," Paulson assured me. "And I'm watching for any new posts, but I can't guarantee that nobody else has seen it."

That meant Anna was in danger from every bounty hunter on the west coast. She had her father's security around her, but I didn't trust them to be enough. What if they didn't know?

"At least they don't have her name. Looks like she went by Annie Taylor. But I did a reverse image search on Google and it isn't good. Anyone with a half a brain cell and an internet connection can probably find out who she really is."

My hands shook and I turned and swept the file and every other piece of useless paper and junk off my desk, hearing metal and glass knock and shatter into the hardwood.

"Keep looking," I growled. "I want everything you can

find on her. Her friends' names. Her boss' name. Phone numbers. Any other aliases she might've used. Where she lived. All of it."

I bent and snatched the photo of Josh from the floor, tearing it in two to separate him from Anna. I thrust the half that depicted Josh at Paulson. "And I want *everything* on this fucker. Family, education, work. His address. Phone number. Socials. Last known location. Fuck, I want the last place he took a shit."

"You got it." Paulson gulped.

"I want my people watching Anna at all times. Talk to my head of security. He knows who to call. I want the best of the best on this. No compromises. I'll handpick the men, you coordinate with them. If anything happens to her, it's on your head, Paulson."

Paulson nodded and left, leaving the copy of the file with me.

I closed, trying to ground myself—shoving every disturbing possibility out of my mind.

What if there were men already on their way to find her? To capture her?

My head spun and I sat down hard on my chair, the caster protesting my weight as I bent forward and pressed my palms into my eye sockets.

I forced myself to picture the beach, like I always did.

The water.

The navy sky.

The moon.

And her there waiting for me.

When my breathing evened out, I pulled the mess of Paulson's file from the floor and set it in my lap, flipping to the pictures of her.

The recent ones of her walking around downtown and eating at restaurants. I thought about seeing her again so much that it still felt like a dream. As though my mind was still the only place she existed even though there was proof right in front of me.

Seeing her vibrant and alive almost made me forget the sheer rage I felt learning about the hit on her. I was going to make Josh regret the day he set eyes on my Anna.

I pulled up the computer program that let me access Anna's phone. Hacking into it had been one of my first orders of business. Her location was in the Vaughn mansion, which comforted me. She should be safe there, with the governor's intense security system.

Clicking again, I accessed the view of her phone screen, my jaw dropping when I saw my own face staring back at me. My name was in the search bar, and she was scrolling through photos of me. A sick smile spread across my face.

I knew my obsession with her wasn't one-sided. After all this time, she was still curious. Still just as starved for me as I was for her.

The top results for me were mostly professional head-shots and photos from work events, me in a suit giving the camera a closed-mouth smile. But eventually, more candid, casual photos started filtering in. Anna paused longer at the pictures of me with other women, my dates for galas and fundraisers. Their names and faces had long blurred from my memory, but they were all stunningly beautiful and dressed to match my Brioni suits.

Anna scrolled down, pausing at a photo of me shirtless on my yacht. The photo was taken by a photographer with a long lens—I didn't give the paparazzo permission, but it hadn't annoyed me enough to force him to take it down.

Anna lingered on that picture for a long time. Minutes seemed to pass. Acting on suspicion, I pressed the tool to give me access to her microphone. The sounds of soft moans and heavy breathing filtered from my speakers. Fuck, I recognized those sounds.

She was touching herself to photos of me.

I groaned aloud, and my cock stiffened instantly in my pants. What I wouldn't give to be there with her, watching her slender fingers move between her legs. I would have buried my face in her, drowned in the scent of her musk.

Unbuttoning my pants, I wrapped my fist around my cock. My hand was a poor substitute for Anna's touch, but being able to hear her moaning, knowing she was thinking of me, had me harder than I'd been in years. I stroked myself slowly at first, but as Anna's breathing quickened, I moved to match her pace.

I ached to press the camera button, but then she'd know. There was no way to access it without the little red light turning on on her end. I had to settle for my own imagination, but with those sounds she was making, it wasn't hard.

I didn't bother remembering the sweet, practically chaste way we'd made love the first time as a pair of broken teenagers in the sand. My fantasies now were far darker.

I was going to own every fucking part of her. I'd fuck her mouth, her pussy, and her ass, claiming her so thoroughly that no other man could ever hope to satisfy her. When I got the chance, I would fuck her throat hard enough to make her gag on it. I pictured wrapping my fingers around her long neck and squeezing until she came, harder than ever.

She'd had a taste of that side of me when we were

nothing but juvenile delinquents. She liked it when I pinched her nipples and dragged my teeth over her slit. She cried out when I fucked her so hard I left bright red on her ass and thighs from our bodies slapping together.

Anna's quick, short gasps meant she was close now. I increased my own pace, wanting to come with her, even if she had no idea I was listening. She cried out, a wordless, blissful scream. That was enough to send me over the edge, spilling into my own hand with a hard, teeth bearing groan. My head was full of nothing but her.

There was no better buzz.

No better high.

Her breathing slowed as she came down, the little sounds hitched at first and then evening out.

If she knew the depths of my obsession, the things I wanted to do to her that were far from sweet, would she run for the hills?

I was going to make her mine again. That much I knew.

But just how much of me could my little siren handle?

7

ANNA

Mom and Dad sat at the head and foot of the table. Her in white linen. Him in his usual black suit. Like a pair of decorative salt and pepper shakers.

Across from me, Steve Draven took a long swallow from his glass of Malbec.

"So, how was your time in Africa?" he asked casually.

I put my fork down on my plate and dabbed the sides of my mouth with my napkin before peering over at him.

"Life-changing," I replied obsequiously, feeling the frost of my father's gaze on me from the seat at the head of the table. I quickly added more detail to my answer. "I'm so glad that I got to see more of the world, but I'm grateful to be home again."

"Hudson, you're very involved in charity, aren't you?" Steve asked. He was a state senator, and I doubted Dad had paid him much attention before. He probably only chose him because he was single, under forty, and attractive enough to look good cheering Dad on from behind a presidential podium.

The poor guy didn't seem to realize that his job here was to seduce me, not suck up to the governor.

Dad cocked his head toward Mom. "Michelle takes the lead on charity work in the family."

"Yes, you're probably too busy with work, Hudson," Steve replied. "I know getting the state budget approved was a nightmare."

Nobody saw me roll my eyes. If there was one thing that got Dad talking, it was budget cuts and whether or not he personally approved of them.

My mother was silently eating her swordfish steak, laughing and gesticulating at the appropriate times to cast my father and me in the most flattering light. His perfect performer.

It made me sick to think that I could be her in just a few years.

...if I let this happen.

Sorry, Rosie. I agreed to dress up, but that was where my promises ended.

I put my fork down and interrupted.

"You know, Steve, there's something you should know about Malawi."

"*Anna*," my father warned, but I could already feel it. The manic urge to scream rose in my throat. Or maybe that was just bile. And I was doing so well, too.

Doing everything just right, like I was taught.

There was only one problem, the Anna Vaughn that left this house six years ago and the one sitting here now, were not the same person anymore.

I couldn't do this.

Even if it meant kissing the security I desperately needed right now goodbye.

If he wanted me to dress a certain way and say certain things while I lived under his roof, then I could do that. I could play the part of the daughter of a future president at parties, when he had company, when I got my Starbucks in town. But I wasn't going to shape the rest of my life in his image. I'd rather choke to death on this stupidly delicious swordfish right here and now.

My pulse raced and my fingertips tingled. I folded them on the table in front of my plate and gave Steve my best smile.

"I never went, actually," I said sweetly. "That's just what we're telling people, for obvious reasons. The truth is, after high school, I became a waitress at what is essentially a high-end titty bar, had a string of bad boyfriends, then came back."

The sound of my mother's knife clanging against her plate rang through the silence. I looked up. My father cleared his throat, choking out an awkward laugh.

"So...you weren't building sustainable housing," Steve said, his words full of jest, like he was on my side and was as desperate as my parents were for me to say 'just kidding.'

"I'm afraid not. Didn't so much as pick up a hammer. I can't take credit for something I never did. If anything, I lost the last six years to bad decisions, and I'll never get them back. If you and I are going to get engaged, you should probably know all the details."

"Engaged?" Steven echoed. He sounded like he'd just swallowed a fly.

"That's why you were invited," I explained, while Dad's face got redder and redder. "Dad doesn't intend to do anything to help your political career. Not if you don't put a ring on it. But I'm guessing a smart guy like you realizes that I'm as much a liability as I am an asset."

I pushed my seat back and stood.

"*Anna. Sit down,*" my father hissed through clenched teeth. My mom looked like she was going to pass out. I clenched my fists, meeting my dad's eyes. He was braced in his seat, holding himself back.

"Please excuse me. I've lost my appetite."

I smiled politely at Steve and walked out of the dining room. My heart thrummed almost painfully. I didn't go upstairs. I went to the great room and slid the doors open to the patio. The brisk sea breeze filled my lungs, immediately invigorating me. I walked over the lawn, and down to the beach, ignoring my father's roaring voice fighting against the wind for me to return this instant.

He wouldn't chase me. He was too proud for that.

Instead, he'd have to figure out some way to convince Steve to keep his mouth shut. Maybe our dinner would be good for Steve's political career after all if the guy had enough balls to reach out and take the low hanging fruit I left for him.

I kicked my shoes off, leaving them behind me to sink my feet into the sand. The beach felt like freedom. The sound of the ocean and the clean, crisp air whispered that I was okay. I'd be okay. Even if dad kicked me out after what I'd just done.

Unconsciously, I wandered down the wide strip of beach, wrapping my arms around myself to stave off the chill of the wind and what waited for me when I eventually returned.

If Hudson Vaughn didn't already combust from the rage, I'd get an earful when I got back. I was ready this time.

I wasn't a kid anymore. He scared me, but I'd faced down scarier men now.

Plodding through the sand, I kicked my feet, wondering how I managed to live away from the ocean for so long. Staring at boats chugging along the Mississippi River just didn't do it for me. I walked down to the water line and let the water wash over my feet, sucking in a breath at the chill.

I ached to go further down the beach. Another half mile and I'd be at that invisible line between luxury and squalor. Right at the spot where Carter and I...

Before I knew it, I was already halfway there, walking until my feet were numb with cold in the water. Until I was *here*.

The houses up the sloping sand away to my right looked a little different. Larger than I remembered. Perhaps remodeled or rebuilt, but this was definitely the place.

I turned to the water, hating how my throat ached as I stared out over the silver capped waves and tried not to think of all the other times I'd come here. Tried not to think of *him*.

"Do you know how many times I came out here hoping I'd see you?"

I screamed, stumbling toward the water. He hurried over to me to help me up, and I swatted his reaching arms away, flailing to get my footing.

"What are you doing here?" I demanded.

He drew up to his full height, nothing more than a black silhouette against the blinding light of the setting sun, but I knew it was him. I knew his voice just as my body knew the pull of his nearness.

"I live here."

8

CARTER

Six Years Ago

"I think I should head home."

"Nah. You definitely shouldn't."

Anna lay next to me in the sand, her head resting on my arm. It was dead. Numb to the fucking bone. But I wouldn't move it if it meant ruining her comfort.

She raised her head and looked down at me coyly, the moon behind her lighting tiny strands of her brown hair to a silvery hue.

"What's that look for?" I asked, gripping her chin and leaning up to try to kiss it away. This was the thing about our little meetings on the beach, they always had to end.

How the best part of my day would always be capped off by the worst part was the most bullshit kind of Catch-22.

"Carter," Anna moaned and I resisted the urge to pull her against me again. "You know I can't stay too long. If I walk into the house tomorrow morning, my dad will literally kill me."

I shook my head. "He'd probably pay someone to do it," I corrected her. "Too afraid to get those girly hands dirty."

She chuckled, swatting me.

"I won't let him touch you," I said, earnest now, though I knew it wasn't violence she feared from him. It was being stuffed into the box he made for her. Forced to mold to the shape he predefined.

I pushed a lock of her hair back behind her ear. She laughed softly, lying back down on the blanket. Her hand came to my shoulder, just inside the neckline of my shirt so she could feel my skin against hers. She absently ran her fingers over the thick scar I had there.

"I don't want to go." She sighed, pushing her face against my shoulder.

"Then don't. Stay with me. We can get up early and you can be back home before—"

"That's not what I meant," she said, sighing. "I mean, it is, but I meant I don't want to go to stupid freaking Yale. I don't want to leave when summer ends."

My turn to sigh.

In truth, I didn't want to think about it. We still had some time until the end of the summer, a little more than a month, but every day, we were getting closer to the day when this would be over. When she would leave and forget I ever existed, too busy with white-collars, pretentious vocabularies, and fatter wallets.

Her dad wanted her to get into Yale on a law school track since she was born. She would be a legacy applicant which would strengthen her application. He was also one of the most powerful politicians in California which wouldn't look bad in that application either. I shrugged.

"Then don't. He can't make you go, can he?"

"He's more persuasive than you think," she said.

"You're eighteen this year. He can't make you do anything."

She fell silent and I wondered if I said the wrong thing. Maybe she just thought I wouldn't understand. I wanted to, but I knew there was a gap there. We were close to the same age and neither of us ever wanted to be at home but that was where our similarities stopped.

Her home was one of the palatial mansions that dotted the coastline in the ritzy neighborhood up the beach. Meanwhile, there had been three drug-related deaths in my neighborhood in the past two months. Her father was Hudson Vaughn, career politician who was running for governor this year. My dad was a violent drunk whose only qualification was his marriage certificate.

But when we were out here, that stuff didn't matter. We both got to forget what was waiting for us at home. We were just Carter and Anna.

"What do you want to do?" I asked her.

"Ideally, if I didn't have to care about what my dad wanted, I'd want to take some time off."

"Off of your busy schedule?" I asked, teasing.

"Just not start college immediately. Maybe take a year to be a little independent for once. Travel. After that, I'd want to go to school for photography."

"That sounds great. You're an incredible photographer. I still have that negative you gave me. Tucked away safe. You'd definitely get in if you applied to CalArts," I said.

"Thanks," she said, biting her lip in that way she knew

drove me mad. "I was thinking...I mean, I could look at schools here. Some of them have photography programs."

"Really?"

I tried to hide the rise of hope from burning through every inch of me. I could never tell her I wanted her to stay. She deserved greatness. She deserved far more than I could ever give her.

"Yeah. Really."

"That's not Yale."

"Yes, but I thought we'd already established that I don't want to go to Yale. I don't have to be what he wants me to be."

"You trying to convince me or yourself?"

"I want to stay here," she said, cutting her gaze my way, her green eyes blazing with certainty. Her throat bobbed. "I want to stay..."

She trailed off, as though there was something else she wasn't saying.

Don't say it. It's so stupid. Don't fucking say it.

"With me?" I asked, glad it was too dark for her to see me turn red.

I could practically hear her smiling.

"I mean, I guess it's nice that you'd be here too."

A giant stupid grin spread on my face, and I was glad she couldn't see that either. Grateful for the forgiving darkness of the beach at night.

I wasn't stupid though, and my smile quickly faltered, a leaden weight pressing on my chest.

She was the rich girl who had everything, including a dad who called the shots on every single breath she took.

"What's your old man gonna say about that?" I asked.

She sighed and I looked over at her. She was staring up

at the sky like it might give her some secret wisdom or maybe grant her a wish.

"I don't care," she said, rolling over and leaning on her elbows so she was looking down at me. "I have to stand up to him one day. Otherwise, it will never end."

"He won't like that," I said. I knew the Hudson Vaughn from the news, but she lived with the real life version. I was all for toppling the evil dictator, especially if it meant we could be together but I couldn't give her the things she had. Not right now. Not today. But with some time, some luck, and a hell of a lot of hard work...

"I don't care what he wants. *He* doesn't care what I want."

I clenched my jaw because no. Fuck that. It was bad enough that he got to call the shots all the time. I didn't want to lie here thinking about him. This was the only place he didn't matter and I wanted to keep it that way, even if one day, he might be the end of us.

"I do," I whispered. "I always will."

9

CARTER

I pressed the balls of my hands into my tired eyes. The pressure felt good. I leaned back in my seat, stretching my back out. A glance at the corner of my computer screen told me the time.

It was eight. What remained of daylight slanted through the floor-to-ceiling windows. I had about two more good hours in me.

That was how it was in the past; nose to the fucking grindstone day after day, but I wasn't fighting anyone anymore. I had more money than I knew how to spend. I didn't have to work like somebody was chasing me anymore, but the old work ethic had stuck. That was the thing about money though. I had had nothing, so I knew that it wasn't permanent. If I could make it, I could lose it too.

I looked over at the photograph on the wall directly across from my desk. Of the beach at night. Grayish white clouds crouched in the navy stillness, but the moon shone brightly through them, illuminating them from within. The silvery light reflected off the water.

The image was captured at exactly the right moment to catch both the waves washing up on the shore and rolling down. Every other wall was bare, no paintings, art, nothing. I wasn't a sentimental guy, but that was just because I never had anything worth keeping until Anna gave me the negative of that photograph. It was a miracle that by the time I had the money to have it properly developed and framed, it wasn't worn off from my constant need to pull it out and stare at it through lamplight.

Why don't you just use a digital camera like a normal person, I had asked her once. The reason was that some people with the most cutting-edge digital cameras couldn't take pictures as good as she took with 20th-century technology. I wondered if she still felt the same way. She was talented.

I was biased, but I was also right.

That picture was the first thing I saw whenever I looked up from my computer. It was impossible to look at it without thinking of her.

A punishment, but also a snapshot of some of the most peaceful nights of my life.

Seeing it day in and day out motivated me like nothing else could.

God, I needed to see the beach tonight. Not just the photo on my wall, or in my mind. I needed to feel the sand. Smell the sea. Anything to bring me the calm I would need to stop myself from getting on the highway, driving to St. Louis and killing this *Josh* asshole without even a lick of real evidence that he was the one who hurt her or put that bulletin out on the dark web.

The massive villa was an investment property but it was also a 3.9 million dollar fuck you to everyone who lived on this end of the beach.

When I was younger, guys like me would get the cops called on them if we hung out within five miles of here. Now, I could take a shit out there if I wanted and nobody could say a word. I just wanted to be near the water. And this was the perfect spot.

Just a little ways past the halfway point, tipping toward the wealthy end. This was where I met her so many times I lost count.

I parked the Ducati and entered the villa, discarding my jacket on the stool in the kitchen knowing it would be hung on a mahogany hanger in the closet before I woke up tomorrow morning. The staff here came and went like ghosts.

That was our beach out there; me and Anna. The best nights of my life were spent twenty yards from the back door. And now a piece of that was mine forever.

The place was way too big for me. I could easily fit a family of seven or eight in the house if I wanted to. Kids had never crossed my mind because typically, they came with a wife, something I'd resigned myself to never having. There was no woman I wanted enough to share my last name with.

To raise children with.

There *was* one once, but I'd gone and ruined that, just like I'd ruined so many things before it.

I wasn't cut out to be a husband. Not anymore. Not after everything I'd done. What I'd become in her absence.

My footsteps echoed through the empty entrance hall as I made my way to the living room. I kicked off my boots and peeled off my socks, opening the door to the verandah that wrapped around the entire back of the house. The smell of diffused sandalwood giving way to ocean brine and cold sand.

Enough of the homes in the neighborhood, mine included, were second or third homes, so the beach was never crowded, even during the day. Not like the northside beaches. With syringes and trash poking out of the sand.

I walked out onto the beach, the sea air refreshing me from the inside out. I stopped just outside my property line, stuck still by the silhouette of a woman interrupting the view.

The immediate association I had made me shake my head. I didn't bother fighting the feeling clawing its way through me as memory after memory assaulted me.

I almost forgot what it was like, feeling something other than numbness and rage.

I remembered lying on the sand with her, walking out on the pier and dangling our legs over the side. The sound of her laugh. The feel of her. I wouldn't trade that summer for all the money in the world.

Except you did exactly that, you ruinous bastard.

Squinting through the darkness, I moved closer, ready to give a gruff nod to whoever it was as I passed them for my usual walk down the shoreline.

My jaw went slack. Even in the dark, even this far away, I knew the way she moved.

Anna shifted her weight onto one foot, pulling her arms tighter around herself with a shiver as a cool wind swept up the shore.

Her skirt billowed. She had to hold her hand to her face against the breeze to stop her hair battering it. It wasn't all that dark, but she hadn't noticed me yet. Her head tilted down to the sand as she turned away from the wind with a scowl on her face. Tension across her shoulders.

It reminded me...

It reminded me of so many other nights where she'd walk down this beach looking exactly like she did now, only younger. With less curves to her body. With shadows carved not quite so deeply beneath her eyes.

The sound of crashing waves disguised the sounds of my approach. I was close enough to kiss her neck before I finally spoke.

"Do you know how many times I came out here hoping I'd see you?"

Anna shrieked, jumping back at least a foot, shoving at my reaching hands as she struggled to regain her footing with a glare.

She wore a conservative blue silk dress, perfectly tailored to her shape but revealing little of her skin. The neckline wasn't even low enough to show her collarbone, while the skirt hung just below her knees. She'd swept her hair up into an elegant updo, looking every inch the perfect governor's daughter.

I wanted to rip that fucking dress in half.

Anna collected herself, straightening her shoulders.

"What are you doing here?" she asked. It sounded more like an accusation than a question.

I peered down the beach, the way she would've had to come and frowned when I didn't see any trace of life. Where were my men?

She shouldn't have been out here alone, and by her lack of pockets or purse, she'd taken off without even her phone to call for help.

Anna, Anna, Anna.

What was I going to do with her?

I made a mental note to call Paulson and remind him his neck only stayed unbroken because he was good at his job. Any more slips like this one and I'd assume his skull didn't need to be connected to his spine anymore.

"I live here," I told her.

I gestured to the villa behind me and her lips formed a perfect O of surprise.

"That's yours," she repeated, then shook her head with a scoff. "Of course it is. Look, Carter, I just came here to think. Whatever you want from me, I'm not in the mood."

"Too bad," I said, my voice dropping an octave all on its own. "You owe me answers, Anna."

"I told you where I went," she said immediately. "Malawi. I would have called, except you made it pretty clear that you didn't want to speak to me again."

I cringed inwardly. If I could wipe away everything I said when we broke up, I would do it. I would have given up my whole fortune, my home, every goddamn thing I owned to erase that day.

But I had bigger concerns. I wanted to confirm, once and for all, that it was Josh who left those bruises on her.

"I'm more interested in learning who hurt you."

She scoffed again, folding her arms across her chest. "Why do you care?"

My eyes narrowed. Things between us ended badly, but how could she pretend like what we shared would ever be really gone? I was never going to stop wanting her. *Never.*

"You know why," I said in a low voice.

She looked at me skeptically, her perfect pink lips pursed, brow raised.

94

I let her see it.

See me.

The truth.

She *did* know why. She just needed reminding.

The tension in her forehead went slack as she read something in my quiet stare, her lips parting in a way that made my cock thicken in my slacks.

"Carter, I—"

I curled my hand around the back of her neck, pulling her to me roughly to crush my mouth against hers.

10

ANNA

Kissing Carter Cole, time stopped existing. The world outside of this patch of sand melted away.

The sweet, eager kisses from my memories melded with the expert, relentless way he kissed now. Every shift of his lips and flick of his tongue lit me on fire. Burning away the memories of any man who touched me in his absence. Carter was everywhere. And I was powerless to escape him.

He kissed me greedily, like he was touch-starved and had been waiting for this moment just as long as I had. It was a beautiful, dangerous lie, but one I wanted so badly to believe.

One of his hands tangled in my hair, tugging at the pins holding my updo in place. The other hand grabbed me by the waist and pulled me hard against him, making me arch into the hollows between our bodies until I was reminded of how fucking perfectly we fit together.

My nipples peaked, rubbing deliciously against his hard chest. Fuck, those shirtless pictures didn't do the reality justice. He felt as strong and solid as the earth itself.

His teeth skimmed my bottom lip and I moaned, unconsciously encouraging him as he bit the soft flesh until I gasped and his grip on me tightened tenfold.

I ran my hands up his arms, feeling the divots of the muscles under the fabric of his shirt. My fingers mapped him, finding the soft parts that had hardened, the lines of his back, the softness of his hair. Every change to him felt right, like he had chiseled away until he became the truest version of himself.

No.

No.

I pulled away and met his icy blue eyes. Suddenly, I was pulled right back to my senior year. Looking into the same eyes on the same beach.

The cold reality crashed down on me and my stomach twisted.

I was kissing the man who broke my heart. Who never apologized or explained any of the cruel things he said. I'd seen the pictures, seen him move from woman to woman.

No matter how much I wanted him to be—this wasn't the same Carter I fell in love with.

Why should I expect him to treat me any differently than he did those pretty models always on his arm?

Our bodies still worked together, but our hearts didn't. They hadn't since the night he tore mine from my chest and left it to dry out in the sand.

Fuck, I should have learned by now.

"We're not doing this," I forced out, pulling from his grasp to stumble back a step.

His eyes narrowed. "Don't, Anna. Don't fucking pull away right when I have you again."

"You don't have me." The words tasted like lies on my tongue. "I don't belong to you."

Carter grabbed my face in his hands, pulling me roughly against him. "Yes, you do. You're fucking *mine*."

He forced his lips against mine again, harsh and unforgiving. Like he was marking me. Claiming me.

My fingers clawed at him, digging into his skin, but my lips parted easily for him. I kissed him back even as I fought him off.

I felt something hot on my fingers, and looked down with horror to see bright red on Carter's neck. Somehow, I'd broken through the skin there.

I'm sorry.

The words were ghosts on my lips. But before I could release them, Carter smiled feral at me. Like he was pleased that I hurt him.

"Go on, my little siren," he said roughly. "I can take it. And so can you."

With that, he shoved me to the ground. The sand embraced the weight of our bodies, Carter heavy on top of me. He shoved his thigh between my legs, rubbing the hard muscle against my pussy. The friction was perfect, and I couldn't hold back my moan.

As he pushed against me, I gasped, feeling the proof of my arousal damp in my panties and knowing any second now he would feel it, too.

I was soaked for him and I hated myself for it.

Hated him.

Wanted him even in my hatred.

I shifted my hips, rubbing myself shamelessly against him.

He used me first, the angry thought pushed through my Carter drugged thoughts.

My turn.

He pulled back, putting his weight on his arms so he could watch me grind against him. It felt so pathetic and childish, chasing my pleasure like this. But Carter's blue eyes blazed as he watched me, meeting every roll of my hip with the rocking of his thigh against my pussy.

My entire body felt hot and needy, like molten metal was creeping through my veins. This beach had some power over us. It always had. Made us elemental, more animal than human.

Carter grabbed at the fabric covering me.

"I hate this fucking dress," he growled.

"So do I," I blurted on a breath before I even made the conscious decision to reply.

With a growl, Carter grabbed the fabric at my neck and ripped it roughly in two. The silk gave way under the force, splitting down the middle, each fine thread snapping against my skin until it fell to either side of me in tatters. My skin pebbled in the cool air, only my ivory lace bra and panties left to cover me from the chill.

Carter licked his lips while he looked down at me. "Fuck. Better than I remembered."

He dragged his fingers from my neck, down over my breastbone to circle my breasts. My nipples tightened so quickly, it almost hurt. Even the lightest touch was enough to make my body desperate for him. Carter shoved down the cups of my bra, lifting my breasts up. He dragged his teeth over one tight nipple, then bit down so hard that I screamed.

I was going to let him take whatever he wanted from

me. Because I knew Carter always gave in equal measure and I needed that right now. I needed a release more than my fingers could provide.

He sucked my other nipple into his mouth, lavishing it with his hot tongue as his other hand traveled low, searing a path down my belly to the top of my panties.

Fuck.

I squirmed beneath him, beside myself with need.

So ready to be his perfect little whore.

Who's my perfect little whore? Josh's words rang in my ears, and I fought to shove them away.

If only he could see me now. Every man who leered at me at the Butterfly Room. Every man he accused me of cheating on him with when I was just a few minutes behind schedule getting home.

And here I was, proving him right. Just letting Carter waltz back into my life and take what he wanted, without so much as an apology. Opening my legs for a man who hurt me worse than Josh ever could've.

I couldn't let this happen.

"Carter," I said weakly as he found my neck with his lips, kissing a hot path back to my mouth.

"Mmm?"

"S-stop. I can't."

His scent filled me. Different than I remembered but somehow still the same. Warm wood, amber, and sea salt. I wanted to bottle it and keep it for the rest of my miserable life as a trophy wife. To remind me what this felt like. What *he* felt like when he wasn't taking a sledgehammer to my heart.

"Carter, please."

He kissed the underside of my jaw, my cheek. I turned

away from him before he could reach my lips and felt him stiffen. Pull back.

"Why can't you?" His voice sounded rough, like he had tapped into some animal side, barely human enough to speak.

My lips parted, but I had no argument for him. Suddenly every reason seemed flimsy. His body over mine just felt so *right*.

And I knew I was weak. Too weak to say no because I'd imagined this moment a thousand times and...

"If you want me to stop, tell me," he said in a husky whisper, sounding almost pained.

I had no words.

I didn't want him to stop.

He lowered his face closer to mine, until our breaths mingled, until our lips just barely brushed. The anticipation made my body tense and shudder. My heart ached and hummed wildly as he hovered there, waiting.

"Last chance," he spoke against my mouth.

I drew in a stuttered breath, but no refusal passed my lips. He swallowed my exhale with a swift, hard kiss and shoved my panties down my thighs, drawing a broken whine from my chest.

He dragged his fingers along my slit, groaning into my mouth as he felt how wet I was.

"So goddamn soaked for me. Your body knows what you really want, Anna."

Carter pressed just the tips of two fingers inside me. It was barely enough to stretch me, but my entire body heated at the intrusion.

I moved my hips for him, trying to pull him in deeper.

"That's right," Carter said roughly. "Show me how

much you want this. Fuck yourself on my hand, Anna. Take what you want. Use me. Use me up until there's nothing left."

So I did. My shame drifted away as I rolled my hips against his fingers. All too soon, I'd stretched too much and I needed more. I whimpered, and like he could read my mind, Carter added another finger. The pressure hurt, but my inner walls gripped his digits tightly, like my body couldn't bear for him to leave.

"Look at you," Carter whispered. "You look so fucking perfect stretched around my fingers."

I looked down too, the image of his fingers disappearing into my slick lips bringing me even closer to the edge. The friction just felt too goddamn good. I clenched around him and electricity gathered in my core. He pressed the heel of his palm against the apex of my pussy, encouraging me to grind against it.

I choked on a cry and squeezed my eyes shut right before I came.

Except Carter pulled his fingers away.

I gasped and he just shook his head.

"I'll let you come, little siren," he murmured. "All you have to do is tell me who hurt you."

My body stiffened, humiliation crashing over me. I couldn't tell him that it was Josh, my ex, who'd left those bruises. A man I'd been stupid enough to trust.

"Nobody," I said. "Nobody hurt me."

Carter shook his head. "You're lying. That's too bad."

Then he crushed his lips to mine, kissing me so fiercely that any thought of Josh vanished. It was just Carter, his presence overwhelming me. His hands were everywhere, his lips dragging along the line of my neck. He moved down my body, suckling at the line of my collarbone while I trembled under him.

His tongue moved along the edge of each breast, then he kissed around each nipple. My heart thudded so hard, he must be able to feel it against his lips. But even though my nipples were diamond hard, he wouldn't touch them, neglecting the place I wanted his mouth most.

"Carter," I whimpered. "Please."

"What do you want?" he asked, the sound vibrating against my skin.

"You know." It was all I could choke out, he'd scrambled my mind so thoroughly.

"Use your words."

Use my words? I could barely remember my own name at this point. Pathetically, I grabbed his head and moved it to my nipples.

"Just this once," he said with a sigh.

He closed his lips around one nipple, sucking gently. Electricity pulsed through me and I buried my fingers in his hair, pressing him closer. It just felt so goddamn good.

Whatever Carter had been doing with all those girls the past six years, it had turned him into a fucking sex god.

His mouth moved lower, pressing open-mouthed kisses along my belly until he was positioned between my thighs. With his eyes fixed on my pussy, he used his fingers to spread apart my lower lips.

"Still perfect," he said, then dragged his tongue from my entrance to my clit. I gasped and my thighs tightened around his head.

Every stroke of Carter's tongue had me trembling, my orgasm building in me with a pounding force. I lay balanced on a sharp edge, and I didn't care if there was anything to catch me when I fell.

Let me break on the rocks if it'll feel this good.

Then, right before I came, Carter pulled his mouth away. My orgasm ebbed immediately, throbbing in my clit, and I cried out in frustration.

This motherfucker.

He knew exactly how close I was. How could he read my body so well, after all this time? I pulled hard at his hair, trying to get him back where I wanted him. He just shook his head.

"Are you ready to tell me who hurt you?" he asked, cocking a brow.

"Nobody," I repeated stubbornly.

"We both know that's not true, Anna."

Tears pricked at my eyes, threatening to spill. How dare he bring me back to that pain, just when I was feeling so good? He didn't have the right. Not when he broke up with me, not when he spent years with no idea what was happening in my life.

"You haven't earned the truth."

I expected Carter's face to fall. I wanted my words to hurt him, too. Instead, he just grinned wickedly.

"I will."

He buried his face in my pussy and fucking *devoured* me. His nose rubbed up against my clit, his tongue burying itself in my entrance. Two fingers shoved inside me, and my inner walls squeezed desperately at them.

My entire body felt like melted gold. Dripping and bleeding into the sand beneath me, scorching anybody who dared touch me. Like I was invincible as long as Carter kept his mouth and hands on me.

The cliff of my orgasm loomed in front of me. It was even steeper, thanks to the two times Carter had brought me to the edge already. I was so fucking close, but I knew he would pull away if I didn't give him what he wanted.

And I needed it.

I couldn't be deprived again.

I knew I'd regret it later, but all I could think about was finally making that fall.

"It was my ex," I breathed. "Josh. He gave me the bruises."

Carter only stopped for a moment, gazing up at me, his eyes full of cold blue fire.

"Good girl."

He closed his lips around my clit and sucked, reigniting my orgasm. That gentle pressure built me up so quickly, I didn't even realize I was falling until I screamed out some unintelligible noise. I saw fireworks as I came fast and hard against his mouth.

Liquid streamed from me, but Carter never stopped lapping it up. He groaned at the taste of it, the vibration of it only extending my orgasm. I had no idea how long I spent coming. The whole world went fuzzy, the line between pleasure and painful reality obliterated.

Eventually, Carter released my clit and pulled back to kneel.

All I could do was lie there like a broken doll. I was boneless, and my muscles had completely stopped working. My chest heaved as I tried to find oxygen. It was like my orgasm had broken the way my body worked.

I barely had the strength to stay awake, let alone make it home. I could see his blurry form at the edge of my vision, pawing at the massive erection in his slacks with a knot between his brows and a tense jaw.

Falling onto his back next to me, he hauled me into his chest and the feeling was so vividly familiar—so vividly comforting, that I didn't fight him.

His fingers played with the tips of my hair. Almost all of my elaborate updo had come undone, sand mixed in with my tangles.

I breathed in the scent of him. The fabric of his shirt was soft against my cheek. Whatever we just shared, it was nothing like the way Carter and I came together six years ago. We were both so young and inexperienced then, completely different from the broken, corrupted versions of us that existed now.

Now, when our bodies touched, our broken places pressed into each other and made us bleed. We hurt each other, and it only made us crave each other more.

And Carter took advantage of that.

I told him about Josh.

Carter manipulated me into handing over my most shameful secret. He knew exactly what buttons to press to make me open up to him. I didn't know who I hated more just now—Carter for tricking me, or myself for giving him the chance to get close again.

I shoved away from him, forcing myself to my feet.

"Where are you going?" he asked sleepily.

"Home," I spat.

"That's not your home and you know it," he called after me, the single word a well-placed blade twisting in my stomach.

I stormed back to the house, clutching the edges of my ruined dress around me and praying nobody saw.

11

ANNA

"I'll probably be here for a while, so you don't need to wait for me."

I tried to meet David's eyes in the rearview mirror. It was hard to do through his dark sunglasses.

"Let me know when you're finished and I'll bring the car around."

I bit my lip and nodded, knowing I wasn't going to win this fight. I thanked David and got out in front of The Drift, Mrs. Wu's art gallery.

Olivia Wu was my art teacher back in high school. She was the first person to notice my interest in photography. The one who showed me work by famous photographers and who taught me how to use a dark room. I used to spend all my free periods in her art room, browsing her black and white photography books and asking her questions about lenses.

She retired from teaching a few years ago and bought a local gallery when it became vacant. I looked it up online, browsing through all the pieces she'd chosen. As the curator, she seemed to favor modern artists, but something in the pieces she showcased had the same feel to some of my work. Evoked similar emotions. At least, I hoped they did.

I planned on dropping a huge check purchasing some art pieces here. I wanted Mrs. Wu to get the commission, and it had the added bonus of probably pissing off my father. He clearly intended me to use my new credit card for clothes, manicures, and lunches with my society friends. A bill for tens of thousands spent at The Drift would probably make his shriveled little heart explode.

Whatever. After his very obvious setup for me with the state senator, he deserved it.

He was barely speaking to me, which was a new but very welcome punishment. I knew it wouldn't last, but I intended to enjoy every second he wasn't shouting at me.

I'd visited The Drift a few times before, back when it still had the old owners. Mrs. Wu had obviously done a lot of renovating when she took over, making the space her own. She'd changed the walls from a distracting teal green to a pale charcoal color, which let the pieces stand out. Her expertly placed lighting drew the eyes to each individual photo, which meant that the smaller, more subtle pieces weren't overwhelmed by the bigger, flashier ones. Each painting or photograph existed in its own, perfect little bubble.

An assistant greeted me at the door, but I told him I would rather browse alone, and he nodded his understanding before backing off.

Mrs. Wu chose an eclectic display that somehow seemed to fit together. There were landscapes with strange, ghostlike shapes hidden in them, next to close-up portraits where the person's face was lit like its own landscape in a way.

I was lost in the photos when I felt a tap on my shoulder. I spun to see Mrs. Wu, wearing funky red glasses and a cool black jumpsuit. She had always seemed like such a grown-up when I was in school, but now I saw that she was only in her early 40s.

"Anna Vaughn!" she said warmly. "I didn't know you were back in town."

"It's good to see you, Mrs. Wu," I said.

She laughed aloud. "Please, call me Olivia. You're an adult now."

"I guess so, even if I don't always feel like one."

"Here's the secret," she said, looking comically around. "You never will. But don't worry, you'll get used to it."

I laughed, then gestured to the space around me. "The gallery is incredible. I love the work you curated here."

Olivia beamed at me. "I'm glad you think so. I try to feature local artists whenever I can. You know, I was just about to make a cup of tea if you want to join me? I'd love to catch up."

I could see in her eyes it was a genuine statement. She was always that way. *Caring.* Genuinely caring about anything and everything in her students' lives and the things they said or didn't say.

I nodded. I was hoping I'd run into her, but this was even better.

"I'd like that."

Her office was a medium-sized room off the gallery's reception. A velvet couch huddled against one wall with a structural coffee table in front of it. The desk was lush oak and art pieces tastefully garnished the walls of the room.

She left for a few minutes, then returned with a classic ceramic teapot. She poured me a cup, which smelled amazing, like orange peels and cinnamon.

"So!" Olivia said cheerfully. "What have you been up to since graduation?"

The familiar heaviness set over me. The lie about building houses haunting me again and again. I had repeated it to so many people, but for some reason it felt wrong to tell my old teacher. Like it was a bigger betrayal of my younger self.

"Oh, I've been doing some traveling," I told her. "Working in St. Louis for a while."

Olivia's eyes scanned my face, like she was searching for something. She must have realized that I don't want to talk about my past, since she politely changed the subject.

"I've been in the gallery for three years now," she said. "I love the work, and I get to guide artists who are more advanced in their careers. But I'll be honest, I miss working with students. Being a mentor was so rewarding."

"Even when you're mentoring a bunch of spoiled kids with their parents' credit cards?"

"Even then. I know there are a few who pursued art as a career. I'd love to see what kind of work they're doing now. I'd love to see your photography, for example. I remember how committed you were. There were a few shots I can still see vividly in my memory. You had that natural eye for it. I always wondered if one day I'd see your portfolio pass my desk."

I felt my cheeks heat with embarrassment. "I can't believe people still remember how into photography I was. Lots of kids had cool hobbies back then."

"But not all of those students had real talent."

Olivia gave me a piercing look over the edge of her teacup. "Trust me. I know the difference."

"I'm not sure how much I did with my talent," I said, glancing down. "I mean, I kept taking photos, but they were just of the people in my life mostly."

"Don't underestimate yourself, Anna. Some of the best art is focused on our personal lives. Did you keep working with film?"

"Whenever I could. I couldn't always—"

I stopped myself before I could tell her I couldn't always afford film. It seemed presumptuous, somehow, to talk about that time now that I had access to unlimited cash.

Olivia sipped her tea and gazed at me thoughtfully. "I'd love to see them, if you ever have the time to bring them by."

"Oh, I don't know, I really don't think they're—"

"Don't worry about what's good. I'm the gallerist— that's my job. Satisfy my curiosity. I'd really love to see what you've made and I think you owe me after promising to keep in touch and then vanishing from the face of the earth for—what is it—six years?"

I laughed hollowly, knowing I couldn't say no.

I knew she wasn't just being nice. She really did want to see my work, no matter if it was shit or not. She'd be honest with me, tell me where I might've gone wrong, where I could improve. She'd praise the things I got right.

I missed that kind of constructive feedback. Didn't realize I was craving it.

"Well, when you guilt trip me like that..." I trailed off.

She smiled coyly. "Fabulous. Shall we make a date then? Say early next week?"

I KNEW IF I THOUGHT ABOUT IT TOO MUCH, I'D CHICKEN OUT. So I went straight home and put every reel of film I'd collected over six years into a grocery bag, then had David drive me to a photoshop to get it all digitized. When I pulled out Dad's credit card to pay extra for the rush job, I didn't feel a moment of guilt.

After I made an appearance at dinner for Mom's sake, I hurried up to my room to review the photos. I clicked through the thousands of photos, giving myself just a few seconds to decide what I was interested in looking at again. I ended up with about four hundred that I didn't hate on sight.

Once I really took the time to look at them, I found myself entranced. I'd captured every woman who worked with me at the Butterfly Room, women who knew me—the real me—better than almost anyone here at home.

There was Vanessa, the 30-year-old single mom who taught me that men tipped more when you wore red lipstick. She loved the camera, and I'd taken dozens of photos of her. There she was painstakingly applying liquid eyeliner, putting Band-Aids on the blisters she got from her six inch heels, video calling her sons to sing them a good-night song.

Then there was Zara, the girl who started on the same day as me. I'd never met anyone who was so tough and vulnerable at the same time. She'd curse out any customer who touched her without permission, and stay stone-faced when we were overwhelmed. But she cried whenever she heard a sappy love song.

Here she was pouring out a line of shots, hiking up her cocktail dress, pulling out twenty dollar bills she stuffed in her bra.

But some of my favorite photos included me. Not me alone, but me slotted into a group shot with my coworkers. There I was, snapping a photo of eight of us just before service, primping in the mirror behind the bar. Or when I posed with Zara, both of us pretending to be Jessica Rabbit.

Maybe that was what made lying about where I'd been so horrible. It was like I denied these women, this life I'd built, every time I pretended to be some house-building do-gooder. Because when I looked back at my time in the Butterfly Room, I didn't feel embarrassed. I felt proud of how hard I worked, and nostalgic for a time when at the end of the day, it felt like I really did something.

I whittled the whole thing down to fifty pictures. My favorite ones implied a mystery or a bigger story, feeling like I captured a moment of a life so complex, you have to imagine the rest of it.

These were women that the rich people in this town would write off immediately, but in these photos, they were powerful and captivating.

Maybe my photos should be seen after all.

12

CARTER

The sand gave way under my feet as I went into my final sprint. I loved the brutality of running on the beach. It looked so serene, but it felt like fucking hell, my muscles straining to balance my weight as the ground shifted underneath me. Sweat streamed down my face even though the wind was cool. Every cell in my body felt ready to combust.

I deserved that pain.

Finally, my watch beeped, marking that my last interval was over. I hunched over, hands on my knees while I breathed in knife-sharp bursts.

In business, I couldn't afford to let guilt make me soft. So I pushed the feelings down, only letting them out with punishing daily workouts.

I made this one especially shitty after what I did to Anna.

I didn't regret using her desire against her. I needed confirmation that Josh was the one who hurt her before I could put my plans in motion.

That didn't make the self-loathing I saw on Anna's face any easier to live with.

She obviously blamed herself for those bruises. I saw it on her face whenever I asked her for a name. Nothing that he'd done to her was her fault, she still felt responsible for it. It only made my revenge fantasies toward Josh get bloodier.

One way or another, I'd make him pay.

The waves crashed against the shore in thick, foamy swaths. There must have been a storm off the coast to make the water so choppy. Just two nights ago, it was calm.

The night I finally tasted Anna again. I hadn't wanted to kiss a woman in six years but three minutes with her on the beach and I couldn't get enough of the feel of her mouth on mine.

Fuck, it'd been years since I lost myself in a woman like that. Sure, I liked my partners getting off, but Anna was different. She was the only one whose pleasure I cared about more than my own. I could have stayed between her thighs, tasting her for fucking days.

It made me think about our first time together on the beach. I was so careful back then. Anna was still a virgin, and I was terrified of hurting her. It was a miracle I didn't spill inside her immediately once I finally felt her tight little pussy squeeze around me. I barely survived a few minutes.

I was anything but careful the other night. Anna made me fucking feral, and I didn't hold back for a second once I got her underneath me. I got everything I wanted—her fucking abuser's name, and her sweet cries as she came all over my face.

My phone dinged, and against all reason, I hoped that it was Anna texting me. Maybe she could sense I was thinking about her. I shoved down my disappointment when it was just my PI, Paulson. I quickly dialed his number, and he picked up on the first ring.

"Hey, boss," Paulson said. He sounded tired. Good. He should have been up all night working after his little slip two nights ago.

"What do you have for me?" I asked impatiently.

"Josh Porter's full biography. I've already emailed it, but I'll give you the highlights. Can't hold down a relationship, can't hold down a job. Parents are loaded, some bigshot corporate lawyers in St. Louis. They've been bankrolling the kid for years now. He should've been in jail with all the women he hit, but they've got connections. They kept him free."

I clenched my jaw so hard that I could practically hear my molars crack. He was the worst kind of scum, the kind who thinks they're better than anyone thanks to their birthright, even if they're so pathetic, they have to prove their power by hitting a woman.

"Where is he?" I growled.

"Working on it," Paulson said. "He left his apartment when Anna snuck out of it. I've got a guy surveilling it, but I doubt he goes back. I think he caught our scent while we were trying to sniff him out and he's running scared. He's been hopping from cheap motel to cheap motel, but we haven't been fast enough to catch him before he moves on. I don't think he knows where Anna is now, since the motels he's staying at are scattered all over the place with the closest one still a state over."

It was wishful thinking and I knew it. Even if Josh was stupid enough not to be able to find her by now, I knew the dark web scum he was probably in contact with would've figured it out and likely filled him in.

No. He was just biding his time. But for what?

"Keep your man there, and three guards on Anna at all times. Other than that, I want all your resources on finding Josh. I don't care what it costs, drop all your other cases and get it done," I hissed.

"Right. You got it, boss," Paulson said, wisely hanging up.

He knew now would be a dangerous time to piss me off.

There was a special place in hell for men cowardly enough to hit their girlfriends. And when I finally got my hands on Josh Porter, I was going to send him there.

13

ANNA

"These are exceptional," Olivia said, gazing at the last of my photo prints.

I flushed with pride. "You really think so?"

"Absolutely. You have the makings of a real collection here, Anna."

I bit my lip, so excited that I practically laughed out loud. My hunch was right—my photos were more than just candids of my friends. They were proof that I really did have talent. I'd brought her a portfolio of my favorite photos and didn't tell her any details about the background.

"There's a real sense of place in here, even without knowing where they come from. Where were these taken, by the way?" she asked.

"The Butterfly Room. It's a St. Louis cocktail bar that's usually full of wealthy businessmen. That's why the women are all dressed in so little. For tips." I took a deep breath, then told her the truth. "That's where I've been. I worked there for a few years."

Olivia's brows rose, and I could tell she was surprised.

"Weren't you in college? You were on that track in high school."

I looked away. "I never ended up going. My plans changed, I guess."

Olivia laughed. "Plans will do that, won't they?"

There was no judgment or contempt in her expression. My shoulders relaxed and relief washed over me. She was the first person from my old life who I *chose* to tell the truth, and it felt so good. I hadn't even realized how much the lying weighed on me.

"Could you do me a favor?" I asked. "If anyone asks, could you not mention my job? My dad has this whole story he's been telling people, and I don't want to cause trouble."

"Of course," Olivia said. "It's none of their business. But your background makes these photos even more interesting, Anna. The governor's daughter, leaving her world of privilege to enter the serving class. Not a lot of people with your upbringing would be open to that."

"It's not like I'm better than these women," I said defiantly.

Olivia raised her hands. "Never said you were. In fact, these pictures position them as your equals. It would make people like your father very uncomfortable, in the way that all good art does."

"So you really think I should try and exhibit?" I asked, excited.

"I do. I'd offer to host it here, but, well, I doubt my clients in town would appreciate it. I'm still new to owning this place, and I couldn't afford to offend people."

"I understand," I said. I knew the way rich people in this town held grudges better than anyone.

"But there is someone I know who could maybe help

you." Olivia grabbed a sheet of paper and scribbled down a phone number. "His name is Jaden Austen. I showed some of his work last year. I don't know him very well, but he has a good eye and last I heard he was looking to take on someone to mentor. Would you be interested in meeting him?"

"Of course!" I said immediately. If I wanted to break into this world, I'd need all the help I could get.

Olivia reached over and squeezed my hand. "I think you should be really proud of these."

The comment should have made me happy, but instead, I felt a prick of pain. I should be hearing those words from my parents, but that would never happen. The only version of me they wanted was the fake one, the one made up entirely of their lies. I was never going to hear Dad say he was proud of me.

No. I refused to let Hudson Vaughn bring me down. Because the truth was, even if I didn't always believe in myself, I did believe in my photos. That was enough.

"Thank you," I told Olivia. "I am proud of them."

MY MEETING WITH OLIVIA LEFT ME FEELING INSPIRED. I YEARNED to get my camera out and play with it, but I'd run out of film a while ago. I looked up the closest photo shop in the area, which was just a ten minute walk away.

It took me almost that long to convince David not to come with me.

"It's just a short walk," I pleaded. "I'll be there and back before you know it. You can still drive me home."

"Your father wants me to stay with you," he said stubbornly.

I sighed. "Please, David. I appreciate you driving me around, but I'm an adult. I just need a break from having my babysitter follow me everywhere."

David's lips twisted as he thought it through. Eventually, he sighed. "Fine. But if you're not back in thirty minutes, I'm coming for you."

The walk to the film store brought me through streets of old warehouses, with crumbling bricks and broken windows. There was an eerie kind of beauty to them. So many places like this were modernized and transformed into breweries or wedding venues. What happened to the places which were truly abandoned?

It was the wisp of an idea that had me aching to get my camera out.

The film store was small, mostly selling vintage cameras and outdated equipment. At least they had more than enough film in stock. I bought a dozen rolls and loaded up the camera in my backpack.

Hurrying back to the warehouses, I got out my camera and checked my watch. I had at least fifteen minutes before David freaked out. More than enough time to get back to those warehouses.

The overgrown bushes and empty sidewalks made it clear that nobody came here anymore. Not even any broken glass or graffiti to suggest teens explored at night.

I started with a few sample shots, playing around with framing. I moved close to the buildings, shooting upward to emphasize their size. Just after I took a round of photos, I felt a strange prickling on the back of my neck.

Someone was watching me.

Pretending to check my focus, I turned around and checked out the sidewalk from where I'd come.

A group of three men were walking directly toward me. They wore baseball caps that left their faces in shadow. Instinct told me these weren't just casual pedestrians. They wanted something from me.

I wasn't going to wait around to find out what.

My heartbeat pounded in my ears while I headed back to the sidewalk. I forced myself not to run. They'd just chase me, and I'd escalate things quicker than I had to.

I caught a flash of movement in my peripheral vision. A guy in a blue hat had run to the opposite side of the street, and was walking just ahead of me. It was like they were trying to herd me somewhere. Behind me, I heard rapid footsteps. The other two following me were moving faster.

Oh my god.

The one on the left, he looked the right height. The right build. It couldn't have been...

He tipped his head up and I breathed a sigh of relief to see that it wasn't Josh, but the look on his face—the piercing way he was looking at me—like predator watching prey told me Josh or not, these men weren't here by accident.

Fuck, I had no choice. I broke into a run, adrenaline pumping through me, powering my muscles to spring as fast as I could.

It wasn't enough.

The guy in the blue hat crossed in front of me, blocking me off, while the other two pushed forward and corralled me against the wall of a warehouse.

I was trapped and my heart sang like caged canary, my

vision sharpening even as dark spots began to burst in my field of view.

One of them held a knife, while the other two didn't have any weapons I could see. I forced myself to take a breath. They were probably just muggers, looking for a payday.

I clutched my camera to my chest.

No. Not my camera.

It was the same one I'd had since I was a teenager. The grips worn. The battery port door held on with a strip of duct tape.

"Here," I said, reaching into my camera bag to pull out my wallet. I tossed it on the ground, but the men didn't move to pick it up. "You can take whatever is in it," I clarified. "Just take it and go."

Blue hat laughed. It was cold and cruel.

"What we want is you, Annie."

He lunged toward me, grabbing my arm while the other two pulled rope out of their pockets. My camera fell heavy against my chest as my arms were wrenched behind me.

I struggled, kicking and elbowing wherever I could, but it was too late. Rough rope tightened around my wrists, pulling tight. Blue hat pulled a hood over my head, and the entire world went black.

The sharp bite of panic nipped at my nerve endings, making me hyperventilate beneath the hood as I tripped over my feet, being pulled along by rough hands.

"No. *No.* Please, you can't. Please *stop. Let me go.*"

They were kidnapping me.

The horrifying thought echoed in my skull.

Kidnapping *Annie.*

I gasped for oxygen, desperate. I heard the squeal of

tires on the street. A car they planned to force me into? Where would they take me?

Was my phone still in my bag? Could it be traced?

Would my father even come looking for me or would he just let his only problem vanish into this black bagged hell and say pretty words at my funeral. Use the pity of the people as a springboard for his campaign.

Oh god.

Oh god.

My throat felt thick with unshed tears and the need to scream.

I felt myself lifted off the ground—then, abruptly, dropped. My hip throbbed in protest and I shifted, trying to squirm away against the rough cracked pavement, feeling tiny stone bite into my elbows and knees.

Grunts and muttered curses filled the air. Nobody touched me. It was like I'd been totally forgotten. I stopped inching away and reached for the hood, yanking it off, blinking into the sunlight.

Six men fought on the sidewalk. The three new ones looked like random strangers. One in a crisp black suit, another in joggers and a loose fitted tank, and the third in jeans and band tee with biceps the size of my thighs.

They must've heard the commotion and come to help.

Fuck, I was the luckiest goddamned girl in the whole world.

I sobbed out a grateful cry, trying to get myself back to my feet without the use of my hands.

The random strangers were pummeling the baseball hat guys, kicking in their faces and slamming them against the hoods of two sleek black cars. Blue hat was already unconscious, and the suit guy loaded him into a car trunk.

"What the hell?"

I fumbled back a step, then another, seeing the chaos in a new light. Noticing details as the men finished subduing my kidnappers.

The one wearing the suit had a gun. I saw it inside his jacket as he threw the body of blue hat guy in the trunk of his car.

And the one that looked like he was just out for a run? He had a pair of brass knuckles on his fist as he landed blow after blow into the face of another blue hat, until blood sprayed from his cheek and little white bits dropped from his mouth.

Teeth.

Those were teeth.

I couldn't move.

The hairs on the back of my neck rose and heat flooded my chest, swiftly replaced with an ice cold that left a clammy sweat in its wake.

The last guy—the one in jeans—he laughed as he held the remaining blue hat in a chokehold until he stopped moving. And at his waist, where his Radiohead tee shirt rode up enough to expose the deep adonis v of his lower abdomen, I saw a flash of silver.

He had a gun, too.

Who were these guys?

Move, Anna.

You need to move.

Blue hat guys might've kidnapped me, but something told me these three were going to do far worse than that.

A knife lay on the ground near my feet and I grabbed it, pressing it between my thighs for leverage, rubbing the rope around my wrists against the blade. It took too many precious seconds to saw through. By the time my hands were free, the clearly-not-random-strangers had already loaded the other unconscious blue hats into the trunk with their friend.

Or were they dead?

Holy shit.

My throat went utterly dry as I pushed back to my feet and made a break for it.

An arm like a tree trunk wrapped around my middle before I got more than five steps, hauling me back.

I clawed at it, screaming. "Let go of me!"

I didn't know what I was expecting, but for the guy to immediately drop his arm was *not* it. I fell forward, scraping my palms on the pavement. Getting back up felt impossible. I wanted to curl up into a little ball and just fucking disappear.

The man who stopped me from running stepped around me and I peered up at him as I fell back onto my ass and clutched my aching palms to my chest.

He was exceptionally tall with smooth dark skin.

"Who the hell are you?" I croaked, keeping an eye on the others in my periphery.

Where the hell did I drop that knife?

Why had I dropped that knife.

Goddamnit, Anna.

"I'm Jack," he said.

Jack?

He extended a hand to me and I recoiled back.

He gave me a hard look. "We aren't going to hurt you. We're here to protect you."

The man, *Jack,* pointed toward the car parked a few

yards away. "They're all locked up and won't be conscious for a while. You're safe."

"Here to protect me?" I repeated. "Then why the fuck do I have no idea who you are?"

This made Jack pause and he shared a look with the other two on the sidewalk. They shrugged at him and he sighed, clearing his throat.

"Look, our employer didn't want to worry you. It's best if you just pretend you never even saw us. It can be like this never happened."

"But those men—"

"Will be dealt with," he finished, interrupting me. "I promise you that. You'll never see them again."

I shivered. Swallowed.

"W-who's your employer?"

"Can't give you a name, Miss Vaughn. But rest easy knowing you have someone looking out for you."

Apparently done with the conversation, Jack turned on his heel and stalked to the driver's side door of the nearest black. "Hopefully you won't be seeing us again any time soon."

He could fucking say that again.

"Want a lift back to the main drag?" the one in the suit asked, seeming completely unfazed with the fact that he had a river of blood staining the left side of his face from forehead to chin.

"Fuck no," the words blurted from my lips and I sealed them shut, feeling the blood drain from my face.

But black suit guy only grinned at my response. "Smart girl. Best not to get into cars with strangers."

"We'll wait here until you're safely back to where you belong, Miss Vaughn," jean guy added, jerking his chin in the direction of the road that would lead me back to David. "Go on, now. It's not safe over here."

I couldn't believe I was just going to walk out of here, but as I turned and left, walking as fast as I could without breaking into a full on sprint, the men didn't come after me. But I could feel their nearness. As if they were following at a distance. Only a few blocks away.

Our employer didn't want to worry you.

Who the hell hired them?

Dad wouldn't be above hiring bodyguards to follow me around. But he'd also probably tell me to my face. Plus, they would have brought David with them. It can't have been him.

There was only one other billionaire in my life who was that presumptuous.

Carter Cole paid to have me followed.

14

CARTER

"Mr. Cole! I didn't expect to see you here."

An older woman who managed a hotel I owned approached me. I couldn't recall her name, but it didn't matter. I had no intention of talking to her.

She hovered several feet away, waiting for me to acknowledge her greeting. I glared at her and saw her face go pale. With a respectful nod, she backed away into the crowd of elegant guests.

I managed to scare away anyone who dared to try and sit down at my table. When I found out Hudson Vaughn had RSVPed to a charity dinner gala, I dropped a hundred thousand on a table of my own. I didn't bother trying to fill it with guests, or even showing up for the meal.

All the action I was interested in started after dessert was served.

That was when guests would start to mingle. A band would play, people would dance. Then, I'd finally get the chance to sneak away with the reason I'd come tonight.

I spotted Anna the minute I entered. Her hair was

lacquered into frozen curls falling over one slender shoulder. Her long-sleeved deep red gown covered every inch of skin, but hugged her figure perfectly. I couldn't stop staring at the curve of her peachy ass. I could still remember how it felt under my hands a few days ago.

Fuck, it had been too long since I touched her.

Unfortunately, I wasn't the only one admiring her. Every straight rich asshole in this whole goddamned estate was staring at my girl. I made a mental list of names, noting anyone who needed their eyeballs plucked out.

Anna tucked her hand into her father's arm while he led her through the crowd. Hudson stopped to speak with every single man under fifty, cutting short conversations with women and married couples. It couldn't be more obvious what he wanted. He planned to marry his daughter off to whoever made the most advantageous match.

I stared as the pair stopped to talk with a tech CEO who recently graced the cover of Time Magazine. He had a reputation as a Silicon Valley playboy, and he obviously wanted Anna as his next conquest. The way he looked at her body, I was surprised his eyes didn't pop out of his head.

It was enough to make me want to destroy him.

Fortunately for him, Anna didn't even notice. She kept looking back at me, rage shining in her green eyes. Clearly, she was still angry that I'd gotten her to admit who hurt her.

Good. Better she be angry at me than flirtatious with anyone else.

I planned to hunt her down, but this was better. I'd wait for her to come to me.

Even when Vaughn introduced Anna to a gold-mining heir and a French ambassador, I barely felt a prick of jealousy. Those men seemed not even to exist to her. They were just obstacles, keeping her busy while she searched for a way to evade her father and come for me.

I leaned back in my chair, satisfied. My cock hardened in my pants every time I caught her emerald eyes flashing at me from across the room.

Anna and I meeting was inevitable, just like everything between us was.

We were like magnets. Always had been. While she was away she'd flipped her magnetic poles to keep me away, but they were turned back now and there was no separating us.

Finally, Vaughn left Anna alone with a real estate titan from Dubai. No doubt, he hoped the two of them would hit it off in Hudson's absence.

Instead, Anna turned away immediately and stormed right to my table. I gazed up at her furious face, my hands steepled in my lap.

"You have some nerve, Carter," she snapped at me.

I shot her an innocent look. "What have I done this time? I'm afraid I can't remember. Take a seat. I'm happy to discuss it."

She shook her head. "I don't want to have this conversation in public."

I raised my brows in approval. "I didn't realize you were so eager to be alone with me."

She huffed. "You wish. Get up, quick, before my dad comes back."

Anna grabbed me by the arm and pulled me to my feet. I had more than enough strength to escape her grasp, but there was something delicious about letting her have the reins.

She brought us to a hallway off the main ballroom. It

was huge, made of marble and spotted with statues. Our footsteps echoed off the high ceiling. A set of velvet ropes clearly marked where the venue planned for guests to stop, but Anna lifted her skirts and stepped over it.

"What if they catch us?" I whispered jokingly.

"Then you'll pay them off. That's what you do these days, isn't it?"

She put her hands on her hips in a gesture of disapproval. It only brought my attention to the curve of them, making me grin at her.

The truth was, I'd give away half my fortune in an instant for a stolen moment with Anna.

She huffed, then turned into a small alcove housing an antique settee. I followed. No one looking down the hallway would see us, but we could still hear the band's music drifting up the hall. Anna turned to me, her face a pretty pink from her misplaced rage.

"You had me followed," she said accusingly.

Ah. So she figured it out.

I thought she was just angry about me finger-fucking her into revealing her secrets. My security detail already reported back what happened to me, with reassurances that Anna was unharmed and only a little shaken up.

I'd been chomping at the bit to see that truth for myself, and this was my first opportunity to do that. The first time she'd left the Vaughn estate since it happened.

They reported she had no idea I sent them, but unsurprisingly, she was clever enough to figure it out anyway.

"Are you even going to deny it?" she pressed.

"No."

Her lips made that beautiful surprised O they always did when I did or said something that shocked her. I wanted to push her to her knees and shove my cock into that perfect circle until she saw stars.

"At least have the fucking decency to look sorry, asshole."

My Anna finally learned how to deliver a curse without blushing. I knew she had it in her. I smirked.

"Why should I? I don't regret it."

She scowled. "You invaded my privacy. You basically stalked me, Carter."

I stepped closer, glaring down at her. "And the men I hired saved you from being attacked." I caressed her jaw. "You should be grateful, little siren."

"Grateful!"

She tore away from my touch.

"You tyrannical, manipulative prick!"

She poked me in the chest.

"You haven't been in my life in *years*. And in case you forgot, you broke up with me. You don't just get to reappear and *have me followed*!"

I grabbed the hand poking me and pulled it against my chest. "Yes, I do. Because you're mine, Anna. You always have been. Remember?"

I pushed down the sleeve of her gown to reveal a small rope burn on her slender wrist. I ran my thumb over the reddened skin, and she winced. Fury burned in my chest.

"Those assholes shouldn't have gotten close enough to touch you," I growled.

I'd need to be more careful. My men should've gotten there faster. They should've seen the others coming a mile away. If they couldn't do their job properly, I'd just have to do it myself. Then I really would be her 'stalker.'

The thought didn't perturb me one bit. She belonged to me and I had every right to protect what was mine.

"I'm fine," she insisted, trying to yank her hand away. "Let me go, Carter. You can't keep doing this. I'm not yours."

I grabbed her by the neck and kissed her. I was as possessive and claiming as I wanted to be, forcing her lips to part for me. I nipped at her lips and beat back her tongue even as she fought me.

Her claws sank into my shoulders, but they weren't trying to scare me away. No. They were pulling me in. She couldn't lie to me; she craved this version of me. The version who would take whatever he wanted. Who would force her to do what she wanted instead of what was expected of her.

I ripped my mouth away from hers. "Still think you're not mine? Because you let me kiss you like I own you."

"You're delusional," she said. The dazed-looking expression on her face betrayed her. I could read exactly what she wanted.

And I was ready to take advantage.

She was terrified to admit it to herself. That I was what she wanted. That this twisted love was why she came home.

Anna Vaughn couldn't accept that she would never be her father's puppet because she craved the sorts of things a life spent in a gilded cage couldn't give her.

She read my stare and as those lips parted, I brushed my thumb up her jaw until it rested against her lips. They parted, just slightly. Just enough.

And I grinned as I sank the digit into her mouth, sliding

the pad of my thumb over her tongue, pushing into the back of her throat.

Her eyes rolled back and a soft curse left my lips as I pushed her down until she was seated on the settee.

She went without more protest than a single gasping breath as my thumb left her mouth, blinking as if waking from a dream.

"I'm so fucking angry with you," she said, her voice breathy as her hands clutched the edges of the seat cushions.

"I know," I crooned, tilting her chin up. "I want to see those pretty green eyes looking up at me."

She glared at me, and I thought she would defy me. She looked equal parts regal and wrathful, like a deposed queen kneeling to her conqueror. The image made my mouth water.

"I hate you."

"I know."

This time when her lips parted for me, I pushed my two middle fingers past them, gliding them over her tongue.

Her knuckles turned white.

I drank in the sight of her. The feel of her tongue on my fingers as I thrust them deeper, testing how far she could go. Her eyes rolled back again and I knew she loved this just as much as I did. Love and hate. They were one and the same for us.

A tightrope we walked on, getting closer to each other with every careful, balanced step.

She looked like sex personified as she tipped her head back, taking my fingers into her throat.

Every muscle in my body tightened as I felt the hot press of her throat closing around my fingers. I groaned, a curse pushing through my clenched teeth as I wrapped my other hand around her pretty neck and squeezed.

She moaned around my fingers, gagging lightly.

The little siren knew what this would do to me. She knew how deliciously gorgeous she'd look. Fuck, she was trying to seduce me, to take back control.

I unbuttoned my pants, pulling out my cock for her. It was already rock hard, pre-cum gathering on the tip for her.

Her dazed eyes drank me in, studying every inch of my length as she licked her lips. Her gaze caught on the small tattoo inked into my hilt. I didn't give her time to figure out what it meant. I snaked a hand around her neck and twisted my fingers into her hair, pressing my tip against her lips. She opened for me, such a good fucking girl.

Her hot little mouth sucked me in and I shuddered as her tongue ran over the underside of my shaft. Her eyes lifted to meet mine, still ablaze with passion concealed as loathing.

I reached down and peeled her left hand from the settee, placing it on my thigh.

"Tap my leg twice if you need me to stop," I said, gritting my teeth. "I'm going to fuck that tight little throat until it's so raw you can't even say my name."

I gave her no more warning before I shoved my cock deep into her mouth. She gagged at the intrusion, saliva swelling at the corners of her lips. Her nails bit down into my thigh, but she didn't tap.

This quickly, I could only fit half of my length into her mouth. I grabbed her gold tipped curls, refusing to let her pull away.

"*Uh, uh,*" I chastised her. "Breathe through your nose, baby. You can take it."

I could see her trying to collect herself, taking a long slow breath in. Both hands now on either of my thighs loosened their grip, and her throat relaxed enough for me to slide in another centimeter.

"Good," I praised her. "That's so good, Anna."

I eased back for her to take another sip of air before pushing back in an extra centimeter.

"That's it," I crooned, caressing her face as her eyes glassed over with unshed tears at my intrusion. "Just another few inches."

I could go slow. For her. Just this once.

"Wider," I coached her. "Good girl. Relax your throat. Yes, just like that."

My fingers in her hair tightened and it was a fight for my life to keep from coming down her throat right there as she moved her throat, allowing me past that little dam and into absolute heaven.

"Fuck," I hissed and I couldn't hold it back anymore.

I shoved into her mouth, forcing the last two inches in until her lips met my groin and she was silent save for the tiniest choking sound as her throat flexed and spasmed against my cock.

It took everything in me to pull out, to analyze her expression, taking in the dopey look in her tear-filled eyes and the way her mouth watered for more of me.

It was all I needed.

I pushed back in, harder now, faster. Anna opened wide for me as I pistoned my hips at a brutal rate. Her mouth filled with saliva, lubricating my slide and spilling over her bottom lip. Tears swelled at the corners of her eyes, threatening to fall.

But she never tapped out.

My beautiful fucking disaster.

I could see how hard she was working to take me, shifting the muscles of her throat, relaxing them. After a minute, her eyes grew hazy. She was drifting into another world, where all she had to do was submit to me and take what I gave her. It made her throat open even more for me.

I groaned loudly, shoving deeper. Her face was a sloppy mess, with her lipstick smeared all over my cock and tears streaming down the side of her face, messing up her make-up. I dragged a finger through her tears and brought it to my mouth, sucking in the salt taste of her.

Her eyes flashed with eagerness. I could still read her after all these years. She loved being used and praised for it.

I could sure as fuck give that to her.

Wrapping a hand around her throat, I forced my entire cock down her throat and stopped. Her muscles milked my tip so sweetly, it took all my strength not to come. Her eyes widened as she struggled to breathe, and I could see the panic in her face.

"It's okay," I soothed her. "Just a few more seconds. You can take it."

I could see her relaxing, accepting it.

Trusting me.

I pulled out and she gasped for breath, her face covered in tears and smeared make-up. She looked so fucking sexy like that, I couldn't wait any longer. I needed to have her. I had to feel that perfect pussy wrapped around my cock right fucking now.

I lifted her and pushed her against the wall, her cheek pressed against the wallpaper. I yanked up her skirt over her hips so I could press my fingers against her panties.

"You're fucking soaked for me, Anna," I whispered against her neck.

Tearing her panties to the side, I spread the moisture and circled her clit. "Admit it," I hissed. "You missed me. You missed *this*."

Anna whimpered and arched her back to press her breasts against the wall. She was so needy, desperate for pressure against her nipples.

I ripped her panties off, the lace disintegrating in my hands. I lined up my cock with her entrance, teasing her with the tip.

"Say it," I growled against her ear, remembering that first time. The way she wanted me so bad. How I'd said maybe we should wait but she was so eager to give herself to me. She wanted me to be her first and her last.

"Please," she begged, just like she did that first time, but now there was no blush in her cheeks. No shy smile in her eyes as she pulled my hips to press against hers.

I want it to be you, she said, biting her lip in the cold sand. *I always want it to be you.*

Slowly, I sank into her. Her perfect pussy felt unreal, as hot and tight as it was our first time.

She whimpered underneath me as I stretched her wide.

"*Shh,*" I murmured. "They'll hear you. Everyone in high society is right down the hall. You don't want them to know I've got perfect Anna Vaughn split open on my cock."

I emphasized the words with a hard thrust, bottoming out inside her. Anna squealed loudly before clamping her lips tight.

I would like nothing more than for every person at this stupid fucking gala to hear her cry out my name as she came on my cock.

"Go on, Anna," I growled, feeling her juices seep down, staining the wallpaper and my thighs. "Let them hear you. Let them see who you belong to."

She whimpered, keeping her lips pressed tight.

I pounded into her. I could feel her tight velvet sheath squeezing me as I slammed into it, over and over. She couldn't hold back her whimpers and they grew louder with every one of my punishing thrusts.

And it dawned on me again that I had her. That she was *mine*.

Every part of her.

This ass. These glorious tits. Her perfect cunt.

And every sound out of her beautiful mouth.

Those were mine, too.

Mine.

I clamped my hand over her mouth, silencing her.

"Did you hear me, Anna?" I muttered. "I meant it when I said you were mine. That means this pussy is mine. All your sweet little cries, they're mine, too. I'm the only one who gets to hear them. All of you is just for me."

Her inner walls fluttered, and I knew she was close. I *needed* her to come on my cock. Shoving my other hand under her skirts, I found her clit and caressed it.

"Come for me, Anna," I demanded.

With a shudder, she obeyed. Her pussy gripped me like a vise, impossibly wet and snug. I followed her right over the edge, my spend filling her in hot spurts. For a few moments, the whole world vanished. The only things left on earth were Anna and me.

We stayed there together, breathing hard while we came back down. I could feel the mixture of our release seeping out of her, coating her thighs. I had the sick urge to shove it back inside her.

We didn't talk about birth control, and I didn't waste time worrying about getting Anna pregnant. But now that her womb was full of my seed, I found that I liked the idea. Anna's belly round with my child, letting anyone who saw her know she was mine.

She couldn't leave me then.

She and I were always destined for each other. Nothing would tie us together more permanently than a baby that looked just like us. The image of her holding our baby sent a wave of something terrifyingly primal through me.

Both Anna and I came from fucked-up families, but that didn't mean that we couldn't create something better.

Of course, Anna wasn't ready to think about that yet. She could barely admit that she belonged to me. Her future was already written in stone, but I'd wait for her to see it for herself.

Reluctantly, I pulled my softening cock out of her. I let her pull away from the wall and turned her around so I could give her the sweet, gentle kiss she'd earned.

"Go to the bathroom and wash your face," I murmured.

"God." Anna raised her hands to her face. "I must look terrible."

"No." I shook my head. "You look so fucking perfect."

So fucking mine.

"I don't want anyone seeing that but me. But you keep this inside of you."

I gripped her pussy in my palm, making her thighs squeeze. "I want it dripping down your legs all night. No matter how many men look at you, I'm the one whose seed is in you. Remember that."

She blushed and looked away from me, her jaw clenching. "This was a mistake, Carter. We're never doing that again."

"That's not your decision to make." I brushed her hair back from her face. "You don't seem to get it, Anna. You made me a promise. You're mine. That means you're mine to take care of, and you're mine to fuck, and you're mine to love."

She scowled at me. "Do you even know what that word means? I don't want you, and I don't want your bodyguards. If they keep following me around, I'll call the police."

"You think the police can help you?" I laughed loudly. "You don't become as rich as I am without having the boys in blue in your back pocket. You aren't safe, Anna, the bodyguards stay. End of discussion."

Something in her hard look softened. "Look, I know I got attacked, but it was random. Just some guys who probably recognized me from the papers and wanted a ransom. Lightning doesn't strike the same place twice. I'll be more careful, just please, call off your dogs."

She still didn't know that her ex had every seedy motherfucker on the west coast on the lookout for her. It was better that way—knowing Anna, she'd probably walk right into his lair to demand he cut it out. She was too softhearted to know when someone was dangerous.

The fact that she'd just let me fuck her was proof of that.

"Here."

I pulled a burner phone out of my pocket and shoved it into her hand. "This has my security team's numbers in it. If you don't want them following you, you can call them and tell them where you're going to be before you get there so they can position themselves discreetly. You won't even know they're there."

"*Carter*."

I smiled. "Yes, Anna?"

I wanted to give her the illusion of choice, but she looked so furious, I half expected her to hiss at me like a wet cat. Instead, she just shoved me back.

"I need you to leave me alone, okay? I can't—we can't keep doing this. Tell your security team to back off. And stop following me to charity events. It's pathetic."

With that, she spun on her heel and stomped away. I followed at a distance to make sure she made it to the bathroom unseen. I wasn't above knocking someone out to expunge the memory of her sex painted face from their minds. That was *my* face.

My chest swelled with satisfaction. Anna might be furious with me, but I just realized she took the phone. And my seed was still deep inside her.

Was she on the pill?

Would she leave my cum inside her like I told her to or would she try to clean it out? I almost wanted to push my way into the women's bathroom to make sure she did as she was told, but that was...

That was fucking crazy, even for me.

I pushed my hands through my hair, gripping it at the root to try to pull the thoughts from my head.

I didn't even want kids. Never really had.

But something changed tonight. As soon as I came inside her, I knew there was nothing in the world that would stop me from planting myself in her so permanently that she could never tear out the roots.

15

ANNA

Pulling my portfolio out of my bag, I nervously flipped through the prints. They were the same ones I showed to Olivia, the ones she swore had promise. But it was one thing showing my work to an old teacher. It was another thing to show them to a real photographer.

I lingered in the hallway outside Jaden Austen's studio. We had an appointment in a few minutes, and I didn't want to be too early. Olivia had done me a favor setting up this meeting, and I didn't want to fuck anything up. I even brought him a good bottle of whiskey to show my appreciation for meeting with me.

Fuck. I hoped he drank. What if he was a recovering alcoholic or something?

I took a deep breath, telling myself that he could just say *thanks but no thanks* if he didn't want it.

It wasn't as if I could get much more embarrassed than I was last night. After I saw Carter at the gala, I planned to ream him out for having me followed. Instead, I let him shove his cock down my throat and fuck me against a wall.

And I loved it.

I fucking hated him. And yet I loved it.

What was wrong with me?

The connection between Carter and me never faded over all our years apart. It just corrupted. When he said obscene things to me, when he touched me wickedly, when he manipulated me...I felt cared for somehow. Like I belonged. At peace. Whatever the opposite of being judged was.

When I felt like the whole word was picking at me as if I were a fresh scab, when I was with Carter it was like their clawed finger couldn't reach me. Not while I was in the clutches of the real monster.

But he didn't pick and poke, trying to make me into some perfected version of myself.

No.

He wanted to ruin me. He wanted to see me let go and fall apart in his hands. He wanted me to be his beautiful disaster and not only would he not judge me for letting myself fall to pieces—he relished it.

Carter didn't seem to be on the verge of discarding me, like he did back in high school. He was claiming me instead.

I sighed, rubbing the tense muscles at the back of my head.

Maybe it wasn't Carter. Maybe I was the one who was fucked up, from years of picking the wrong men and letting them abuse me. Every time I gave into Carter, I chose the guy who wouldn't treat me right. Keeping the pattern alive.

Well, that was done. Next time Carter showed up—and I had no doubt that would be soon—I was walking away. No more living in the past. It was time to think about my future.

And the first step to rebuilding my life was taking this meeting with Jaden.

I'd left the house an hour earlier than I originally planned, so I could sneak out the back door, swipe the keys to the car David was always driving me around in and take a roundabout route to the studio. Hopefully, I'd evaded all my bodyguards—Dad's and Carter's.

If my father knew I was going to show these photos—images that proved I wasn't in Malawi—to anyone outside our home, he would lose his shit.

My watch's minute hand clicked to the hour.

Okay, Anna, head in the game.

I pasted on a smile and knocked.

The studio door swung open seconds later, revealing a tall, smiling man behind it. Jaden was slender and wiry, and his dirty blond curls tangled wildly, like all his extra creative energy was released through them.

"Hey, you must be Olivia's friend, Anna. So glad you could make it. Come in, come in." He ushered me inside the spacious, brightly lit space.

"This is for you," I said, handing him the expensive bottle. "I hope you like whiskey."

"Damn. That's a good bottle right there. Thank you. I'll have to save it for a special occasion."

I beamed at him and he gave me an encouraging, easy grin. "Have a look around while I put this away."

There were several framed photographs on the walls, mostly portraits. Everything made my little collection of photos that I thought were good enough to show feel like a five-year-old's finger paintings.

"These are incredible," I said when Jaden returned, stopping to look at one.

"Thank you," he said. "I try to keep my best work on display. Remind myself that even if I feel like a fraud, at least I have proof that I was good *once*."

I laughed. "Wait a minute. I was told that once I became successful, I'd stop feeling like an imposter."

"Wow. Don't know who told you that, but it's not true. You'll always doubt yourself. But it's a good thing, right? It gives you a reason to keep working."

I could feel the muscles in my shoulders relaxing. I was so nervous about impressing this professional, but Jaden was easy to talk to. He felt more like a peer than a mentor and I felt myself relax a little.

Jaden showed me around his studio. It was inviting and roomy with a lounge area separate from the office and shooting spaces. Against the far wall which had two large windows was a fancy coffee station complete with an espresso machine that he deemed an *essential* business investment with a wink.

He answered all my questions when I wanted to know what his equipment was called and how he liked to set up for different kinds of shots. The studio was mainly for product and portrait shoots, where he also did his personal work and sometimes ran workshops.

His scanners, printers, and computers looked intimidatingly high-tech. I looked over his camera collection.

"How many of these do you actually use?" I asked.

"All of them. I'm kind of a tech-head. Right now, I'm really into this Sony a7RV."

He picked up the Sony, pointed it at me and snapped a photo. I flinched back, looking down.

"What's the matter? You don't like getting your picture taken?"

I shook my head. "I'm usually the friend who volunteers to take the picture so I don't have to be in it."

"Shame. I mean, the camera loves you."

His hand came up and brushed back a lock of my hair.

I pulled away immediately. Even after years working at the Butterfly Room, I still couldn't get used to strangers touching me. It took a long time for me to get comfortable enough for a touch to feel right.

And Jaden touching my hair like that *definitely* didn't feel right.

Olivia said this meeting was supposed to be for me to make professional contacts. But maybe Jaden misunderstood. Could he think this was a set-up? My entire body felt icy and awkward. If he tried to touch me again, I didn't know if I could just brush it off.

Then, Jaden took several steps back, giving me space, and I realized I was being completely ridiculous and over-thinking the tiny gesture.

He probably fixed the hair of a thousand girls who he took a photo of in his career.

"Should we take a look at your photos?"

"Oh. Right. Yeah. Yeah, of course," I said, laughing at myself.

He directed me to the lounge area where we sat side by side on one of the sofas. He picked up a shot, thumbing the edge of the paper while examining it in complete silence. I looked at the side of his face, seeing nothing but pure concentration.

"So?" I asked, choosing to ask before I wore a hole in the hem of my dress.

"These are exceptional," he said in a low voice. "You're

able to capture so much energy in the shots. Is this in a strip club?"

"No, a cocktail bar I worked at." I'd already told Olivia the truth, it just felt right to be honest. "But a customer did offer this woman two hundred bucks if she'd finish out her shift in her underwear."

Jaden's eyes widened. "That's terrible! How demeaning."

"Not to Trista!" I said, laughing. "That two hundred bucks meant she could take cabs home for the rest of the week. I probably would have done the same thing."

Jaden shook his head. "You're something else, Anna. Photographers want to show the world as it is, but so few of us actually live in it."

"It's not that hard. If you want to try working at the Butterfly Room, I'll be your reference. I'll warn you, though. You better be ready to spend the night in five-inch heels and get your ass pinched at least three times before midnight."

He laughed and leaned back against the back of the couch. He was such a tall and big guy that he took up a lot of space without even meaning to. That was why when he stretched his hand out and rested it on my left thigh, the closest one to him, the motion seemed almost natural.

I looked down at his hand, wrapped around my thigh where the hem of my dress had ridden up, too stunned to move.

My heart raced with something hotter and stronger than just discomfort.

"Jaden," I said, my voice sounding like I was trying to talk under water to my own ears.

"*Hm?*"

"I think maybe you have the wrong idea."

I shifted in my seat, and he slowly retracted his hand. "Oh. I thought there was a vibe here. We were joking around, and you're a beautiful woman..."

"I have a boyfriend." The words of the lie fell over each other on their way out of my mouth.

"Just one?" he pressed, his lips raised in a smirk.

His hand touched my thigh again, fingertips running along the side of my knee.

A chill ran up my spine as I jerked away.

Steeling myself, lifting my chin and fixing him with a stare that I hoped was all business, and no fear, I lifted his hand from my thigh and set it on the cushion next to me.

"Jaden, my love life isn't a topic I'm comfortable discussing with you. We just met. I really hope there hasn't been any misunderstanding. I'm here because I want to get into the industry, and because Olivia said you might be able to help me do that."

My fingers clutched my portfolio book like I could use it as an anchor to draw me up out of this shitstorm.

Jaden worked his jaw, considering me before he replied. "All right," he said finally, sitting up straighter on the couch. "I know why you're here, and I am willing to help. You've got natural talent, but you have a lot more to learn before you're ready for an exhibit. Work with me for six months, and I'll teach you everything I know."

I bit my lip, uncertain now.

Six months with this guy?

If he'd made this offer to me five minutes ago, I'd have been over the damn moon, but now? Now, I wasn't so sure.

"Work with you? What would I be doing, exactly?"

His lips pursed in thought.

"Call it a *personal assistant* job. You would assist me on shoots, help me out in here," he said, sweeping his arm to gesture towards the shooting areas.

I swallowed, wanting what he was offering so badly I was already thinking that maybe I could be willing to forget his advances a few minutes ago.

"That would be really helpful," I said on a breathy exhale, trying to set my nerves back at ease. "Would there be any salary?"

Already, I was imagining myself in a small apartment somewhere closer to the other end of town. A place all of my own, where Dad wouldn't be looming over my shoulder all the time.

"I'd give you work experience, teach you the ropes, help you set up your presence and network."

I watched his eyes drop from my face and make their way down my body. My white dress covered me from collar to knee so he wasn't getting a good look at anything, and I refused to squirm. Maybe he was appreciating the way the light from the tall windows was brightening the fabric with an almost silver hue. He was a photographer after all and this fabric really did capture the light.

His eyes came back up.

What he just finished saying finally registered in my mind and my mood fell. "So, *nothing*. There wouldn't be any pay."

His nose wrinkled slightly as he scoffed. "If you think giving you what you want is nothing. But we can talk about a fee for helping on shoots for higher tier clients."

I was almost afraid to ask but better to have everything hashed out now. "What would you be getting out of this arrangement?"

If he said anything other than a helping hand...

Jaden's disgruntled expression morphed into a smile.

"A pretty photographer's assistant who won't hesitate to show me her appreciation from time to time."

I dug my nails into the overpriced leather folio and set my jaw.

This motherfucker.

Jaden reached to tangle his fingers in my hair again. I ducked back.

Ugh.

Fire burned in my gut, the heat spreading up to my cheeks as I jumped to my feet.

Screw this guy.

I was going to tell Olivia exactly what kind of man he was so she *never* sent another girl up here to be mentored by this jackass.

"I'm out of here."

"Let's crack open that bottle you brought when you came," he said, standing.

"You do that," I said, gathering my pictures, trying to be gentle with them as I tucked them back into the portfolio book.

"I guess you aren't as interested in photography as Olivia made me believe."

I spun around.

"Funny, I thought you had me here because you shared that interest, guess we're both disappointed, then."

His brows went up, and he hacked a harsh laugh.

"I don't gain anything by holding a spoiled rich girl's hand as she tries to make it on her own," he snarled, taking a step closer.

I wasn't short, and I was in heels, but he still towered

over me. His form was like the moon blocking out the sun during an eclipse, the shadow of him falling over my face.

It reminded me of someone else. Someone I never wanted to see again.

I fought the urge to cower.

"You're right. I am a spoiled rich girl," I spat back. "I expect crazy things like respect, decency, and minimum fucking wage."

Jaden's eyes darkened. "Is that all it costs for me to get you out of the dress? I imagined something in the two hundred dollar range by the look of that strip club."

His hand flashed out to grab my shoulder, and all of a sudden I was back in my St. Louis apartment with Josh. His fist slamming against my ribs, tearing out chunks of my hair. Me trying to fight back, then being shoved to the ground. I ripped out of his grasp and slipped, knocking my head into the edge of the coffee table so hard I saw stars.

"You okay, baby?"

I muttered a curse, reaching up to touch the aching point at the base of my skull but when I peeled my eyes open, Jaden was there. Hovering over me. Almost on top of me.

"Let me see," he said in a dangerous whisper, reaching for my face. My head spun and when I tried to bat his hand away it connected with nothing but air.

His hand went around the back of my neck, lifting me as I heard a familiar sound.

Was that...a zipper?

I blinked, trying to get the dark spots out of my eyes as he whispered unintelligible words it sounded like I was hearing under water.

"There. You're okay. Let me make it better."

The overpowering scent of him in my nose and his touch on my collar shocked me back to reality.

I pushed at his hands, but he worked past them. Stronger. So much stronger.

I couldn't win against him.

Just like I couldn't win against Josh.

My eyes pricked and a ball formed in my throat.

"I-I'm fine," I said, finally regaining some clarity as Jaden gripped my right side, his hand on my rib cage, his thumb brushing the underside of my breast though my dress. "You don't need to—"

"Shh, it's okay."

No. No, it wasn't okay.

"No, I need to go. I need to go. Just," I grunted, trying to get my legs out from under him, trying to get up. "Get off me."

A loud knock cracked through the air and Jaden's probing touch stilled on the swell of my left tit.

"Open this *fucking* door," someone shouted, their voice muffled through the door but terrifying enough to make my skin crawl.

The handle swung up and down.

The next knocks sounded more like kicks.

Jaden jumped away from me, and I used the opportunity to scramble awkwardly to my feet and collect my shit. Clearly, Jaden had pissed someone else off. They wouldn't be here for me. I'd just scoot past them and get the fuck out of—

"Who the hell is that?" Jaden whisper-shouted. His wild eyes looked around the studio, then at me, an accusation in them.

"No idea," I said on a breath. "But it's your problem. Not mine."

Jaden staggered toward the door, hesitated, and spun, his previously calm demeanor shattered. The banging continued. My hackles rose.

Wait. Maybe it was my problem.

Carter's bodyguards?

Maybe they had followed me.

I swallowed.

More banging.

God damn it.

"Who the fuck did you give my address to?" he was shouting now, stepping into my path to stop me from opening the door. God, my head was throbbing. I needed to get out of here.

"Move."

"Fuck no. You're not opening that door. I'm—I'm calling the cops."

I tried to make for the door again as he reached for his phone, but he snatched my wrist, yanking me back.

"*Ow*," I hissed, feeling something pull painfully in the joint.

The next bang on the door was so loud it sounded like a gunshot in the room as the hinges rattled. And the next one saw the whole thing busted from the frame as the warped metal caved in and hung uselessly from its hinges.

Carter shoved through, his eyes glimmering with a dangerous rage. He might have been dressed like a CEO, but he looked like an avenging god ready to destroy an entire city with sulfur and fire for its sins.

"Who the fuck are you?"

Carter didn't even acknowledge him. His gaze zeroed in

on Jaden's hand still wrapped around my wrist and something in his expression darkened.

Jaden must've noticed too because he dropped my wrist as if burned by it, acting as if he'd never touched me.

"Look, man, I don't know what you think—"

"Shut your pathetic mouth."

Jaden sealed his lips.

Carter's eyes connected with mine, the dangerous glimmer in his exploding into hot flames at something he found in my stare.

Carter cleared the space between himself and Jaden in barely two strides, twisting his fist into the front of Jaden's shirt, shoving him backward until his back connected with a photo on the wall, shattering the glass frame.

"*What did you do?*"

"Nothing!" Jaden said, pleading. "We were talking, that's it. I offered her a job, man."

"Then why the fuck is her whole body shaking? *Hmm?*"

"Carter, I—"

"Did he touch you?"

When he turned the full force of his stare on me, I couldn't speak. I felt my throat bob. I wanted to say no to stop him. To stop this. But I couldn't.

Jaden had touched me. Then I noticed the silver nibs of his fly wide open. His top button undone. Carter followed my gaze and saw it, too.

He hadn't just touched me. He'd intended to do far worse while I was still dazed from smashing my head on his stupid fucking table.

Carter turned back to stare at him, pressing him harder into the broken frame until I heard the glass creak and shatter some more.

Jaden's mouth opened and closed. He looked like a big, stupid goldfish. Apparently he couldn't come up with an explanation, so he looked at me. "Tell him!" Jaden pleaded. "Tell him nothing happened."

My lips parted, but I couldn't force any words out.

My silence was all Carter needed to assume the worst.

He pulled back his fist, ready to strike. I could see it happen, see Jaden's nose shattering and his blood splashing all over Carter's shirt. Jaden might be tall, but he didn't stand a chance against Carter's wrath.

I had to stop this.

"Carter, stop!"

My voice was small and throaty, but he heard it. His head swung my direction, his eyes wild and unseeing. A man possessed. I couldn't move. I watched him, afraid but refusing to show it.

"My car is outside," he said in a deadpan tone. "Get in and lock the doors. I'll be down as soon as I'm finished teaching this asshole the consequences of touching what's mine."

Jaden let out a low sound, muttering something I couldn't hear. He tried to shove Carter off, but Carter just pulled him forward and slammed him into the glass again, hard enough that his head knocked into the frame and he went down in a dazed heap on the floor.

My heart skittered to a gallop, thrumming in my ears.

"Anna, look at me."

I did.

"What did I say?"

"*Umm...*"

"Go to the car. It's an Aston Martin parked right outside. Lock the doors. Wait for me."

He nodded, waiting for me to confirm I heard him as Jaden groaned on the floor.

And I remembered.

All the rumors about him. I hadn't believed them. Not really. Not until right now.

He climbed a mountain of corpses to get to the top.

Swallowing, I turned and walked out, making for the elevator, trying to even out my breathing.

Down the hall, from the mangled entrance to Jaden's studio, I heard a sharp, disturbing *snap* and Jaden's scream of pain and decided I couldn't wait for the elevator.

I ran for the stairs, clutching my portfolio to my chest as I took them two at a time, just needing to get away. Far away from whatever was happening upstairs.

I didn't look back until I walked down all five floors of the building. Pressure constricted my lungs and every breath I took felt hot.

Outside, I sank against the wall, helpless against the feelings crashing down on me. Time collapsed along with my body. I might have been calming myself down for a minute or an hour. Finally, my breaths slowed and the world shifted back into focus. I chanced a look over my shoulder in time for Carter to emerge from the building.

"Anna, I asked you to wait in the car, love," he said, moving toward me.

Red. There was red on his knuckles. On his collar. On his cheek.

Jaden's blood.

I dodged his seeking eyes as he stopped in front of me, but I could do nothing to avoid the wood and amber scent of his cologne, or how it made me shiver.

"Did he..." Carter's voice vibrated with lethal urgency.

I shook my head. "No. he didn't—it didn't get that far."

I felt more than saw him relax, but only a fraction. I sighed. "Carter, what are you doing here?"

He shook his head, face still twisted in frustration. "After what happened, *that's* what you want to say to me?"

"I told you to leave me alone. Instead, you showed up and interrupted a business meeting."

"That wasn't business," he spat. "That fucking scumbag attacked you."

"I was handling it!"

"You were white as a sheet and shaking, Anna! You were in no condition to fight him off and you damn well know it. *God*, why you keep insisting on putting yourself in danger is beyond my fucking ability to understand. You're smart enough to slip my men but not smart enough to see that you *need* protection. It's...*it's infuriating.*"

He rubbed his palm over his mouth, brushing the six o'clock shadow there as he fought for a measure of calm.

About at least one thing, I knew he was right. I'd flashed back to Josh's abuse and completely fallen apart in there. I'd curled into myself. I was placating a man who aimed to take advantage of me. Who knows what Jaden might have been able to do if Carter hadn't showed up?

But I wasn't going to thank the bastard for following me. It would only encourage him to be more controlling, and I'd had enough of men thinking they could run my life.

Carter cradled my face in his hand and I hated how much it made me want to cry.

"Come home with me," he murmured. "Let me take care of you."

I wanted so badly to give up control and let him do just that. Somehow, he always seemed to know how to make me feel good. I could still feel Jaden's unwanted hands on my thigh, still had the memories of Josh suffocating me. Carter could make that all go away.

All I'd have to do was break my commitment to myself. Forget the girl I was trying to be when I left home and give him the reins.

Just this morning, I swore I'd cut things off between Carter and me. I had to focus on the future, not live in the past. No matter how tempting that past might be.

You're a big girl, Anna. Buck the fuck up.

I shook my head. "No. I'm not going anywhere with you, Carter."

Drawing on all my strength, I turned away from him. The car was just down the block. I walked toward it, digging into my bag to find the keys. My hands were shaking so hard, I dropped them in the gutter.

Fuck.

I bent to dig them out with a curse on my lips and stood, rushing to find the button to unlock the doors.

Carter came up behind me, settling his hands on my shoulders. "You're in no condition to drive."

"I'll be fine. Just go home, Carter."

"Anna, put the keys away."

I unlocked the door and reached for the handle.

"*Anna.*"

No sooner had I gotten the door open than he picked me up, tore my camera from around my neck, and threw me over his shoulder, the keys dropping out of my hand onto the sidewalk. My portfolio scattering onto the road.

"Let me down! Let go of me, you prick!" I screamed, hair in my face as I battered against his back. "*Carter!*"

I kicked and thrashed, but he pulled my knees tight

against his chest, locking them in place, carrying me as easily as if I were a sack of flour, back toward his ridiculous, fancy car. I might as well have been clawing at a brick wall.

Carter pressed a button on his keys and the back trunk opened. My eyes widened as I realized with horrifying certainty what he was about to do.

"Don't you dare!" I warned.

Carter didn't listen.

He swung me from his shoulder, somehow managing to get me into the trunk without tossing me. I moved fast, pushing myself up, but he ripped something from the bottom of the hatch and slammed it shut before I could force my way out.

I was trapped.

He fucking put me in his trunk.

I was so fucking mad I could have spat fire.

"You can't just kidnap me!"

If he heard me, he ignored it.

I felt around in the dark, searching for the trunk release and groaning loudly in frustration when I realized that was what he'd ripped off the hatch before locking me in here.

"Carter!"

I felt the jar of the driver side door slamming closed and the thrum of the engine as it came to life.

"*Ughhh*," I screamed through my teeth, giving the hatch one last hard kick and hoping I dented it as he drove off.

16

CARTER

Normally, driving along the oceanside highway was the highlight at the end of my workday.

Of course, it was harder to relax when I could hear Anna's fists pounding against the trunk door. I should have bound her hands with my tie so she couldn't hurt herself. She was already shaken up enough from earlier, and she was only going to upset herself more.

This wasn't how I pictured bringing Anna to my home for the first time, but desperate times called for kidnapping the love of your life.

When Paulson called me this morning, telling me Anna had slipped out of his surveillance, I knew in my gut that something had gone wrong. Fortunately, Anna brought her phone with her, with all my tracking measures on it. I canceled all my meetings and drove right to her.

My hand tightened on the steering wheel as I remembered how I found her. Trembling and terrified, lost so far inside of herself that I could only see the phantom of her in her eyes. She didn't have to tell me what happened; it was obvious that Jaden made a pass at her.

That he touched *my* little siren.

The rage I felt could have destroyed fucking worlds.

To be honest, I couldn't remember if the filth was still breathing when I left.

I broke every finger on his right hand one by one.

By the time I broke the last one, he was delirious with pain and hyperventilating. His vocal cords too frayed to keep screaming. I might've left him like that if he hadn't said what he did after I was finished.

"She's just some rich slut, man," he'd croaked as I turned to walk away. "Are you really going to go to prison for some—"

I hadn't let him finish repeating that heresy.

I wasn't going to go to prison. I had friends in high places and powerful enemies in my back pocket. But I'd spend a life sentence behind bars if it meant I could systematically destroy every man who ever hurt her. Whoever touched her. Whoever had the fucking idiocy to think for one second that she belonged to them.

I'd go with a smile.

I left Jaden slumped and motionless on the floor, pausing only to make a quick call to my good pal Ruarc Monroe's cleanup team before I left to follow my girl.

If Jaden survived and still had at least some mental capacity, he'd leave the state before I could come back and truly sate my frustrations.

But he'd have to wait.

Anna needed me.

I saw where she went in that studio and it wasn't a good place. I remembered the darkest moments of our nights on the beach. The moments where she looked at the water like it might be a relief to walk into the midnight crosscurrent and let herself be taken under rather than go home.

After I brought her back from that place, she needed to be punished.

She couldn't keep putting herself in danger.

She couldn't keep slipping her guards.

And there was a part of me that wanted to punish her for more than that. I wanted to punish her for what she did six years ago.

Anna Vaughn acted like I ripped her heart out and walked away unscathed.

But no. When I ripped her heart out, I cut mine from my chest with it and buried them both in the sand. And every day I couldn't find her was another day our hearts were left to decay in the dirt.

When I reached the road to my villa, I turned in smoothly. The gates opened automatically for my car, and my chest flooded with satisfaction when they closed behind me. Now, Anna was safe inside my impregnable security system. Nobody could hurt her here.

For now, Anna was all mine.

I parked and turned off the engine, but was greeted with silence. Apparently, Anna was done screaming and trying to destroy my three hundred thousand dollar car.

She was probably saving her energy to fight me off as soon as she was freed.

I opened the trunk, ready for her to start hissing and scratching. Instead, she ignored me entirely, reaching past my outstretched hand to grip the rim of the trunk and push herself to her feet.

Her hair was mussed, and her white dress was all twisted. Bedraggled as she looked, she still sneered at me like the queen she was.

"We're at my villa," I explained, retracting my hand. "Are you going to walk inside with me, or do I have to throw you over my shoulder again?"

"I'll walk."

I re-extended a hand to help her step down but she ignored me again, stubbornly clambering out of the trunk and straightening her dress.

She stumbled a little on the landing, but brushed it off. Head high, she strolled right up to the front door of my villa with a stomp in every step.

I felt a rush of satisfaction, seeing Anna open the door to my home. It was her home, too, even if she didn't know it yet. Everything I had was always going to be hers.

We entered the foyer, and I saw Anna's eyes catch on the white sculptural art hanging from the ceiling. With her photographer's eye, I knew she'd be entranced by my substantial art collection. I grinned, thinking about the massive paintings, sculptures, and lightwork waiting for her.

Ignoring the staircase going upstairs, Anna moved forward into the living room which I barely ever used. Nobody came to my house. I didn't have *friends*—nobody I trusted enough to invite here. I didn't bring women here either. Didn't want them getting the idea that they might be welcome to come back.

Yet I knew Anna would love it. Subconsciously, I built the whole place with her in mind just as I built myself. Laying brick after brick with red-stained mortar until I was everything Hudson Vaughn told me I would never be and more.

As Anna looked at the architecture, I could hear the gasp she tried to swallow. She was impressed, even if she didn't want to be. Her heels clacked on the wooden floor, as she slowly made her way further inside, looking up at the ceiling and moldings. Her eyes widened as she took in the warm wood, the walls of windows with seaside views, the luxurious couches of butter-soft leather.

Before I bought this villa, I visited all the most expensive homes in the city with my architect and decorator. I'd even gotten a look at Hudson Vaughn's house while he and Michelle were traveling. I might not have Anna's eye for design, but I had a mission.

Whatever they had, I wanted better.

I bought the biggest property available on the same beach as the Vaughns then ordered my team to build the most spectacular home in town. The result was a modern, luxurious villa with extensive balconies. Looking out the window to the right, I could see my infinity pool and personal tennis court. To the left, the stone garden and closed-in gazebo big enough to fit a football team for dinner.

And right ahead of us, through the bay windows: the beach. Just how we left it six years ago.

Anna took it all in thoughtfully.

"Big house," she said noncommittally, an edge still in her voice. "People might think you're compensating for something."

A smile tugged at my lips.

"I think you know that I'm well-equipped in all areas," I said, brushing my hand over her lower back.

Anna leapt back at the touch. She gasped in a shaky breath, and the blood drained from her face.

I frowned. "What's wrong?"

Anna didn't answer. She stumbled back another few steps, her green eyes fixed on some distant spot. It was like she'd collapsed in on herself again and I promised myself that if the fucker who touched her in that studio wasn't dead, I'd go back there and finish him the first chance I got.

But now wasn't the time to dwell on him. I had to take care of my little siren.

"Sit down," I told her gently. "Let me get you a glass of water."

She sank down on the couch while I moved quickly to the kitchen and filled her a glass.

Anna's eyes were squeezed shut when I returned. She was trying to force back her tears, but I wanted them to fall. She should trust me enough to be fragile in front of me. I knelt in front of her and pressed the glass of water into her hands.

"Drink."

She took a deep breath and obeyed, but not before cutting me a sharp glare.

I rubbed my thumb over her knee in soft, comforting circles and this time she didn't pull away.

"I know you're going to anyway, but please don't," she whispered.

"Don't what?"

"Don't lecture me about trusting Jaden. I already feel like enough of an idiot without you—"

"You weren't an idiot."

I surged up onto the couch and pulled her into my lap,

wrapping my arms around her. She sunk into my embrace, tucking her face into the crook of my arm.

She sobbed silently, soaking the fabric of my shirt.

"You weren't an idiot," I repeated firmly. "It wasn't your fault."

"But I always do this. I trust the wrong people, and they take advantage," her voice was so low, I could barely hear it. "And it's your fault."

I hugged her tighter to me and she sniffed, digging her fingernails into my arm like she wasn't sure if she wanted to pull me closer or hurt me. I was fine with either as long as she didn't leave.

She sniffed. "It all started with *you*."

Something in my stomach tightened because I knew she could be right. I broke her heart just like I was told to and then she went off trying to fill the void I left behind with anyone who could put a temporary bandage on the pain.

I did this.

"I'm sorry," I muttered into her hair. "I'm sorry, Anna."

I should have known that her reaction was about more than just the photographer. She was still processing memories of the asshole who abused her.

I felt in awe of the woman in my arms. She was so goddamn brave, trying to rebuild her own life after what she'd been through. Strong enough to put herself back in the cage she left knowing she could leave again when she needed to.

A week ago, I watched with fury as she crawled back to her father, letting him parade her around, lie about where she'd been, try to marry her off to men who were pathetically unworthy of her.

Now, I knew how much she needed me. I would protect her from everything.

I held Anna tight until her tears stopped flowing. Her breaths slowed, and her body relaxed against mine. Even after she stopped crying, she made no attempt to move.

"How are you feeling?" I asked.

"Better," she said, sighing as she pulled out of my embrace. "But I'm not going to thank you. Not after you threw me in your trunk. I can't believe you did that."

Then she really wasn't going to believe this.

"I'm glad you're feeling better," I echoed. "Because I'm going to need to punish you for that little stunt this morning."

Her whole body stiffened.

"I'm not punishing you for trusting Jaden," I said, stroking her hair. "But I will have to punish you for evading your bodyguards. For going off on your own after I warned you that you needed protecting."

"Punish me?" Her eyes narrowed and when I didn't balk, they widened. "You're serious."

"Yes, Anna."

Her throat bobbed and she worried the edge of her dress between her fingers.

She wasn't refusing, I realized with a lick of electricity flicking down my spine, a column of white fire that went straight to my greedy cock.

She wants this.

Maybe even needs it.

"Do you trust me?"

A little knot formed between her brows, but she didn't answer me.

I felt myself frown.

174

She might not be able to trust me with her heart just yet, but as I drew the back of my index finger down her arm, provoking a shiver, I knew she understood my meaning.

Do you trust me with your body?

Anna nodded tentatively, flinching as if admitting it in that small motion was some sort of betrayal of herself when in fact it was acceptance. I just needed to show her.

I reached out to push her hair back from her face, tucking it behind her ear before wrapping my fingers around the back of her neck, guiding her to bend forward until she was lying over my lap.

Her back arched with anticipation, her hips propped up over my thighs while her face sunk into the couch cushion at my side.

I dragged up the hem of her sundress to pile at the small of her back and as the air kissed her round ass, she sucked in a gasp and curled her fingers into the sofa cushions.

Unlike the dangerous lace number she hid beneath her clothes at the last charity event, this time my Anna wore sensible taupe briefs. No sexy underwear for her business meeting, where she didn't expect to see *me*.

Such a good girl.

I hummed in approval while I dragged my hand over the juicy curve of her ass. Anna shivered when I drew the tip of my index finger along the line of where the silky panties met her upper thigh.

"I'm going to punish you now, Anna. Do you understand?"

"Yes," she replies, her voice muffled by the cushions.

I hooked my fingers over the edge of her panties and slowly dragged them down to puddle around her thighs.

Her pretty little pussy was already glistening for me, inviting my fingers to trace it.

But that would have to wait.

My cock jumped beneath her and I knew she felt it as she twitched, arching her back further, pressing her face tighter to the cushions.

I raised my hand and brought it down on her left cheek, the satisfying *slap* of my palm cracking on her ass dragging a groan from my throat.

Anna winced at the impact, but otherwise sat silently. That wouldn't do.

"I want to hear you, Anna," I purred. "I need to know the message is sinking in."

I spanked her again on the other cheek. This time, she let out a small yelp. My cock throbbed at the sound. I know she could feel how hard I was getting against her stomach.

"There you go, little siren."

I rubbed out the sting, satisfied as her pale flesh started to bloom with red.

I hit her again and she gasped before moaning loudly.

With each blow, Anna was louder, releasing all the pain and fear as she let go.

She stopped tensing between strikes, her muscles relaxing the more I painted her cheeks red.

She looked so gorgeous, so *alive*. Her pussy was so wet, I could see her juices leaking onto her thighs. Onto my designer sofa.

Fuck, I wanted to bury my face between her legs and stay there for days. I loved her like this, all messy and undone.

I was tempted not to let her go. I could force her to stay in my villa and let me take care of her. I'd get her all the photography supplies she needed and keep her safe from her ex. At night, I'd fill her pretty cunt with my cum again and again. Just breed her until my seed took and her belly swelled.

The image of her with my baby in her practically made me feral, my veins burning and teeth grinding with unspent desire.

When I delivered her the final spank, Anna shrieked my name, her voice watery as it echoed against the high ceilings. I lightly massaged her ass.

"You took that so well," I told her. "Your ass looks gorgeous, all pink for me. How do you feel?"

"I feel...calm," she said, betraying herself with a sniffle. "Why do I feel calm?"

"Of course you do, baby."

I duck my head to press a kiss between her shoulder blades. "This is *right*. We're *right* together."

She turned her head to the side, and I could see that little knot trying to reform between her eyes. I ached to smooth it back out.

Stop doubting us, little siren.

For one fleeting second I thought she was going to say something else. Ask me a question I wasn't sure I could answer. One she hadn't asked me since she rematerialized in my life.

Why.

Why did I break her heart?

Before she could summon up the courage to ask questions I couldn't answer, I wiped an errant tear from her cheek. "Now, it's time for your reward."

"I get a reward?"

I could hear the teasing in her voice.

"Yes."

I parted her legs with my hands and finally let myself touch her wet cunt.

Anna gasped, her thighs instinctively trying to close around my hand. I took my time exploring every crease, watching as my fingers got wetter until they glistened with her arousal.

Without warning, I plunged two fingers inside her.

She keened, her back arching at the sensation as I began to pump my fingers slowly in and out. Her pussy gripped me tight, trying to keep me deep inside her. I watched my Anna wriggle and moan deliciously while I finger-fucked her.

"Show me," I muttered. "Come on my fingers and show me how much you love me touching you."

I hooked a finger downward to press against the raised spot inside her, and Anna's eyes turned down, fluttering to nothing but slits as she took the pleasure I gave just as well as she took her punishment.

Her little sounds started to bloom into a crescendo, and I pushed her there, working her sweet little cunt until it was a tool of my destruction just as much as it was an instrument of hers.

"That's my good fucking girl. So fucking wet for me. I can feel you milking my fingers, little siren."

The more I talked, the more I felt her walls shudder flex around my fingers. She liked this. Good. Because I would never tire of praising my future wife.

Her gasps turned to cries and she squirmed against the force of her pleasure, trying to escape it.

I leaned my forearm across her back, pressing her

down, holding her still while I finger fucked her pussy until she was screaming.

"Oh god, Carter!"

Her thighs clenched, and I felt the exact moment she came, her slippery cunt squeezing me tight, spasming, quivering as she fought through her orgasm, legs shaking.

Mine. I gave that to her.

And I wasn't stopping there.

No fucking way.

I barely gave her half a minute to come down before pulling her up for a rough kiss on the mouth.

Guiding her off my lap and shakily to her feet, I leaned over my knees to watch her. "Take your dress off."

I shrugged out of my jacket and tossed it away, steepling my fingers against my lips as her bright eyes flicked over me, drinking me in as if I were a dream personified.

If she didn't take that dress off right fucking—

She reached behind her neck to unzip the top before reaching for the hem to pull it up over her head, revealing inch by inch more and more of my territory.

A landscape I fully fucking intended to capture, cultivate, and build my forever home on.

I undid the buttons on my shirt and pulled it off. Her gaze felt like a physical touch as she traced the lines of my muscles and the shadows of my tattoos.

"You're beautiful," she said, sounding dazed.

I smirked. My body was muscular, but it was also scarred. Some of the scars Anna had already seen, remnants of my childhood. Others were fresher, thicker. I had lived a violent life, and my skin was the proof of it.

Her brows lowered as she took in some of the ink on my

right arm and I wondered if she was putting together their meaning.

The ship heading into a storm, like the lyrics of the song she declared *our song* when we were seventeen.

The shattered diamond for the one time she joked about wishing she could smash every diamond her father insisted on buying her and forcing her to wear.

The jellyfish that stung me when we took a midnight swim and she insisted she *had* to pee on it or I would die.

There was very little ink on my body that wasn't in some way tied to *her*. Each tattoo reminded me of my goal, kept my eyes on the prize: become a man even more powerful than Hudson Vaughn. A man he couldn't touch. A man who could protect his daughter better than any other man on this fucking planet.

It felt obscene to be shirtless next to Anna, with her perfect posture and willowy figure. But she bore marks of violence, too. The bruises on her back were almost healed, but still yellow. Her wrists were red from the ropes that had tied them.

She wouldn't scar, not physically. With time, her skin would heal. But she would carry that violence with her for the rest of her life.

The urge to imprison her in my villa surged up again. Here, no one could hurt her.

No one except me.

With her dress discarded, Anna kicked off her panties and unhooked the matching sensible bra, her breasts dropping into soft, heavy peaks that I wanted to get my mouth on more than I wanted air.

Her hands were on me before I could get my pants off.

"I wanted to touch you before," she said, sliding onto

my lap, drawing her fingernails over my heart. "But you wouldn't let me."

"You can touch me now," I promised. This was her reward and I wouldn't put a limit on it. Not like the others. "Everywhere. As much as you want."

She did, her hands slowly mapping my body, teaching me lessons in patience I didn't ask to learn, but would swallow if it meant I could keep her once I was a learned man.

My little siren lingered on every scar she'd never seen. It was almost like she'd memorized me as I once was, and wanted to remap everything she missed.

When she ran her fingers down the V of my hip bones, I gritted my teeth to stop myself from grabbing her. It was her turn to use me just how she wanted.

Anna started undoing my belt, her movements painfully slow. If it weren't for her own quickened breath, I'd think she was torturing me. Finally, she loosened the buckle and undid the button underneath. She pulled down my pants and underwear, my cock springing free, hard as granite for her.

"What does this symbol mean?" she asked, tracing the sharp intertwined lines at the base of my cock, making me clench my teeth.

I smirked at her. If she didn't see it, it meant she wasn't ready to. "I'll tell you sometime."

She bit her lip and looked up at me through her lashes.

"Tell me what you want, Anna, and it's yours."

A muscle in her jaw ticked and something desperate and vulnerable crossed her eyes.

"You."

That was all I needed to hear. I pushed us up to standing, wrapping her legs around my waist, using my cock like a shelf under her warm, wet cunt to hold her up as I pressed her against the glass windows overlooking the beach and stole a vicious kiss from her lips, biting her lower lip until I heard her whimper.

Fuck. I would never get tired of kissing her.

Grabbing her wrists, I let her legs drop and spun her to face the water, grabbing onto the swell of her hips.

"You see our beach?" I muttered, nipping her ear.

"Yes," she said with a hitch in her voice. "It hasn't changed."

"Nothing really does."

Lining up my cock, I slowly slid inside her. We both groaned at the friction.

Nothing had changed. Anna and I are just as good together as we ever were, just as right.

She was still mine.

I took my time pulling out and easing back in, filling her.

She stretched beautifully around me and made small little sighs and whimpers.

Once, it took a substantial amount of work to get my length fully buried in her heat. That first time and the times after it, we'd needed to work it in inch by delicious inch. It was torture and I spent most nights without her training for our next encounter with my fist and her image painted on the back of my eyelids.

But now...

Now she took me so well. Every thick inch with only little whimpers of pain-laced pleasure as she adjusted. As I hit that spot so deep in her I doubted any other man had ever touched it.

Watching my cock slide in and out of her made my thighs shake and my back tense with the need to plant that fucking flag on conquered ground, but I held back.

In front of us, the ocean crashed against the sand in huge, unstoppable waves. That beach was an intrinsic part of Anna and I, and neither of us could ever rip it out. We were violence and force, water clashing with the earth. Elemental.

Inevitable.

Her walls trembled around me and I knew she was close. I lowered my hand between us to strum her clit, and my fingers were instantly soaked in her.

"Carter," she gasped. "I'm going to..."

"I know, baby." I kissed her neck roughly. "Me, too."

Anna came violently at the admission, clenching around my cock as she threw her head back onto my shoulder and brokenly moaned a string of curses.

That was all I needed to fall over the edge with her, my spend pumping into her in strong spurts. I groaned and lowered my face to her neck, burying my face in her trademark scent as I rode the aftershocks of the quake still quieting inside me.

I summoned enough strength to pull out of her with a grimace, wishing I could stay buried in her forever.

Carrying her over to the couch, I pulled her down onto the cushions with me, tucking her in against my chest, contouring my body to hers.

She still fit so perfectly against me, her head tucked just under my chin. We lay there quietly until our breaths synced. I waited to soften, but my cock barely lost any of its steel as we lay like that.

I felt our releases leaking out of her where she was

pressed to my upper thigh and suppressed a scowl. Shifting, I reached to steer my cock back between her thighs.

She wriggled, sighing sleepily. "Carter, I—"

"Shh," I whispered against her neck. "Just let me keep it in a little longer."

My little siren didn't protest again as I slipped back into her warmth, not allowing myself to give in to the urge to take her again. I envisioned the wide head of my cock pushing my seed as deep as it could go, keeping it there for as long as it needed to stay to fulfill its purpose.

I wanted to ask her if she was on birth control, but I wasn't sure what I'd do if I didn't like the answer. Was it the pill? Did she keep it on her? Maybe in her purse in the chauffeur's car? I could get rid of it. But what if it was one of those IUDs?

Could I pull it out without her noticing?

I shivered at the thought, mixed feelings of disgust at myself and primal satisfaction warring for dominion.

"What are you thinking?," Anna murmured, shifting slightly so I could see her face but not enough to dislodge my cock.

"You're perfect."

I propped myself up on an elbow to study her in the aftermath. Her skin was pretty and flushed, our joined bodies glistening with sweat and her release. I could see the liquid rolling down onto her thighs, a mix of both our cum. I frowned, pulling my cock out only long enough to catch the roll of pearlescent liquid with my tip and push it back up inside her.

Her eyes narrowed. "What are you doing?"

"I want you to keep my seed inside you," I said honestly.

"Why?" she asked, raising a brow, sounding amused. Unworried.

IUD then. Must be.

I didn't answer; she wasn't ready to hear the truth yet.

Anna sighed, apparently writing it off as just some new facet of my obsession with her. She played with her hair and gazed out at the ocean while I angled my hips to better lock my hilt against her and wondered what the chances were of getting pregnant with one of those things inside her.

"Oh shit," she said, trying to move, but I held her against me, not letting her go. Not yet. "Carter, my photos. When you picked me up I dropped them all over the—"

"I got them."

"You what?"

"I picked them up after I put you in the trunk. They're in my car."

She sagged back down against me, falling silent for a minute before breaking the silence again.

"Are you going to keep me here?" she asked, her voice distant, as if she wouldn't be all that opposed to it.

I refused to let myself hope.

She looked wary, uncertain of what she wanted my answer to be.

I was tempted to drag her up to my bedroom, throw her in and lock the door. I could keep her forever, making sure she's safe, from her ex's hired kidnappers and her father's manipulative plans.

But that's not how I wanted her. I wanted Anna to choose me. Like I chose her.

Already, she was drawing closer to me. She'd let me see

her broken, vulnerable, and crying. She'd let me spank her. Inevitably, she'd figure out that I was what she needed.

"You can stay here as long as you want," I offered.

Anna bit her lower lip. "I think I want to go home."

The fire in my veins turned to ice, and I shielded the still regrowing thing in my chest from the frost.

"Dad has security there, and I...I need some time to think. I won't slip your bodyguards again the next time I go out."

Letting my relief chip away at my disappointment, I dipped my head and nodded against her cheek, sighing. "I'll drive you home, then," I vowed. "In a little while."

17

ANNA

Six Years Ago

Why was I curling my hair? The wind was just going to mess it up anyway. I freed the freshly spiraled lock of hair from the curler's clamp, then surveyed my progress in the mirror. About three-fifths of my head was done already, might as well keep going.

It was so dark, he wouldn't even notice.

Whatever, I wanted to look nice. It was a special occasion.

I sandwiched another lock of my hair between the heated prongs. I stared at my reflection, zeroing in on the spot where my nose met my cheek. I missed a spot. I put down the curler and looked through the mess of bottles, tubes, pencils, and pots on my vanity, knocking over the foundation I was looking for. The cylindrical bottle fell and rolled off the edge of the surface, taking a lip gloss and eyeliner tube with it.

"Come *on*," I sighed, sliding down to the ground and

picking them up. Something caught on my curler, bringing it to the floor too, only before grazing my arm as it came down. I yelped, clambering back to my feet, knocking the vanity hard enough to knock down some more makeup. I snatched the curler off the ground where it landed way too close to the white plush carpet under my chair.

The red welt on my skin stung. I frowned, calling for Rosie. Moments later, she knocked, then poked her head into the door.

"Let me see."

She turned off the curler before examining the damage. She tutted, telling me to wait. When she reappeared, she had the little first aid kit she kept in the kitchen. She led me to the bathroom and instructed me to hold my arm under cold water for a while.

She rifled through the kit for the Neosporin while I frowned at my reflection. The makeup was... fine. The hair was going to have to change. I looked at the water flowing over my scalded skin. All this just to have sex for the first time?

"Where are you headed tonight?" Rosie asked, coming over and turning the water off.

"Uh, nowhere. I was just trying out the curler."

"Right before bed?" she asked, dabbing me dry with a hand towel. I shrugged, ignoring the heat in my cheeks.

"I wanted to see how it worked. It's new."

It wasn't.

"The make-up too?" she asked.

"Umm." I squeaked.

She motioned at my face.

"Are you trying out the makeup too?"

My face bloomed bright red. Why did I even try lying to

her? I felt like I had to do it because I didn't like to disappoint her but if she knew the truth anyway, what was the point?

"I... *uh*... I just haven't washed it off yet. I wanted to head out to Summer's house but I changed my mind so I'm just gonna wash it off before bed."

"*Hm*," she grunted, with a twinkle in her eye. She knew. She always knew. She never called me on it, but she always knew.

She put a thick coat of Neosporin on the burn and wrapped it loosely in gauze, telling me not to touch it. I thanked her and she left the room, allowing me to keep pretending that I wasn't going to sneak out later to have sex with Carter.

I shuffled back to my vanity and slumped in the seat, wondering what now?

Was this an omen?

Abort mission.

The planets weren't aligned.

It was a warning.

I was going to go out there tonight and embarrass myself.

Bad sex doesn't exist for guys. There's literally no way to mess it up, if Summer was to be believed. It wasn't like I could argue with her. She was the one who'd lost her virginity last year. I fixed my foundation in the mirror.

Tonight was the night. I wanted to do this with him. We'd kissed. He had felt... *stuff*, over my clothes but we never really went further. Carter was happy to wait. In fact, he preferred it. Even said it shouldn't be him. It should be someone else. Someone better for me. Softer. Someone I wouldn't regret.

It was why he never pushed things, but I didn't want to wait anymore.

Want wasn't the right word. I *couldn't* wait anymore. It was like I was burning every time I was with him. Burning and aching and just barely able to stop myself from begging him to take me.

Which was exactly what I planned to do tonight.

He couldn't say no.

Summer said they never said no.

I finished my hair and makeup, then waited until the lights went out downstairs, before escaping out of my window and texting Carter to tell him I was on the way.

I ran out onto the beach, my blood buzzing and doubts rushing in only to be scattered by the wind.

Kicking my feet through the sand, I walked until I made out Carter's form down the beach. I sped up, working my way to a full on sprint with a laugh on my lips as he beckoned me forward.

I barreled into him, knocking him back a step as I wrapped my arms around his middle and pressed my face into his shirt, realizing too late that all the work I did in the mirror probably just got ruined.

Couldn't remember why I cared.

Carter wouldn't.

He dropped the blanket that was under his arm. The one he almost always brought for us to lie on and watch the waves.

"Whoa," he said, pulling me back to arm's length to get a look at my face. "What's the occasion? You look..."

"I know. I totally overdid it."

He moved his warm hands to my face, dragging me in

for a kiss that I felt all the way to my bare toes curling in the sand.

"I was going to say beautiful."

He chuckled, pulling me in so our bodies were flush again. He smelled faintly of sea salt and heady musk and that thing that was just *Carter*. Like if warmth could be captured in a bottle and sold.

I ran my fingers through the messy mop of dark brown curls on his head. He had enviable natural waves that I'd burned myself tonight trying to mimic.

"Is there a reason you're all..." he trailed off, gesturing to all of me when I pulled away. I shrugged, playing coy.

"Can't I just be excited to see you?" I asked.

He laughed. He was in a good mood tonight. Good. He lived in a warzone at home so I did whatever I could to get a smile on his face. We spread the blanket on the sand and stretched out on it side by side. I rested my head on his chest. His t-shirt was soft and faded. I listened to the rhythmic thud of his heart.

"How's your mom today?"

He sucked a deep breath into his lungs, swelling his chest.

"Not better but not worse either," he said.

"That's... good right?"

His hand snaked into my hair, fingertips stroking over my scalp.

"I don't know anymore. It's so fucked up. I don't know what to do."

I bit my lip. I'd been thinking about asking my father to do something but that would be difficult considering my father didn't even know Carter existed.

Carter's mom had been sick for months. Cervical

cancer. The hospital bills were so high, they'd be buried under them any day now. As if that wasn't enough, his father was responsible for the reason why he didn't want to take his shirt off the first night we went swimming.

I'd seen them now. The bruises. The scars.

He took the abuse from his father so that the bastard would spare his mother. He'd always done it, got in between them, but now more than ever he refused to let the piece of shit touch her. She was too weak. Too fragile as her illness grew inside her.

I ached for him. It hurt so much to see him hurting.

He didn't know it yet, but I'd been working to put money away. Little bits here and there withdrawn from Daddy's credit card, stuffed under my mattress. When I had enough to make a difference, I'd make him take it.

Then he wouldn't have to work so much and his mom could get more of the treatment she desperately needed. As it was, I knew after this round of chemo, they wouldn't be able to afford the next one.

"Carter?" I prodded when he didn't reply.

"I mean, yeah. I'm glad she's feeling all right, but I know it won't last," he said.

"Don't say that."

He sighed into the wind.

"Do you think the cops have let your dad out yet?"

They always did when he inevitably found himself being belligerent at a bar and getting himself arrested and thrown in the drunk tank. Which was exactly where he'd wound up a couple days ago.

"Don't know. Don't care," he said flatly.

He left after a fight two days ago. That night, he came to

the beach with a busted lip and finger marks around his neck, his eyes bloodshot.

I'd been so terrified, I couldn't sleep when I went home.

I begged him not to go back and he listened, staying with a friend, but I knew he would have to go home eventually. For his mom who despite everything refused to leave with him.

I'd never understand that.

My arm wrapped protectively around his middle and my eyes squeezed shut. I wanted to protect him.

I came from home every night, he came from his job waiting tables. Right after school, before he started at the restaurant, he had another job at a garage.

The last time I offered him money he had looked at me like I slapped him. But that was before his mom was diagnosed. Now, he might take it. I hoped he would take it.

"Let's hope he stays there," I said, knowing he wouldn't. He never did.

"I've thought about that."

I raised my head and looked at him.

"Thought about what?"

It was dark tonight so I could barely see him but I knew his brows were pulled down over his eyes. His lip curled when he talked about his father.

"I've thought about the day when the cops will show up at the house. Sometime I imagine they'll come with a court summons that will put him behind bars for years or even for life.

Other times I imagine they'll say some shit to my mom like, 'We're so sorry, ma'am, Frank Cole was found dead from an automobile accident. Looks like he was drinking."

His throat bobbed and his chin shook as he said the

next imagined line. "'We're going to need you to come identify the body'."

My mouth fell open but I didn't say anything. Frank Cole deserved to die a slow, painful death after what he had done to his son and wife. I didn't want to admit it to myself or to Carter, but I'd imagined something similar. Or even just him leaving, abandoning them.

They'd be better off, even if it meant Carter had to kill himself working. At least there wouldn't be someone hurting him every night when he dragged his tired feet home after a shift. And selfishly...then I wouldn't need to worry so much about him.

"I'm really sorry. You don't deserve what he's done to you."

"You sure?" he said, laughing darkly.

"Yes, I'm sure." I leaned down and planted a kiss on his lips.

He was the first person I'd ever kissed and I was starting to think I'd be okay with it if he was the last one, too.

"You're a good person, Carter Cole. No matter what that...*asshole* says."

He raised his brows, a tiny teasing smirk on his lips. He always teased me for that—my inability to curse without blushing. I really meant it, though.

Frank Cole was more than an asshole. I didn't think there was a bad enough word for what he was, but if I found it, I would say it without so much as a blink.

"I'm not as good as you make me out to be, Anna."

I brushed his hair back. His eyes were a limpid, warmer shade of blue when it was bright enough to see the gold in them.

"You're good *to me*."

"That's because I like you. I don't like Frank."

"Nobody likes him."

"I want my own father to die. Who wants that kind of shit?"

"He deserves to die."

I surprised myself with how strongly the words came out, without any doubt.

Carter looked away.

"You don't get it. I want it to *hurt*," he said as if pushing the words past some dam he used to keep them hedged in.

"When he's dying, in pain, I want him to think about everything he did to me and my ma. I want his last moments on earth to be his worst."

A chill ran over me.

He'd never said anything like this before. Hinted at it, but admitting it out loud...

I could see he meant it.

And I didn't know how I was supposed to feel.

No, wait. Carter's words from another night replayed in my mind. He was talking about something else, but they rang true now all the same.

Don't think about how you're supposed to feel, Anna. Just feel how you want to.

It didn't bother me, I realized. In fact, I hoped Frank died badly, too, even if that made me more of a bad person than I ever believed I could be.

I thought about the thick scars that were scattered across Carter's chest and back. They were too random to have come from an accident. They were scars because Frank liked to test how hot the fireplace poker was on his body.

That dark laugh again. "Fuck. Maybe I'm more like him than I thought."

195

"You're nothing like him," I snapped.

He grimaced, hugging me close. "Let's hope so."

I felt his cool fingertips as his hands burrowed under my hoodie, wrapping around my waist. They lingered there for a long time. Both of us listening to the sounds of the sea washing over the shore, just being here. In this moment. Away from the vastly different circles of hell we resided in.

Soon, his touch turned from light and thoughtful to something else. He slipped his palm against my skin, gripping my waist until I felt him shudder.

I took the invitation to throw my leg over him, straddling his body. He was long and lean. His arms muscular from his mechanic job.

"What are you doing?" He cocked his head, staring up at me with banked coals in his stare and tension in his jaw. I could feel him beneath me. That hardness through his dark denim jeans.

I angled my hips to grind into him, rolling them over the bulge with my lower lip caught between my teeth.

A small sound escaped his mouth and his hands tightened around my waist.

"*Anna,* you shouldn't—"

"I..."

He looked up at me with a question in his eyes.

"I-I brought condoms."

He stared at me, silent. Was that horror in his stare?

My mouth went dry, but I stayed where I was.

They never say no.

"I want it to be you."

"You shouldn't."

My brows knitted. This wasn't what he was meant to say. He was meant to rip my clothes off and ravish me. My confidence began to fall like a plane shot out of the sky, spiraling down, down, *down.*

"Well, I do. I've thought about it," I swallowed. "A lot."

His jaw clenched.

"I can't take it back if you change your mind."

The coals in his stare turned to straight fire.

He wasn't going to deny me. I could tell. I just needed to push him a little more. A little harder.

I settled heavier against his erection, making my skirt bunch up around my hip as my satin panties pressed against him, making his fingers dig harder into my waist.

"*Fuck,* Anna," he hissed, throwing his head back.

I grinned wickedly.

"If you don't want me, then just say it," I pressed, giving my hips another roll that made his legs shift, pressing into the sand beneath the blanket.

"Stop doing that," he said between his teeth, and something in his tone brought me out of the haze of my lust. I froze.

"I thought... you really don't want to...oh my god, just— just forget I said anything."

Tears stung my eyes as I moved to get off him, already knowing I might never recover from this, but he didn't let me move more than an inch, holding me in place.

"Before," Carter blurted, staring at me with a madness in his gaze bordering on insanity. "Before, you said you wanted to wait. You said you wanted to save yourself—"

"Forget what I said. I changed my mind."

He groaned, shutting his eyes to take a long breath before he opened them to speak again.

"Anna Vaughn, if you think for one fucking second I don't want you, you are criminally insane."

My stomach flipped, coming alive with that feeling only Carter could provoke.

"But if we're doing this, I want you to enjoy it. I want to give you something better than *this*." he motioned to the beach.

I thought sex on the beach at night was romantic, not that I'd ever tried it. I'd never thought it was a big deal before. And we'd only ever seen one other person out here this late in all these months. No one would see us. No one would know.

"What about if we tried…"

"What?" he asked.

I want to give you a blowjob sounded horrible in my head. Childish.

It would sound worse out loud.

Carter followed my gaze and seemed to pick up on what I was asking. I'd touched him, but I'd never tasted him, and right now the thought of trying made my mouth water and my skin prickle with nerves.

"Do you know how?"

I shook my head. "But I want to do it."

He held my gaze for a long time.

"I'll tell you what to do," he said finally. "But I get to taste you first."

18

CARTER

G ray clouds filling a navy sky.

The full moon peeking out from behind them.

The dark ocean creeping in. Creeping out.

I sat back in my office chair, staring at Anna's photograph. Even after years of examining it, I was still able to find new depths to it. New meanings. For years, all I had was this photo and my memories. I examined them constantly, looking for any angle I could have missed, like I could find proof that I would see her again.

When Anna came back to my life, she was infinitely more complex than those memories. She had survived so much, and it made her stronger, but more wary. Some of her innocence had faded, but none of her goodness.

She fascinated me more than ever. Even though so much changed, she was still *mine*. The link between us had never broken. But she would need to learn to trust me with more than her body.

I needed her to trust me like she used to. Before everything was ruined.

I had changed her perception of me, so she could still think of me as some kind of hero.

My thoughts were interrupted by my cell ringing. I frowned when I saw Derek Hobbes' name on the caller ID. There was only an hour until midnight. He'd never called me outside of business hours before.

"Yes?" I said, picking up the phone.

On the other line, Hobbes took a long breath. "I'm sorry for the late call, Carter. Unfortunately, I've spoken with my family, and we decided we don't want to sell. I wanted to let you know personally."

Acid churned in my stomach. My purchase of Hobbes Construction was supposed to be all but complete.

"Care to explain why?"

"You offered a very good deal," Hobbes said, coughing to cover the wobble in his voice. "But I heard from an old friend who advised me strongly against it. I had no choice but to listen."

My focus narrowed to those two words. *No choice*. Sounded like Hobbes' "old friend" gave him more than advice. I had a suspicion I knew who he was.

It was only a matter of time until he found out where his precious daughter was spending her time. Just like he'd figured it out last time.

"That's a shame. Does this 'friend' have a name?"

Hobbes was silent for a long beat. "I just can't do it, Carter," he said finally. "Please understand. If it were up to me, I'd sell it to you. All I want is to retire."

My teeth ground together. This had Hudson Vaugn's fingerprints all over it. Of course, a little coward like Hobbes would bow to the governor. Normally, I'd lean on Hobbes until he collapsed. I didn't let anybody run my business for me, much less Hudson *fucking* Vaughn. But now, there were more important pieces in play.

Like Anna.

If Hudson Vaughn was declaring war, I wouldn't waste energy on Hobbes.

"That's unfortunate. Call me when you find your balls, Hobbes. I'll be waiting."

Then I hung up on him, ending the conversation there.

I sighed, gazing up at Anna's photograph on my office wall. I closed my eyes and pictured a full moon, searching for some meager sense of serenity. Hudson had already ruined my life once, and apparently he wasn't finished meddling in it.

There were few fucks to give about the failing construction company, but if he intended to brake check every one of my campaigns, I'd be too busy putting out fires to spend all my time between his daughter's thighs.

Except, I learned early on that everything I had could be taken away at a moment's notice. I invested early and I invested young. I could live off those investment portfolios and offshore accounts comfortably for the rest of my life. There were billions there, tucked safely away from any legal bullshit Hudson Vaughn could sling my way.

Any, save for one vital piece of evidence he could use against me. But would it even hold up after all this time? And did he even have the balls to use it?

He had to know I'd retaliate. I wouldn't go down unless I took him with me.

I wouldn't leave Anna in his hands.

I was interrupted when my phone rang again.

The number wasn't saved. I frowned, my thumb hovering over the red decline icon. I had more than one phone number, obviously, and this one only went out to my close associates and home staff.

Curiosity nagged at me.

Could it be...

I hit the button and brought the phone to my ear, saying nothing, waiting.

"Stay away from her," said a deep, gruff voice.

No preamble, no greeting, nothing.

A man with a plan.

Focused.

If it were anyone else, I could respect it. I didn't though. I didn't respect anything about Hudson Vaughn.

"Who gave you this number, old man?"

His steely baritone used to scare me half to death when I was still nothing more than a kid, barely twenty.

We didn't speak more than a handful of times, but the short conversations we had were immortalized in my memory. Seared into my mind so well, he might as well have used a hot fireplace poker like my old man used to.

The message was the same, just with a different purpose.

Worthless.

Pathetic.

A waste of skin.

A quick chill ran over me. Anna's ex might've left physical bruises on my girl, but Hudson had hurt her, too. He cared too much about appearances to mark her on the outside, but I knew she had just as many scars as I had. Different ones. The kind that made it feel impossible to just to exist. Made even breathing a chore.

"Leave her alone," Hudson repeated. I tipped my head back, in the mood for a little fun.

I licked my lips. "No. I don't think I will."

He balked.

"Excuse me?"

"I said 'no.'"

I heard movement. Scraping, like the sound of a chair across the floor. Hudson Vaughn standing to his full height.

"Did you forget, boy? That money you took came with strings."

"So you weren't just trying to help an underprivileged youth pay for his ma's hospital bills?"

"Leave. Her. Alone."

"*No.*"

"Who the fuck do you think you are?" he snarled.

I was getting under his skin. It was surprisingly thin for a politician. With that job, you would think he was comfortable with a little ribbing.

"Ask Anna who I am. She knows better than anyone."

"You're a dirty, worthless piece of trash just like your father. You wouldn't be able to so much as walk past that building you work in without being arrested if it wasn't for my help."

He might as well have taken that line right out of the Frank Cole playbook.

When I was a dirty, worthless piece of trash who wouldn't be welcome to clean the floors of the building I worked in, maybe his words would have hit different.

I wasn't a broke, desperate kid with a sick mother, scared that I'd be homeless the next month. He wasn't as powerful as he thought anymore, not over me and not over his daughter.

"If you're done, I'm sure both of us have better things to do tonight," I said. "I can think of at least *one* on my end."

A low sound almost like a growl came down the line, and I wondered why he made it so fucking easy to find just the right buttons. The man, for all his success, had a lot to learn with this sort of business.

"I know what you said to her. Why do you think she'll give you a chance? You broke her heart. I saw her when she came home, Carter. Do you really think she'll forgive you?"

My teeth ground together. Cold snaked around my neck. What did he know? She wasn't close to him. She wouldn't come crying to him about what happened between us. I swayed, losing my footing in the ring.

"Why don't you ask her, Vaughn? This time, she might even tell you the truth."

"You will leave my daughter alone or I'll—"

"You'll what? Tell the police what I did *six fucking years ago?*" I scoffed. "I have every judge up the entire mother fucking coast in my back pocket."

"No," he replied, dripping venom. "I'll tell *her.* I'll tell Anna."

My blood practically froze in my veins.

Anna was smart enough to know what I was capable of, and strong enough to bear knowing it. But seeing it would be different.

She hadn't wanted to see what I did to Jaden, but she seemed fine enough knowing—*accepting*—that I hurt him. Killed him, actually. The cleanup crew got rid of the evidence and made it look like he skipped town, running scared.

I hadn't told Anna that he was dead. I was happy to let her believe what Jaden's closest clients and friends whispered to the tabloids. She didn't need to know.

Knowing might change her perception of me and we'd already come so far.

Seeing.

Seeing could destroy everything. And Hudson could make her see.

I couldn't take that chance.

"So? Will you be a good dog and keep your distance? Stay away from her until I get her engaged, and I'll have Hobbes sell you his company. Plus a $10 million bonus for every year before she's got the ring on her finger and a baby in her belly."

The metal case on my phone groaned as my grip tightened on it, my head filling with steam so hard to see through all I could think of was reaching through the phone and strangling Hudson Vaughn where he stood until his windpipe snapped under my thumbs.

I wanted to tell him to fuck off. No amount of money on earth could make me stay away from my girl. Not this time.

$10 million was a laughable nothing to me. And now that I knew about his feeble revenge plans, I could shut him down before he sabotaged every business arrangement I had.

But he still held the trump card.

Anna couldn't know what I did to my father.

She wasn't ready for that part of me, yet. It would ruin everything, and I'd already done enough of that.

As much as I loathed letting Hudson Vaugn think he won, I had to buy time to convince Anna to trust me again.

So I said nothing.

Hudson laughed. "That's what I thought. Even after all these years, you can still be bought."

Before he could say anything else, I hung up.

My fingertips felt numb, all the blood in my body collecting into this ball of white hot rage in my chest that made it hard to breathe. Fuck. I could drown in it.

I staggered to the window, throwing it open. The moon was nothing but a sliver slit in the sky tonight, but feeling its light on my face and inhaling the salt breeze into my lungs, I sighed.

I'd find a way.

We would always find a way.

ANNA

A brisk sea breeze blew past me, billowing through my loose dress. The sun's first light warmed my back, and sand pressed under my toes. The water lapped calmly on the sand and the soft dawn light cast a warm glow on the beach.

I decided.

I was never leaving the ocean again.

"Can I have you two walking through the surf, Summer?"

She was yawning but nodded.

"Sure, what do you want me to do with my arms?"

She pushed up from the rock where she was sitting with her boyfriend.

James was a six-foot-tall med student who had not only agreed to join Summer's photoshoot without question, but he also brought her coffee and two different dress shirts in case the one he had on clashed with her outfit or didn't photograph right.

"Umm... maybe, like, *frolic* a little? Try and look natural, though. Just give me some movement."

Summer obediently took James' hand and led him to the edge of the water. I followed them into the water, making sure I caught a good shot of them as she playfully pulled him along to a slow run, kicking up water.

I wanted the natural sandstone bluffs in the background of the shot, so I had to angle it just right. This beach wasn't large, just a sandy crescent bordered by rocky cliffs on each side, but the small cove in the morning with no one around was breathtakingly beautiful. The blue water sluicing over the rocks and sand was probably the kind of peaceful you experienced when you died.

I'd always thought so, anyway.

In some of my bleaker moments, I didn't think drowning would be such a bad way to go.

Summer stopped to pull James in for a quick kiss before spinning out with his hand still in hers. I snapped every facet of the movement, knowing in every shot she would look absolutely gorgeous.

I suspected that she saw an engagement on the horizon and wanted to have some professional photos ready for the big day.

It was almost...*unsettling* watching them.

Things seemed so easy between them.

Unforced. Unhurried. Unfrantic.

Just...*easy*.

Was this what it was supposed to be like?

James let go of Summer's hand and splashed water at her. I snapped a couple of shots, shaking off the sour thoughts. I caught a shot of the water midair and Summer at just the moment before she covered her face with her hands.

James grabbed Summer around the waist and hoisted her up to his chest. She wrapped her arms around his neck, squealing. I was about to take the shot but my finger stopped midway, almost jarred by the intimacy as he let her slip lower so their faces were inches apart.

He said something to her, too soft for me to hear which made her laugh. She threw her head back. *Click.* And then she kissed him.

I looked up from behind my camera with a fake sneer. "You guys are disgusting."

Summer looked over first.

"What? You said frolic. This is frolicking," she said, her feigned pout unable to hide the smirk pulling at her lips.

"Okay," I said over a laugh. "Well, I think we're good. You can stop frolicking now."

"You're going to look so hot in these photos, babe," James said, coming up out of the water with Summer.

His arm went around her waist and he pulled her into him. The movement was so fluid and automatic, like he was blinking, or swatting a fly away when it landed on his leg. They were so incredibly in sync and natural together. It was adorable and yes I was jealous.

But only of some parts.

"I bet my girl Anna can make a street cat look like a lion if she wanted to," Summer said with a giggle.

"Well you are *far* from a street cat," he joked, and she raised her hands, curling them into claws.

His other arm went around her, and he pressed a kiss to her forehead, erasing her faux feline snarl.

Summer and James really were adorable together. They

were playful, flirtatious, respectful, and kind. Why couldn't I just be attracted to guys like James?

Instead, bad guys seemed to draw me in like a moth to a fucking blowtorch.

And then there was Carter, who literally threw me in the trunk of his car two days ago. I should have been running for the hills, but instead, I was obsessing about when I could see him again. I tossed and turned all night, remembering how relaxed I felt when he spanked me.

If anyone else threw me over their shoulder and locked me in their trunk, I'd have been traumatized.

So then why wasn't I?

I was angry. So *so* fucking angry at first, until I realized I should've been scared and sat there in the dark closed-in space wondering why I wasn't.

Why when he said he needed to punish me, I got *excited*.

God, what was wrong with me?

"I don't know about you, Anna, but I need breakfast," Summer said, interrupting my thoughts.

As if on cue, my stomach growled.

"What if I said I had a mean souffle pancake recipe that I want to try out on you two?" James asked.

Okay, so he was perfect.

I would roll my eyes if I wasn't so happy for Summer.

James gave me his address and I got into the car with David to drive me to his apartment, knowing Carter's men wouldn't be far behind us, even if I couldn't see them.

James and Summer didn't live together but arrived together that morning. He lived in a condo not far from the medical center. David took me to his address, no questions asked. I knew that that address was all he would need to put together an entire dossier on James if my dad wanted to know where I was and with whom.

No need to worry, though. Daddy would take one look at James' file before giving it his stamp of approval. This was exactly the kind of man he'd approve of.

David had had to collect the car I left outside of Jaden's studio. I was under no illusions he would keep my indiscretions to himself when I'd needed to explain where I left it. So, when my dad asked where I'd been, I didn't lie.

I didn't need to protect Carter anymore.

And I knew it would piss him off.

It brought me an insane amount of joy to watch his face pale and slacken as I told him, 'Oh, I was with an old friend. Carter. Remember him? I think that *pathetic boy* might be wealthier than you now, *Dad*.'

God, he hated Carter back then. He still hated him now. I saw the hostility every time they were forced to make nice at events and the feelings were mutual.

I closed my eyes, pressing my face against the cool glass of the window.

Why had I stayed when he let me out of the trunk?

I was still so fucking weak. Still his little toy. I barely knew my own name when I was with him.

Inside me, somewhere deeper, I felt an ache.

I saw his face between my legs, brown eyes like liquid amber the first time he tasted me.

And later, when he took my last first and they all officially belonged to him.

It all came back, but the ache bled for the ugly parts.

The memory of his face twisted in anger and contempt as he told me he didn't give a shit about me. I was just a worthless fuck. The wrenching pain of that moment and the darkness in the aftermath. I almost didn't survive it.

After I left home, even with the money I'd been squirreling away for Carter to keep me fed and sheltered for a while, I was so. Damn. cold.

So empty.

It was a good thing there was no ocean in Missouri, or I'd have thrown myself in it.

I needed to stop. When we were together, it was easy to forget what he did, but after...

It was all I could remember. If I let him get his claws in me again, he'd really tear me apart this time.

Upstairs in James' condo, Summer and I sat at the barstools at his breakfast bar picking at chocolate chips and berries as he put together the soufflé pancakes, hunching over his phone to confirm the recipe with each step.

"So how did the meeting with that photographer go?" Summer asked, sipping her mimosa.

I made a barfing sound.

"What was that?" she asked with a laugh, cocking her head with a crinkle to her eyes.

"It was a flop," I explained, remembering Jaden's hand on my thigh.

I grimaced.

Apparently, he'd taken off. I'd looked it up yesterday, terrified I might find a headline that read 'Celebrity Photographer Found Dead in His Midtown Studio,' but instead there was only a short article that read 'Celebrity Clients Left to Flounder in Wake of Photographer Shutting Down his Midtown Studio Without Notice.'

Good. He should run. I didn't want to think about what Carter might do to him if he'd stayed.

"What happened?"

"He thought that us working together meant he was going to get *favors*," I admitted.

Summer rolled her eyes, groaning. "*Men.*"

"*Men,*" I agreed, glad she wasn't prying anymore into what happened.

"They're all the same, aren't they?"

"Who are all the same, honey?" James asked, tuning into the conversation.

Summer recounted my story.

"This guy who offered to help Anna with her photography just did it to try and get in her pants. And I meant most men, Jamesy. Not you, obviously."

"He what?" James actually looked genuinely disgusted. "What an asshole."

He served up the thick, fluffy pancakes, telling us to wait for him to grab the whipped cream from the fridge, then dolloping out a helping for each of us. "I'm sorry that happened to you."

"Yeah. So that's dead in the water. I'm on my own now. Again."

"Will breakfast help?"

I laughed. It was a good start.

This was probably the most 'normal' meal in 'normal' company I'd had since I got home.

"Bon appétit," James said, staying on the other side of the breakfast bar. I noticed his eyes on us as we tried our pancakes, anxiously jumping between me, then Summer, then back again. Summer took a bite, then gasped.

"Oh my god, babe, this is delicious."

"Yeah?" A wide smile spread across his face.

I tried mine, slicing through the fluffy pancake, getting

a bit of the cream. It melted in my mouth. I hummed with pleasure, getting another bite, spearing some berries for some sweet tartness.

"That's insane, how did you get it so fluffy?"

"A chef never shares his secrets," he said with mock seriousness, tossing the dish towel over his shoulder. "But I'm glad you like them."

We paused to eat, discussing how he got the cakes so thick but so light at the same time. Summer conspiratorially promised to swipe the recipe link from his phone and send it to me when he wasn't looking.

"Can I ask you something?" James hedged after washing the pan and utensils.

I piled some more berries on my plate. "Sure, fire away."

"The guy in the black suit driving the Mercedes with the blacked-out windows," he said, trailing off. I sipped my coffee.

"That's not a question."

"Is that one of the perks of being the governor's daughter?" he asked.

"I guess. He's not my personal driver, though. He drives my dad and mother around too sometimes."

"*Of course*, a driver just for you would be way too extravagant. Sharing one with your family is so much more economical."

I laughed. "Touché. I don't make the rules. I just live there. Truly, I'd rather get around alone, but it's not up to me. Security, you know?"

"I'm surprised he's that worried about threats. Governor Vaughn's pretty well-liked."

By some people.

But I knew James was right, as shocking as it was.

None of Hudson's misdeeds had seen the light of day and his competition was comparatively worse. He had curated his life so carefully that even his approval rating and credit score didn't ever dare to disappoint him.

Instead of explaining that my driver was really just a babysitter, Dad's little way of controlling me after the disappearing act I pulled six years ago, I said, "Did he have your vote the last time he ran?"

James laughed.

"I was out of state then, so I didn't get the chance to, but if he was running again, he'd have it for sure."

Maybe James wasn't perfect after all.

"He's gonna try for the presidency eventually so maybe you can make good on that promise then," I said, hating how the words left my mouth so easily. The perfect response from the perfect daughter of the perfect future POTUS.

"Oh really?"

"Yeah. Career politician. He doesn't really have the skills to do anything else."

"Not like Anna," Summer said proudly. "I can't wait to see the photos from this morning. I wish you'd show me some of the ones you took in Malawi."

I looked down at my hands. I still hadn't told Summer the truth. Part of me was scared she'd be pissed at me for lying to her, but another part was afraid she'd judge me. Where I came from, women didn't grow up to work at cock-tail lounges.

They studied medicine or law or journalism with very little variation and when the time came, they shelved that achievement for their *real* life goal: trophy wife.

The worst part was, I *wanted* to show Summer my

photos. She'd been so supportive of me since I got back. I wished I could pull out my portfolio and show her everything.

Wishing got me nowhere.

You know what? *Fuck it*.

Why couldn't I show her? Why couldn't she know the truth?

Olivia Wu knew. Jaden Austen knew. Why stop there?

I suspected Summer and James could handle the truth and keep it to themselves.

If they didn't?

Oopsie. Guess Daddy wouldn't be able to use me as his precious doll anymore.

"Okay, so don't hate me," I said cautiously, earning myself a wrinkled look from Summer. "But I can't show you any photos from Malawi...because I never went."

Summer frowned. "What do you mean, you never went? You were gone for six years."

I took a deep breath. "I was in St. Louis, actually. I wasn't building houses. I was a cocktail waitress."

James and Summer exchanged glances.

She barked a laugh, putting her hand on mine, waiting for me to say I was joking.

I didn't.

She stopped laughing.

"Oh," she chirped. "So...maybe start at the beginning?"

I ended up spilling the whole story. My job at the Butterfly Room, how I left St. Louis after a bad breakup, and Dad's insistence that once I got back, I had to stick to his fake story about charity work. I glossed over exactly why Josh and I broke up, but otherwise, I told them everything.

When I was done, James started laughing. He had a

huge, deep chortle that filled the room and managed to completely disarm me at the same time.

"Oh man," he said between guffaws. "Your dad is *nuts*. He didn't just make up a backstory. He rewrote you to make you into freaking Mother Teresa. Fuck that noise. What a jerk. He does *not* have my vote anymore, by the way."

I gave him an apologetic look for my earlier 'performance.'

"The house-building story *was* a bit over-the-top," Summer admitted. "Considering that back when we were kids, you couldn't even figure out my Lego blocks."

"Hey! My Lego buildings weren't supposed to be structurally sound," I said with mock offense. "They were supposed to be creative expressions of my imagination."

Summer shook her head. "Thank God you were lying. Those poor Malawians had enough problems without you being their architect."

She did *not* just say that.

"So? Can we see the real photos?" James prompted.

I nodded and took out my portfolio. I carried it almost everywhere with me now, in a little satchel bag with my wallet and phone. I was too afraid to leave them at home. Unable to imagine my father's rage if he found them.

"Oh shit, you actually, like, have them on you?" Summer chuckled with eager surprise.

Summer and James flipped through and carefully examined each photo, pointing out what they liked and asking stories about some of the women.

"Wow," James said finally. "You weren't kidding. She's *good*."

"Really freaking good," Summer said loyally. "Seriously, Anna. These are amazing. You should be so proud."

My heart swelled. I didn't realize how much I needed to hear her praise. Jaden's attack had rattled me, but so had his words. When he called me a spoiled rich girl with a hobby, I actually started doubting my talent. I needed a real friend like Summer to pull me out of it.

And I realized that was what she was all along. A real friend. I just hadn't been able to see it because I didn't want to.

"You totally have to submit these for exhibit. I bet there are a hundred galleries who would love to host this."

"Oh god. No way. These are okay, but they aren't that good. I...I have a long way to go before I get to that point, I think."

"Are these the negatives?" she pointed to the envelope, spilling film onto the counter. I didn't trust leaving those at home, either.

I nodded.

"So cool. I haven't seen film like this since I was a kid. Can I...?"

"Sure, just, carefully."

She pushed up from her chair, taking the envelope to the window to look at the captured images with the light from the afternoon sun.

"I doubt many people use film like that anymore," James mused, looking at Summer how I wanted people to someday look at my art.

"There are more of us than you might think."

20

CARTER

People said the beach was peaceful. Those people were idiots.

Seagulls squawked loudly as they fought over the carcass of a crab. Waves crashed against the beach, pounding broken shells into sand.

Some days the crosscurrent was so strong, it dragged people out so far they had no hope of finding the surface, swimming back to shore.

Boats sunk in ocean storms. Entire crews lost to the abyss of blue.

Then there was what lurked beneath the surface. Things that could sting and bite and poison and kill.

All nature was brutal.

Beautiful, but brutal.

It was why I liked it here. I felt at home among the self-destructive landscape. Among the beasts and the broken shells.

After Hudson Vaughn's attempt to blackmail me, I was

hot-headed and ready to draw blood from the first person to look at me wrong.

I hadn't slept since, which probably wasn't helping.

This did, though.

Our beach called to me. As soon as I could break away from work this afternoon, I came straight here, parking myself in the sand where the blood of Anna's lost virginity once stained the sand.

Crazy to think how long ago that was. We were just two vulnerable teens marked by their fathers' cruelty, sharing secrets and creating a bond that would become completely unbreakable.

Anna was so perfect when I brought her to my villa, letting me hold her, letting me punish her, letting me fuck her. It ate me knowing my seed wasn't in her right now. Wasn't in her at all times. Fuck, I wanted to fill her with it so completely that no form of contraception would work against the battalion of it.

I was distracted by the buzz of my cell. Sighing, I pulled it out and answered Paulson's call.

"What?"

"I've got news, and you're not going to like it."

"Tell me."

"Remember, I'm just the messenger."

He was stalling. Paulson's self-preservation tactics were really starting to annoy me.

"Spit it out," I growled.

"Fine," he said, sighing. "Your girl's ex never stopped putting up bounties for her on the dark web. They were buried deep and my guys didn't find them until they'd been up awhile. We took them all down, but there were some replies on the posts."

An icy dagger twisted in my gut.

"What kind of replies?"

"Information sharing mostly. Her...her real name was used several times."

Jesus fuck.

I squeezed my eyes shut, digging the edge of my cell into my temple, needing the bite of pain to level me out as dark spots fought for cruel dominion over my eyes.

"Anything else," I barely got out through my teeth.

A pause. "Yeah. I'm sorry, Carter. There was a photo a user posted in reply to one of the bulletins. One taken at a charity gala. You were also in the frame. The image puts her here. So we assume whoever is looking to collect on this bounty now has a good idea of her location."

My vision went black with rage.

That pathetic piece of shit.

Josh Porter was as good as dead. It was only a matter of time. I'd do worse to him than what I did to my father and that was some of the most twisted shit I'd ever done in my life.

"*Find him,*" I ordered Paulson. "Find him *now*. Move the fucking world if you have to. I want three times as many men out there looking for him and anyone else who replied to the ads. I want them stopped before they cross the state line. How many men do you have on her now?"

"Three."

"Double it."

"Got it."

"And Paulson?"

"Yeah, boss?"

I could feel my face twitching, feel the anger coming off me in waves strong enough that even the sea seemed to be receding into itself, not wanting to come too far onto shore.

"If another bulletin goes up and you don't have it taken down in the same fucking second, I will cleave your head from your shoulders and hollow out your skull to make a fucking ashtray out of it, you feel me?"

"I do. I have someone on it around the clock."

I stood and jabbed the button to end the call, quickly opening the app that tracked Anna's phone. She was in town, but a good twenty minute drive away. I had to move fast. Who knew how many people might have seen those ads by now?

I sprinted back to the villa. My muscles burned as I crossed the sand, my breath coming in ragged gasps.

As I threw myself into the car and set the GPS, I forced myself to clear my mind long enough to *think.*

I accessed the audio on Anna's phone, and three voices floated out. One, I recognized as Anna's, and another as her friend Summer's. There was also a third male voice I didn't know.

Fuck.

Who the hell was it?

From what I could hear, muffled likely through her purse, everyone's tones seemed relaxed, but I couldn't trust it.

He could be biding his time, trying to get Anna alone. Posing as someone trustworthy. An electrician or a plumber or a fucking vacuum salesman.

I kept the sound on while I started driving, playing it through the Aston's speakers to try to capture more of what they were saying.

Every muffled word, every laugh from Anna reassured me that she was alive, at least for now.

How long had that ad been up?

Fuck. I should have asked Paulson.

Was it long enough for someone to get here? To find her?

My grip tightened on the steering wheel. I had to get to Anna *now* if I wanted to save her. Summer was just as innocent and harmless as Anna, so she'd be no protection against an intruder. My bodyguards were stationed outside, but even they weren't infallible. An expert, someone ex-military or CIA could manage to get around them.

And with a payday like the one Josh was offering, I knew it was possible all kinds wanted a piece of the pie. The first ones who tried were nothing but a bunch of young thugs in baseball caps looking for a quick buck.

Their corpses now lay bloated at the bottom of the ocean. Food for the fishes.

I drove as fast as I could without killing myself. It took me half the projected time to reach the destination, which turned out to be a modern-looking condo building.

I skimmed the names on the doorbells, hoping to see one I'd recognize. Thank God, one stuck out.

James O'Callahan.

I remembered him from Paulson's files on the people close to Anna. He was Summer's current boyfriend. This was his apartment.

Was it his voice on the other end of Anna's phone?

I left the door open, rushing from the car at the very front of the building, seeing two men in the distance, speaking in hushed tones into their earbuds. I recognized them as mine. One pulled his weapon, his head moving on a swivel at something he heard on the other end of his earpiece.

I almost called to them, but an older woman exited the building with a dog, and I used the advantage to get in without busting the double glass paned doors. I held one open for her, forcing a fake smile as my phone rang again.

Grinding my teeth, I pulled it to my ear.

"Go."

"We got a lead on a group of mercenaries headed into the city to collect," Paulson rushed to say. "My guys are checking their last known location and tracing them from there. Looks like they're somewhere in the east end but moving fast. We lost them on Fifth."

I was in the east end. This fucking condo was east end.

Anna.

I didn't bother waiting for the elevator. I sprinted up four flights of stairs, the image of Anna's fear-filled face driving me to move faster than I ever had. My heart pounded, repeating her name.

Anna. Anna. Anna.

I tore into the hallway, skidding past apartment 404, backtracking, gripping the frame as I threw a booted foot into the door.

The wood cracked easily, letting me stride right into the open concept kitchen and living room. A girlish scream pierced the air and I whipped my head to the left to find three sets of wide eyes taking me in from a kitchen island. Anna's quickly turned icy, even as her cheeks flushed pink.

"Dude, what the hell?" James demanded. "Who the fuck are you?"

I ignored him, heading straight for my little siren, who

had hopped off a stool to greet me. She was perfectly intact, and relief washed over me in waves.

Her palms met my chest and she shoved, making me falter a step.

"*Anna.*"

She shoved at my chest again, a vulgar expression on her face.

"*Out,*" she hissed. "You can't just go around breaking down people's doors whenever. The. Fucking. Mood. Strikes!"

She punctuated each word with another shove until I caught her wrists.

"Anna. Anna, *stop.*"

I hushed her, pulling her in by her wrists to cradle her face with my free hand, needing to feel her.

Her lips twitched in annoyance. Fuck, she was so adorable when she was angry.

She struggled against my grip on her, muttering that I was an inconsiderate asshole.

Behind her, James moved around the countertop, and I flicked my gaze to him, fixing him with a look that made him stop in his tracks. His throat bobbed.

Prey recognizing a predator.

I'd eat that boy alive if he moved another inch.

Nothing was coming between us.

"Carter, can we do this out—"

My lips crashed down on hers, stealing a kiss. My fingers wove into her hair, and I focused on the feeling of her soft body arching against mine. Her lips parted and I felt the hitch in her breath as I swept in. Felt her melt for me, even now, even with anger still knotting the skin between her brows.

I grunted as a sharp sting bit into my bottom lip. As *she* bit into my bottom lip.

Pulling back, I prodded the injury with my tongue, grinning as I tasted earth and copper.

"Enough." She dropped her arms heavily, pulling down hard and swift enough to break my hold. "What the hell is going on, Carter?"

"You think that's her ex?" Summer's voice floated to me from where she was whispering with James.

"I don't know. Should we, like, call the cops or something?"

"Um, Anna..." Summer called tentatively, a wince in her expression. "Who's your friend?"

Anna steeled herself before turning to face Summer and her boyfriend. "I am *so* sorry, you guys. He has absolutely no manners, but he's harmless."

I scoffed.

So did James.

"And, *uh*," James lifted a brow. "What is this *harmless* friend doing in my condo, exactly?"

He had put his body in front of Summer's, as if I were a danger to the only girl who'd shown my Anna any real kindness since she came home.

"Carter?" Anna pressed, her hands on her hips.

James blew out a sigh, and I tracked his stare to the mangled door to his condo.

Anna glared at me pointedly.

"Send me the bill for the door," I told him, tugging a business card from the inside pocket of my jacket. He recoiled as I approached but took it.

I turned to find Anna still glaring.

What was I missing?

Right.

I cleared my throat and turned back to James. "Apologies for bursting in like this, it was imperative that I spoke to Anna."

I didn't wait for James to reply before turning and arching a brow at Anna.

Better? I asked her wordlessly.

She rolled her eyes, growling to herself. "Next time use the doorbell like a normal person."

"Or the handle," James added. "It wasn't even locked."

Of course it wasn't.

I resisted the urge to break James' nose.

Who the fuck just left their door unlocked? Especially with two beautiful women inside. What was wrong with people?

"We're still waiting for an explanation, Carter."

I caught Summer mouthing something to Anna that looked like *he's hot,* but she schooled herself the instant she felt me looking, studiously looking anywhere else.

The weight of the gun tucked in the back of my pants from the Aston's glove compartment grounded me as I stalked to the wide bay windows and peered outside.

The others whispered in my absence as I pulled my phone to my ear and dialed Paulson, alternating between checking the parking area and the broken door for any sign of approaching mercenaries.

Paulson answered on the first ring like a good dog. "Status?"

"We have a tail on them in midtown. We'll have them within the hour."

I sagged.

"Want us to dispose—"

"No," I hissed. "I'll do it myself."

I pocketed the cell and went to the kitchen island, making James and Summer disperse as I pulled Anna's portfolio together and gathered the rest of her things into her bag.

"Grab anything else you brought," I said. "We're leaving."

"Anna?" Summer hedged, her voice growing higher in pitch. "This isn't the guy from St. L—"

My girl shook her head, rushing over to snatch her bag and camera from my hands. "No, Summer, everything's fine. Like I said, this one just has *no manners*."

"Does this one have a name?"

"Carter Cole," James supplied, reading it off the business card between his fingers.

"Why does that sound so familiar?" Summer mused and then her eyes brightened and her lips popped open. "Oh my god, this isn't the one that—"

"*Summer*," Anna warned.

Summer squealed, completely unaware that if I didn't have a veritable army out there scaring off every mercenary aiming to claim the bounty on my girl, they'd be dealing with a very different sort of villain right now.

"I thought you said he was—"

"Summer!"

She mimed zipping her lips, but made a gesture at Anna holding her hands about nine inches apart with a wince and despite myself, I almost laughed.

So she had told someone about me.

Or at least one part of me.

She didn't meet her friend's eyes as she huffed, hitching

her bag higher on her shoulder. "James, thank you so much for the amazing breakfast."

Wait. This fucker cooked for her?

"And Summer, I'll have the photos from the shoot fully edited and in your inbox as soon as I can."

"Okay, yeah, no rush. Are you sure you're good going with—"

"Yeah," Anna rushed to say as I caught her elbow between my fingers and started to drag her to the door with me, helping her step over the broken pieces despite her trying to pull from my grasp. "I'm totally fine. Sorry about this again, by the way. Buy a really, *really* expensive door, James, he can afford it."

There's my girl.

"You take care of my girl, Carter Cole," Summer called after me. "If you break her heart again, girl code says I get to key your car and slash your tires."

As threats went, it wasn't one of the more frightening I'd ever received. But the fierce look in Summer's eyes pleased me. Anna deserved friends who looked after her, who saw her for the treasure she was.

ANNA ASKED ME WHAT WAS GOING ON TWICE MORE BEFORE I GOT her out of the building, into my car, and across town to my villa.

I could make up some bullshit about wanting her to be comfortable on my sofa before I told her, but the truth was, I just wanted her within the walls of my impenetrable villa so she couldn't run away once she knew the truth.

She strode through the foyer, straight into the kitchen, pulling open every cupboard until she found a glass and filled it with water.

"Okay, you got me here," she said as she finished the glass and set it in the sink. "Are you going to tell me why you just completely embarrassed me in front of my friends and made a complete ass of yourself?"

"Sit."

Her nostrils flared, but she did as she was told, crossing the hardwood floor to the sofa where I had my way with her just days ago. The evidence of what we did had already been cleaned away and I found myself wanting to put it back.

"I think I've been pretty patient, Carter." She sat, looking up at me. "Start talking or I'm going home."

I slipped into the seat next to her, my thigh pressing against hers.

"I've been looking into your ex."

She groaned. "Carter, I didn't want you going after him. It's exactly why I didn't want to tell you his name in the first place."

"I had no choice, Anna. My PI reported that several weeks ago, Josh placed ads on the dark web, offering a reward for anyone who could deliver you alive."

Her face turned ashen, eyes alive with shock and fear and everything I was trying to protect her from.

"He wouldn't. Why would he? It had to be some—some kind of—"

"My team removed the ads as soon as they could. That's why I've had my men following you. It was a precaution in case anyone..."

I couldn't finish the sentence.

"More ads were posted recently, and they weren't taken down as quickly as they should've been. It *won't* happen again, but it looks like your real identity and location were broadcast to anyone who might've viewed the bulletin."

Anna balled her hands on her knees. She hunched over, like she was trying to make herself smaller. Like if she got lower, the smoke from this dumpster fire couldn't suffocate her.

She pushed a hand against her chest, breathing fast.

Before I knew it, my hand was rubbing slow circles in her back.

"Breathe, Anna. Just breathe. I'm going to keep you safe."

"I knew Josh was messed up," she murmured after a minute. " But I never imagined he would do something like this. This is..."

"A coward's move."

"And the dark web? What even *is* that?"

"You don't want to know."

She fought for control of her breathing again and something cracked in my chest.

"Why would he..."

"So he could have total control. So he could feel like he owned you."

"Oh, God. I can't even think about that," Anna said, shuddering.

I pulled her tight against me and she didn't fight it, burrowing into my side. "It's all right. He won't get his hands on you. I'll find him first."

Anna stiffened. When she met my eyes, her gaze was full of reproach. "Wait. You didn't even tell me. You've known all this time and you didn't tell me."

"I didn't want to worry you," I explained. "And between me and your father, you were well protected."

She stood abruptly, turning to face me with a hard expression on her face. "But you didn't think I deserved to know what was happening? I could have made different choices, Carter. I wouldn't have snuck off by myself or put myself in danger. This is *my* life, not yours!"

My stomach twisted with some unknown emotion.

Anna paced across my living room. I could see her anger rising with each step.

You're going to lose her.

Fix it.

Fix it.

"I didn't want you obsessing about your ex," I said and the words were coming out all wrong. "That's why he did all this. Because he wanted you to be afraid. I didn't want him to win."

She laughed, but the sound was hollow. "I can't believe I actually thought for one second I could trust you. That you were different. God, you're just like him."

Anger surged through me. What did I do to deserve to be compared to that piece of shit? Yes, Anna was mine, but I didn't try to push her down and make her smaller. I was giving her everything she wanted. What she needed. Even if she didn't see it that way.

"Take it back," I said through gritted teeth.

"I won't. You think you get *sooo* many brownie points for hiring some retired mall cops to watch me?"

They were far from that and she knew it, but I let her go on.

"No, you're a real hero."

She needed to watch her tone.

"You're only hiding things from me and trying to control every part of my life. No biggie, right Carter?"

She poked me hard in the chest.

"Don't try and pretend you're not a manipulative prick just like all the rest of them."

That, I was guilty of, but I wouldn't apologize. I was doing what I needed to do to make her safe and make her see where she belonged.

Who she belonged with.

I'd do far worse.

"I did what I needed to. I won't apologize."

"Of course you won't. You don't care about what I want. You only care about what you think you deserve."

This is not how you keep her, Carter.

I tapped my fingertips on the arm of the sofa, racing to find the right words. The ones that would make her see. Make her *stay*.

"Maybe I messed up a bit," I admitted. "I could've told you what was happening and I chose not to. If you want the truth, fine, you have it. From here on, ask me anything you want to know and I'll tell you, just know that you may not like the answers."

Her brows furrowed and her jaw flexed as she thought through what I imagined was a thousand questions she wanted answers to. There was only one I wouldn't give her.

"Are you keeping any other secrets from me?"

"I once came to see you on the beach straight from the ER. I woke up in the emergency room and ripped out the IV before they could—"

"That's not what I meant and you know it," she interrupted. "Is there anything else you're hiding from me *now*. Since I got home."

Dodged that bullet. But I'd have to eat another one.

"All right. Yes. I had my PI look into you as soon as you were back in town."

She didn't look surprised, more vindicated than anything. Like I was confirming something for her she already knew and judged.

"Your dad did a pretty good job erasing every trace of you from existence after you left. For years, I had no idea where you were. If you were even alive. We only got a few leads on where you were after you were already on your way back."

"You really had no right to invade my privacy like that."

"I know for a fact that you would have done the same thing if you had the money and our roles were reversed," I said and her eyes narrowed. "You were just as curious about me as I was about you. I know you kept up with me online. Searching for me, looking at my pictures."

Her jaw dropped.

There it was. My other dirty little secret.

"How could you possibly know..."

I saw the moment it dawned on her and lifted my chin in the face of her icy glare.

"You hacked into my phone, didn't you? Into my search history?"

Her cheeks turned an absolutely delicious shade of pink.

"Yes," I replied simply. "I could also mirror the screen and when it was necessary, I listened to your live audio."

She looked like she couldn't decide whether to laugh or scream. Blinking like an owl. Opening and closing her mouth like some kind of adorable amphibian.

She wasn't surprised I had an investigator looking into her past, but she was shocked at this?

I didn't see all that much difference.

"When...*necessary*?"

I pressed my lips together. Touché.

"Okay. Not *always* when necessary."

She backed away another step, almost tripping on the coffee table. I lurched to catch her but she gave me a look that could've curdled dairy and I sat back down. For now.

"What the actual fuck, Carter?"

I steepled my fingers, pressing them to my lips to sigh against them.

"I'm a possessive man, Anna," I said, drinking in every inch of her.

She shivered at the attention, betraying her misplaced rage.

"You're so fucked up," she said, almost to herself as she shook her head.

"*Yes*. Yes, I am."

I pushed to my feet and slowly closed the gap between us, not stopping until I was inches away and her calves were pressed into the edge of the coffee table.

"I'm not ashamed of what I am or what I want, Anna. I know I can be controlling and overpowering. I want things from you that are definitely fucked up. It's because I want all of you."

I ran my thumb over her lower lip, and her breath hitched.

"I want to consume your every thought. I want to know exactly where you are, always. I want to ruin you for anyone else, and make you come so hard, your memories of anyone before me are wiped from that beautiful mind. I want to tie you to me in every way humanly possible."

I let my hand fall down her chest, to her stomach.

I could feel her pulse tap-tapping against my hand. Speeding like a runaway train. "Can you accept that, Anna? Can you accept all of me?"

When I moved to brush my thumb over her hip, she smacked it away.

"Don't touch me."

I removed my hand, but didn't dare take another step away. If she wanted space from me, she was going to have to take it herself.

After a second, she scoffed, giving me a half-hearted shove before going to get her bag from the kitchen. "I'm going home."

She stormed down the hall, digging her phone from her purse, presumably to call for a ride.

I got ahead of her, planting myself between her and the door. "You're not going anywhere right now, Anna."

Not until I got the call from Paulson saying he caught the bastards that came into town to get my girl. Maybe not even then.

"Yes, I am. *Move.*"

She shifted right, and I blocked her path again.

"You can't just do things like this! You can't just hack my phone and look into my past and listen to my private conversations and check my fucking search history. It's fucked. *Ugh*, this is so fucked, just *move.*"

Anna feigned left and then darted right, ducking under the arm I threw out to stop her, but I used that arm to curl around her waist instead, hauling her back.

She let out a frustrated scream, fighting out of my grip to turn the full force of her fury on me. "*I'm going.*"

This time, when she pivoted to continue down the hall, I didn't stop her.

"Lyle, initiate lockdown."

Anna stopped dead in her tracks, twisting her head to me with shock and confusion all over her face, but just until the electronic voice of my smarthome's AI replied.

"Initiating lockdown."

Her eyes went round as saucers.

She bolted for the door, but the metallic sounds of locks engaging on every exit in the villa echoed like fifty hammers striking iron. Then came the whir of the emergency shutters coming down over the windows. I had to admit, it was impressive if a little dramatic.

I hadn't needed to use this little feature since buying the place, but a glorious satisfaction came over me as the house sealed itself from anything and everything that could hurt my little siren.

Anna pulled on the door handle, fighting with the locking mechanism.

"Shall I alert the authorities, Mr. Cole?" Lyle, the AI controlling the house asked and Anna stopped fighting with the door, looking up at the ceiling like she was trying to find the source of the voice, her chest heaving.

"That won't be necessary, Lyle."

"Lyle!" Anna shouted. "Lyle, open the front door."

Lyle didn't reply.

"It's coded to my voice, Anna. You aren't leaving until I say you're leaving."

21

ANNA

I tried the patio door and the door to the side garden before moving to the windows that didn't look like windows at all anymore.

They looked like something out of a sci-fi movie. Hard gray metal everywhere there should've been natural light.

I banged my fist against the cold slats, making it rattle.

"Anna, stop. You'll only hurt yourself."

Snatching my empty glass from the kitchen, I threw it at the metal, making broken shards rain all over Carter's expensive rug. "*Make it open.*"

The bastard didn't so much as move or even open his mouth to speak, his ocean eyes watching me warily, like a cobra ready to strike.

My phone. I could call—

No sooner did I have it back in my hand than Carter was there snatching it from my fingers. "Face it, Anna. You're staying. At least for now. Let me—"

"Let you? *Let you?* I'm not letting you do anything, Carter. You just *do* whatever the fuck you want."

I tried to get my phone back, but he held it higher than I could reach and I wouldn't play that game with him. Spinning on my heel, I went to claw some more at the metal enclosure, sure there must be a chink in its armor I could use to get free.

"Anna, *don't*—"

I hissed as a shard of glass bit into the bottom of my foot, burrowing itself in deep.

"*Fuck.*"

"Goddamn it, Anna."

He caught the back of my knees, swinging me up into his arms without any warning whatsoever. I yelped, reflexively grabbing around his neck.

"Put me down."

"No."

I pushed away from his chest.

"Anna, stop, or I'll throw you over my shoulder."

I redoubled my efforts and kicked my feet.

He gave me a dangerous look before easily maneuvering me so I was over his shoulder, the bulge of it digging into my stomach.

"*God*, you are just the worst fucking...fucking..."

I couldn't even come up with a word dirty enough or angry enough for what he was.

But as he carried me up the stairs, I felt the fight going out of me and something far worse than anger started to take root.

Because when those fucking shutters went down, I didn't feel caged. Not really. I felt safe. Safe *with him*. And that was a dangerous feeling. I couldn't feel that. Couldn't *want* that. I'd just get hurt.

I knew how this ended. When he got tired of me, he'd throw me away. Just like he did six years ago.

The bit of fight I lost somewhere on the main floor reignited as we got to the top of the landing and Carter pushed into a bedroom.

I dug an elbow into his back, earning myself a pained grunt before I was unceremoniously tossed down onto a bed. The plush silk covered duvet swallowed me whole and I had to fight it to get free, the lure to stay wrapped in it and just cry so strong I almost couldn't resist.

"Oh, no you don't."

Carter caught my ankle before I could clamber from the bed and tugged me back across the covers until he had me right in the middle of it. He flipped me onto my back and pressed his weight into my middle as he struggled with something on the bed.

"Stop fucking squirming," he spat, wrenching my leg toward the edge of the bed. Something whispered over my ankle and then pulled tight.

Oh god.

"Carter? Carter, what the hell are you doing?"

He shifted over me and jerked my free leg easily to the other edge, cuffing that ankle, too.

As soon as he was off me, I was up, reaching for my ankles, but my fingers barely managed to grasp the restraints before I was thrust back, my right arm yanked high above my head, and my wrist bound.

I pulled on the restraint. It was a thick band of soft fabric with a metal lock.

What the fuck was this?

I gasped as he snatched my last free appendage and

bound it in place, standing back to survey his handiwork with a growing hunger in his eyes.

"You can't just—"

"I already did, little siren. Nobody gets to hurt you, not even yourself."

As if on cue, the cut in my foot throbbed painfully, and I was all too aware of the feeling of the glass trespassing beneath my skin.

I hissed in a breath and looked down, pulling on the restraints, trying to see the damage.

Carter walked from the room, and I shouted after him.

"What, are you just going to leave me like this? Carter! *Carter!*"

He came back before I broke sound records screaming his name, a first aid kit in his hands as he knelt at the foot of the bed.

"Just *relax,* would you. I need to clean this before it gets infected."

I didn't even want to look at him. Didn't want him to see the hot tears pooling in my eyes. I stared at the ceiling instead, knowing that until he was good and ready nothing I said was going to convince him to untie these restraints and let me go home.

He set to cleaning the area around the cut and gently prodding my heel to ease the glass out.

I let my head fall to the right, noticing the room for the first time as he plucked the glass out, making me hiss, and started to apply pressure to stop the bleeding.

It had to be Carter's bedroom. I could see his outfit for tomorrow laid out by some household staff no doubt. His collection of watches on the nightstand. But other than his belongings, this room didn't say *Carter Cole.*

There were sheer curtains framing the now-metal-gated windows, though the sound of waves crashing on the beach still managed to drift through. I focused on that sound, on the room, as the throbbing in my heel subsided.

If you'd asked me to imagine Carter's room, I would have pictured something dark and moody. With walls that were emerald green or navy blue instead of this lime washed sand. This whole space looked like something I might've designed for myself, not for someone like him.

"It wasn't very deep," he said as he finished winding the gauze around my foot.

I could feel his eyes on me, but I wouldn't give him the satisfaction of looking at him. A long moment passed between us before finally, he sighed.

"*Maybe* I shouldn't have hacked your phone's audio."

"You think?"

Another heavy sigh.

"If that's an apology, then I'm a fucking circus clown."

"Look at me."

I didn't.

"Please."

I frowned, letting my head fall the other way. He never said please.

"I'm no good at this Anna. I don't date. I don't...do this with people. I'm never going to be..."

"Normal?" I supplied.

He gave me a pointed look, but responded anyway. "No. Probably not. I don't know how to be that guy, Anna. Not anymore. This is me. But I *am* trying."

I rattled my restraints. "*This* is trying?"

"No, this is me not letting you hurt yourself trying to

put yourself right back into the danger I just pulled you out of."

"This is kidnapping, you know. A criminal offense."

"You going to have me arrested?"

I snorted. "As if it would stick. I know all about your friends in high places."

"Ah. That. Redditors really think they're the sleuths of the interwebs."

I rolled my eyes. Of course he saw every Reddit thread I poured over about his meteoric rise to success.

"Are you angry that I looked at your history, or angry that I know you were looking for *me* every time you grabbed your phone at night?"

Both, I thought, but didn't reply.

"That's what I thought. Anna, why can't you admit that you want this—that you want *me* just as fucking badly as I want you?"

His hand on my heel shifted, pushing up to my calf, his calluses against the smooth skin there making goosebumps rise all over my body.

My pulse fluttered.

I worked to shut it the fuck up, but as his hand shifted higher, I couldn't get that canary back in the cage and felt my lips part on a breathy sigh.

I squeezed my eyes shut.

You are not going to let him do this.

"*Anna*," he said, his voice a husky whisper that begged me to open my eyes. I squeezed them tighter.

The mattress shifted and stars exploded behind my eyelids at the anticipation.

Tell him to stop.

My traitorous lips stayed shut, forcing me to breathe

heavy and fast through my nose as I felt the presence of his body hovering just above mine.

His nose brushed my cheek.

"Tell me you hate this," he whispered in my ear.

"You're unbelievable," I replied, the *able* turning into a sharp chirp as he lowered his hips against mine.

"Do you feel how fucking hard I am for you, little siren?"

So hard, he might tear through those Brioni slacks. I tried to move, to press my thighs together, but couldn't.

I did manage to hold in my moan, but my eyes flashed open to find him watching me intently, our faces a breath apart.

There was an edge of vulnerability to his blue eyes that disarmed me, melting away whatever was left of all that pointless rage.

"Let me make you feel good. Call it"—he flicked my nose with his—"my way of apologizing."

"I—"

Why couldn't I just say it?

"N-no," I mumbled.

"Sorry, was that a 'no'?"

He was fucking teasing me. After the shit he pulled today.

Meanwhile, out there, there could be a hundred dangerous humans trying to get their hands on me to deliver me back to Josh.

God. I didn't want to think about that.

I didn't want to think about any of it.

"Hey."

I looked up at him.

"Don't be afraid. Not of me."

"I'm not."

But I should be.

He grinned at that and ground his erection against my pussy in a way that made me convulse around him, unable to hold back my sounds of pleasure this time.

"There she is," he dipped his head to the crook of my neck, kissing along the sensitive flesh there. "I'm going to fuck you now, little siren. Make you forget all the reasons you were angry."

With every roll of his hips, I lost more and more of my sense, my greedy cunt beginning to pulse and ache with a need so strong I resolved to just lie there and let him do whatever he wanted to me.

I wanted to forget all the bad. Just for a while.

And he was going to do it anyway.

Carter wasted no time tearing my clothes off and throwing them on the floor in tattered heaps, leaving me naked in front of him.

I shivered, not from the cool air, but from the way his eyes raked over me. Devouring me.

He pressed one hand on my chest, between my breasts, keeping me flat on the bed. With the other, he tugged on my hair, pulling my head to the side so he could have total access to my neck.

He scattered hot, open-mouthed kisses across the sensitive skin until I moaned for him.

"You love it when I take what I want from you, don't you, little siren?"

I clenched my teeth against a reply because the one word answer that shouted in my mind was *yes*.

Yes.

I loved it. I loved every dirty, depraved second of it. And

I hated that I loved it, but soon, Carter would make me forget that, too.

"You don't have to answer me, Anna. I already know your truth."

He shifted from me, and I opened my eyes to find him slowly undressing beside the bed. I made no secret of watching his every movement, keeping my expression as placid as I could. I was still angry with him. He didn't deserve to know how much his body turned me on. This was my small way of getting back at him.

Carter settled between my legs and snatched my pussy in his fist, making me hiss.

"Don't play hard to get with me, baby." He ground the heel of his palm over my mound, spreading my wetness in a way that felt so fucking good. "This doesn't lie."

He reached behind us, fiddling with the strap on my left leg, not uncuffing it, but loosening it enough that he could get the leg over his shoulder, lifting and angling my hips.

His warm hands felt so big as he reached beneath me, gripping the cheeks of my ass with a shuddering groan.

"You have the most perfect ass I've ever seen," Carter said. "I think I've been obsessed with it since I first saw you in a swimsuit. Now, it's mine."

I quivered at what I thought he was implying. *Planning.*

Carter gathered my wetness against his fingertips and pushed it lower. I jerked as his fingers passed the wetness to a different entrance.

My cheeks flamed hot and I snapped my attention to Carter who was looking at my ass like it was the entrance to the cave of fucking wonders.

Oh god.

He repeated the motion, gathering more wetness to

fully soak my other entrance, but when he pressed a digit to the tight hole, I jerked away instinctively.

"*Wait.*"

"I told you, Anna. You're mine. That means all of you. Even *this*," Carter said, punctuating the last word by slipping the tip of a digit into the warm channel. It burned and something in my stomach flipped and tightened.

"It'll hurt a bit at first, but you'll like it."

"I don't think I—"

"Has anyone ever fucked you here before?"

"No," I said on a breath. "I've never even had fingers in me there. I don't think I'll like it."

I'd always been curious what other women saw in anal sex because I couldn't see the appeal. The one time I'd been drunk enough to consider it I asked my boyfriend at the time if he wanted to try it, and he seemed genuinely grossed out by the idea. It turned me off of ever wanting to try again.

He'd made me feel ashamed for even thinking about it, but somehow this felt completely different with Carter. There was no part of me, no matter how twisted or broken, that he hadn't embraced. He owned all of me.

That was the thing about loving someone who was fucked up. There was nothing you could ever do to scare them.

Carter moaned, sounding pleased. "Fuck. I love that. I'll be the first one to claim your ass, too."

He'd stolen all my other firsts. Why not this one?

He circled the ring of muscles with his fingers. It felt strange, but the more he touched me, the more I felt my body relax, arching into his touch.

"That's it. Breathe," Carter said. "I need you to relax."

Reflexively, I stiffened, but his hand on my stomach settled me as he inserted the tip of his finger again. I felt my muscles clench around him, and my entire body froze, adjusting to the new sensation.

Closing my eyes, I took a deep breath in, then one out. My muscles loosened enough to let him slide in just a bit further. Slowly, he worked his finger in while his other hand slid down my belly, his fingers tap-tapping on my clit before starting slow circles there.

My wetness eased his way, but it still felt strange and intrusive.

"Good girl," he said when he finally worked the whole finger inside. "You're stretching so beautifully for me."

My body softened at the praise. Some instinctive part of me still loved pleasing him.

"I'm going to make sure this feels good for you, just like I promised."

His fingers on my pussy stroked rhythmically, starting a slow, steady build, making me hot all over.

Unfamiliar pleasure built around the finger filling my ass. My breath quickened as I tried to make sense of where the pleasure was coming from.

He began to ease a second finger inside of me and my hands twisted in the soft duvet, my teeth clenching at the feeling of being stretched where I'd never been touched before.

"How does that feel, little siren?"

"T-too much."

"You're overthinking it. Just let go. Let me take care of you. I know what you can take. I need you to trust me."

I nodded and closed my eyes. I could feel my orgasm building while Carter played with my clit. His expert fingers sent lightning flashing through my veins. I focused on that pleasure as he thrust the second finger into my ass, making my back arch off the bed.

"That's it, Anna."

A fiery heat raged in my core as my orgasm built around the searing pain and the delirious pleasure.

He started to pump his fingers in my ass and sped up the other ones on my pussy. The dual sensation was...was...

Fuck. It was *good*.

"*Yes.* Chase it, baby."

My moans came faster, heavier.

"Fuck. You're so goddamned sexy like this, little siren. I can't wait to get inside you. Come on, yes, that's it, *come for your king.*"

He pinched my clit sharply, and the heat inside me combusted. I'd never had an orgasm like this, where it felt like my pleasure came from everywhere. My entire body shook as it bulldozed over me, and I felt a strange, increased sensation in my ass. It took me a moment to realize Carter had slipped a third finger inside me.

"Fuck," he muttered as I hiccupped, coming down with stars still in my eyes. "Your ass looks so pretty, stretching around my fingers."

He increased his pace, dragging his fingers back and forth through my puckered hole while his other hand stayed on my pussy, holding it like he couldn't bear to let go.

I moaned, feeling totally overwhelmed as I clenched around his digits, the burn all but gone now.

His fingers slipped out of me, and I immediately missed them. When I lifted my heavy head, I saw him pumping his cock into his fist, coating it with my wetness.

It wasn't going to fit.

Nope.

Not going to happen.

"Relax," he said, smiling wickedly, reading my mind like he always did. "It'll fit. And I'll make you love it."

He pulled my leg back over his shoulder, angling his cock to line it up with my ass.

My heart thudded in my ears, and I flexed against my restraints, distantly hearing them rattle as they snagged, holding me in place.

Fuck. I loved that, too.

I'd never been tied up like this, didn't think I'd like it. But Carter always knew what I liked. How did he always know before even I did?

He pressed his broad head against the ring of muscles. I bit my lip, throwing my head back to brace for the intrusion.

Carter slowly forced the end of his cock past my entrance. I remembered Carter telling me to take deep breaths, so I closed my eyes and focused. In and out. In and out. Slowly, I felt my body adjust to the strange sensation.

"Fuck," he moaned. "You're taking me so well, baby. Just seven more inches."

"*What?*" I gasped, a bolt of fear-laced dread racing through my veins.

We were only *two inches* in?

He licked his lips. "You doubting yourself, baby?"

"Carter, there's n-no way—"

"There is. I'll show you."

"*Oh fuck.*"

I rolled my eyes up to the ceiling as he slid deeper into my ass, and I held my breath.

"Hey, I need you breathing, little siren. Unclench."

I tried to do what he said. I really did.

"There. You're taking me so beautifully. Almost there. Four more."

Once again, his praise was like honey to my veins. My muscles expanded to let him press in another inch. I felt so impossibly full, but somehow I *did* want more. I wanted to take all of him.

He stopped, letting me adjust with a grimace on his face that told me it was taking every ounce of his willpower not to split me in half.

"*More,*" I whimpered. "I want more."

His eyes turned black.

Carter leaned down over me with my leg still hooked over his shoulder, using the leverage of his knees against the mattress to thrust deeper.

This time, he didn't stop. His cock opened me inch by inch. I breathed hard as my muscles rearranged themselves around the intrusion.

"Ah. Oh god. *Oh fuck. Fuck, Carter.*"

"Almost there," Carter said in a strained tone, bowing his head to his own pleasure as he lost control and slammed the rest of the way in. His hilt slapped against my cheeks and all the air pressed out of my lungs in a strangled cry as tears stung my eyes.

My muscles burned at the stretch, pain rippling through me, but the heat inside me had spread. The aftereffects of my orgasm were still with me, still making everything tinted in a hazy, rose-colored hue.

"Fuck, Anna," he grunted. "*So...goddamn...tight.* You're mine. All mine."

He brought his fingers back to my clit, stroking it as he

shifted his hips back, dragging his thick cock from my hole only to slam back inside. The pain gave way to an electric heat coursing through me.

He fucked my ass, just like he promised he would. It felt like something bigger than sex.

It felt like a promise I didn't know I was making.

His hand at my hip squeezed hard, and all my thoughts vanished as I gave into him. My entire world collapsed to the feeling of Carter's cock driving into my most private place. There was no more pain. All I felt was an all-consuming need. I was a live wire, ready to spark at any moment.

Carter never stopped moving inside me. His thrusts came faster with each stroke, harder, until each one was more merciless than the last, and I loved every moment of it. No part of my body resisted him anymore. I was his to fuck exactly as he wanted.

"*Mine*," he spat through his teeth.

Yours, my traitorous thoughts echoed.

"Oh my god, Carter, I'm going to come," I said, barely recognizing my own voice for the high pitch.

He moved his fingers on my clit and I could've fucking smacked him, but when he stuck two digits into my soaked cunt and continued rubbing my clit with his thumb, I screamed in pleasure.

The feeling of being filled in two holes while he played with my clit was just...just *too much.*

Hot liquid seared down my cheeks as I shattered. I was full and empty at the same time, overwhelmed with a feeling I wasn't sure I could survive. I closed my eyes and saw lightning, storm clouds and a full moon over the beach.

Carter cursed, and through the haze of my mind-altering pleasure I saw him bearing his teeth.

He was going to come, too.

I licked my lips, still shaking with my own aftershocks, blinking to clear my vision enough to watch him.

He pulled out at the last possible second, gripping his shaft, rubbing it viciously as he began to come. Hot ropes of come splattered over my pussy, making me hum with pride.

Carter's expression struck me, reminding me of the boy on the beach. There he was. Disarmed. The mask dropped.

He'd been here all along.

He panted as he finished, his throat bobbing and eyelids heavy as he lowered his eyes to admire his art.

Carter's tongue rolled over his lower lip as he reached between us, and I felt his fingers dragging over my mound. By the time I realized what he was doing, it was too late. He pushed his gathered seed from where it landed into my pussy.

Shit.

I couldn't remember if I'd taken my pill this morning.

Fuck, had I remembered yesterday?

There was just so much going on that—

"Carter, wait, stop."

He didn't even look at me.

I tried to pull myself away from him but the restraints held me in place.

"Carter! I said stop. I can't remember if I took my pill this morning."

He froze and the look he gave me burned with the heat of a thousand suns.

"Good."

What!?

He held my slackened leg in place, locking it over his arm as he stuffed every drop of his spend into my pussy despite my thrashing.

"Are you insane? I could get pregnant!"

"I know."

I stopped fighting, remembering the existence of pharmacies. Of Plan B. And resolved to sit still as he finished, trying to figure out why this would turn him on.

He said he never wanted kids.

I was the one who wanted a big family. For my kids to grow up with siblings to keep each other company and stand up for one another.

It didn't make sense.

I sighed.

"Are you done?"

He cocked his head, double checking my pussy. "I am."

"Want to explain?"

He shrugged. "I think it's pretty self-explanatory. I want to tie myself to you in every way. In the ways that can't be broken."

Carter studied the frown on my face and set my leg down on the mattress, coming to lie next to me.

We lay together a long time in silence.

After a while, Carter untied me and gathered me into his arms. I was only distantly aware as he lifted me and carried me from the room, too spent to think anymore. He set me down on a plush chair and covered me with a blanket in an excessively large bathroom as he filled an equally obnoxiously sized tub.

He helped me into the water when it was ready and settled himself onto the rim. The bubbles smelled like ylang-ylang and vanilla. As if he'd known one day, some-how, I would be here in his house. In his tub.

I sighed, giving myself to the comforting warmth of the water. So, *so* tired.

"Stay the night," he said, swirling his fingers in the water.

I didn't reply.

"Please."

His stormy eyes searched mine, and I felt myself let go.

"I'll stay."

His lips tugged up triumphantly.

"But tomorrow you're taking me home. That's the deal. I won't trade one cage for another, Carter."

He recoiled as if slapped, thinking.

"Alright. But your cell stays with you at all times."

22

CARTER

Six Years Ago

"You feeling okay, Ma?"

I cracked the door open wide enough to look inside the room. The body-shaped lump on the bed didn't move. I stopped, watching her until I could see the slight rise and fall of her breathing.

"Ma? You awake?"

She wasn't. I knew she wasn't. She was exhausted all the time again. I could leave for school and find her right there at the end of the day, after coming home from work, not knowing whether she moved at all the entire time.

I placed the bowl of chicken broth and the slices of soft toasted bread on the nightstand.

"Ma, wake up. You need to eat something."

I stroked her hair, then gently shook her shoulder. Her bones poked through her clothes, the comforter, and into my hand. Her eyes squeezed tighter, making lines on her

257

face that weren't there even three months ago, then they opened, squinting at me.

"Carter?"

"No, it's Pierce Brosnan, Ma, who do you think?" I asked.

She loved those old 007 movies. When she wasn't sleeping or at the hospital for treatments, she was watching them on repeat, finding comfort with her favorite Hollywood heartthrob.

Ma smiled weakly, but her eyes closed again.

"You should really eat."

"Just leave it on the nightstand," she mumbled, her voice barely stronger than a whisper.

It was soup; once it got cold, she'd have a reason not to eat it anymore. She was already so thin and her energy levels were in the toilet. Skipping meals was just going to make it harder. Guilt bubbled in the pit of my stomach. Besides rent, food, and gas, I was saving everything I had for her treatment. It had been six and a half months since her last round of chemo and radiation and she needed another one... *three months ago.*

But at this rate, it would take me ten more years just to pay for the first one.

It didn't help that Dad was drinking and gambling his much better wages away before I could get my hands on even a dime.

"I can't leave until you eat something. You're going to make me late for work," I lied. I didn't have a shift tonight even though I'd been begging to take some off the hands of the other waitstaff at the restaurant.

Pretty soon, I would have to consider alternatives to make more money faster. I promised Anna nothing illegal, but I wasn't sure I could keep that promise if it meant losing Ma like this.

She sighed, pressing her face into her pillow. When the fatigue started a little over a year ago, it didn't seem like that big a deal. *Just a little more tired than usual, I'll just have some more coffee.*

The pain started and she thought it was just early menopause symptoms. I thought she was too young for that but we let it slide. Chances were it *was* menopause, even if it was a little early. The jump from menopause to *cancer* was so absurd, neither of us considered it.

She opted for hormone treatment to combat it because it was cheaper than surgery and radiation. She wasn't that advanced yet and at the start, we were hopeful.

I got another job to help pay for the treatment while keeping things running at home. It wasn't like her free-loading husband was helping. I would have picked up the slack anyway, but it was just kind of funny the way he had enough money to get hammered but I had to pick up the rent because he wasn't making enough money to cover it.

It was harder now with him arrested. They'd never kept him so long before, but I counted every day spent without his presence here a blessing, even if it meant I might need to consider dropping out of school to get a third job.

Another promise I'd have to break.

Ma shuffled under the comforter, rolling heavily onto her back. Her face contorted from the effort. I looked away. It made my chest ache. I wanted to give her privacy but I also just couldn't watch.

I always knew that one day I'd have to bury my parents. I just never thought I'd have to watch her waste away for months in front of me before it finally happened. I didn't think it would happen before I was even the legal age to drink.

Dread crawled up my back and wrapped around my neck, filling my head and expanding like a horror-movie red balloon.

"I made soup. That gross canned chicken noodle one you love that's mostly broth—"

A sharp knock sounded at the door. A chill froze my muscles, but then I realized he had a key. Dad wouldn't knock, he'd just let himself in. Unless he'd lost it.

"Just a sec, ma, let me see who that is. Eat, okay. When I come back, I want to see at least half of that gone."

She nodded woodenly. Her eyes were closed again and her expression peaceful. I whipped my head away, a wrenching in my chest.

I pulled the door open, exasperated, seeing an unfamiliar man standing on the other side. He was tall, that was the first thing I noticed. Then, I saw the suit. I'd never worn a suit in my life, but I knew when I was looking at a good one. It was gray and looked like it was cut to his exact fit, not one of those sloppy rental ones that made guys look like little boys trying on their dad's clothes.

His hair was black mostly but the temples were graying. Still, his posture and vibe didn't say *old man*. They said he was loaded and his mouth, pulled down in a deep frown, said he was pissed.

Just a wild guess; he didn't live in this neighborhood.

"Can I help you?" I asked, my tone clipped.

His cold blue eyes swept down, then back up, sizing me up.

"You're still home. Not working tonight at Sally's?"

I frowned, my hand tightening on the doorknob. He

knew where I worked. Something in his face struck me as familiar, and I had a sinking in my gut I didn't want to explore.

If *he* was here, it didn't mean anything good and I couldn't take any more bad right now.

"Look, I think you have the wrong house or something."

I started to close the door in his face, but his hand smacked the wood, keeping it open.

"I know who you are, boy."

"Okay..."

And what? I wasn't afraid he'd try to force his way into the house. There was nothing to steal in there and he would have done it already. But I didn't like his energy. Didn't want him anywhere near my Ma.

I pulled the door in so he couldn't see into the apartment. He noticed, trying to peer inside over my head.

"Are you home alone?"

"I don't know who you are or why you're here but I'm going to have to ask you respectfully to fuck off."

He smirked, leaning his weight back like he wanted to get a better look at me.

"I never trusted her to pick the right guy but you're worse than I expected."

Play dumb.

"Who are you talking about?"

"You're Carter Cole, you're the loser who's been dating my daughter."

Well, there it is.

I had to say, getting a look at the man for myself, he didn't disappoint. He was every inch the monster Anna painted him to be.

"That's me," I snarked. "Anna's not here, if you're looking for her."

"I know where she is, and I know where she goes when she sneaks out at night. I've known for weeks."

"Yeah, well we've been meeting each other for months so I guess you're a little slow on the uptake, old man."

His expression flashed with something that made my stomach sour, but I forced myself to stand taller. I wasn't about to let this jackass of a father keep me away from the one good thing in my life, but I needed to tread more carefully. I didn't want to get Anna in any more trouble with him than she already might've been.

I'd already told him something he might not have already known. I wouldn't give him anything else to use against her.

"That stops now. You're going to break up with her."

His statement was so abrupt that I laughed.

What the fuck did he think he was doing?

This was clearly a man that was used to getting what he wanted. But he wouldn't be getting it this time.

"Yeah. Sure. Okay. I'll make sure I do that." I flashed him a sarcastic smile.

His haughty stare held like fused steel.

"You think this is a joke?"

He took a deep breath, straightening up like he forgot who he was for a second. Anna told me about her dad and all I knew was that he made her life a living hell. I knew I wasn't the kind of guy she would usually end up with but shit, miracles happened every day. I had her. I wasn't going to let her go that easily.

"I'm going to say it one more time. Stay away from my daughter. She's not..." He looked me up and down again.

His lip curled like he wanted to spit. "You're not good enough for her."

Yeah, when was he going to tell me something I didn't know? She was a beautiful, rich girl with the world at her feet. I was just a poor kid who struck gold on the beach.

"Okay, well, thanks for dropping by. If that's all...?"

I indicated the door and his hand still keeping it open.

He leaned in. "How's your mother doing, Carter?"

My hand tightened on the doorknob.

"My mother is none of your business."

"I know she's sick. Cancer, right? Shame. Treatment often buries people under debt. Struggling to keep your heads above water?"

His eyes shone with twisted false empathy.

"What is this? What are you trying to pull bringing her into it?"

"I already told you. But I can see you'll take a little extra convincing. I can respect that and I'm a fair man. Some people might say I'm a *generous* man. Your mother? She can get the treatment she needs."

My eyes stung from the whiplash, going wide.

"What?"

"Surgery, radiation, recovery, everything. Pick the hospital. She'll have some of the best doctors in the country. Leave my daughter alone and your mom won't just survive this, she'll come out stronger than she ever was."

My throat thickened and I fought past the burn.

The thud in my chest was loud enough to hear in my ears. It hurt. I didn't think he was lying to me, but it was too good to be true. If he was serious...

I could fix the worst thing in my life, but to do it, I'd have to give up the best thing. I'd have to give up *her*.

I felt like I was in one of my mom's dumb movies where a rich guy swaggered up with a bag of cash to bribe someone into doing what he wanted. In the movies, it was kind of funny, it was fake. On set, someone yelled cut, the actors got out of costume and they went home to their normal lives.

No. This was my normal life. When I shut the door, my mom would still have cancer. He would still be a powerful, rich asshole who could use his money to get things no one else could. That suit and money didn't fool me. I didn't want his charity, especially when it came with strings.

He didn't control me with it, and he didn't control Anna.

She'd hate me if I did this.

And I couldn't stand the thought of that.

Anger ran in currents up and down my spine, spreading through my limbs.

"No."

The words came out barely more than a vibration in my chest.

"Are you kidd—"

"I said *no*. Your bribes aren't welcome here."

His brows came down over his eyes. If they were cold before, they were frozen now. His arrogant air darkened into pure hostility.

"Listen, you good for nothing little piece of shit. What the hell do you think is going to happen with her? *Hm*? You think you're good enough for her? You think she'll *marry* you? One day, she's gonna learn to like the taste of the silver spoon in her mouth, and she's going to leave you."

"If you thought that was true, I don't know why you bothered coming here."

He broadened in the doorway, making himself look bigger, like a wild animal about to attack. His eyes blackened like coal. I didn't so much as flinch.

Men like him didn't get their hands dirty. I stared him down, daring him to touch me. I bet he hit like a girl.

"Carter?" Down the hall, I heard my Ma weakly call my name.

I needed him gone before my mom got enough strength to get out of bed. She could not know that this happened.

"Mr. Vaughn. Can't say it's been a pleasure to meet you. Now please remove your hand from my door before I'm forced to remove it for you."

His hand slipped from the battered wooden pane.

I slammed the door, locking it as soon as he did.

Air shuddered out of my lungs and my knees buckled. Sweat broke out over my body. My hands shook.

What the fuck. I counted to fifty, then opened the door. He was gone, but down the street, a sleek black sedan was idling against the sidewalk. So out of place among the other older model vehicles with duct tape holding up their fenders and wires holding up their mufflers.

I couldn't see into the tinted windows, but I knew Hudson Vaughn wouldn't be in that vehicle. He'd be long gone, but he clearly wasn't done with me.

"Carter?"

"*Hmm?*"

I looked up at her from where I was laying on my back. Anna was sitting next to me, hands resting on my abdomen. The wind breezing in over the ocean blew through the loose wisps of her hair that weren't tied back in her bun.

"Do you think that taller people have a shorter lifespan?"

I chuckled, nudging her with my elbow. She would do that sometimes, tee up a question and then ask the most existential shit I had ever heard in my life. But then other times she'd just ask me what kind of meal I'd like to be turned into if I had been born a chicken.

Nuggets, of course. But only if I was to be eaten with sweet and sour dipping sauce.

"You're going to have to tell me how you got to that hypothesis," I said.

"Well, I think they would expend more energy trying to maintain more... mass. So, over time that would reasonably degrade the metabolism and stuff, right?"

I frowned, laughing harder.

"I don't think that's how it works."

"I mean, big dogs don't live as long as smaller dogs," she said with a shrug and I wasn't sure if that was even true but I wouldn't fight her on it.

"Okay but small planes crash more often than big ones," I argued.

She slid her hand under my shirt. Her fingers were cold but I didn't mind when she did that. She could touch me anywhere she wanted. Being out here with Anna, there was very little that could kill my mood. I hadn't said a word about her father paying me a visit the day before and it seemed he hadn't told her, either. I knew for a fact she would've said something if he had.

It felt...wrong. Not telling her. But she'd only worry.

And she had enough to worry about.

"Touche. I'll have to think about it some more."

I chuckled. "Don't hurt yourself."

She gave me a little punch to the gut and I mimicked losing air, making her laugh.

"Okay, Subject change, then. What's one thing you wanted to do this summer that hasn't happened yet?"

I sighed, reflecting on the trainwreck that was my life. I always tried to tell myself that things could get worse.

My dad was an abusive drunk? Yeah, but he hadn't been to the house for a week and a half, and fingers crossed, maybe he'd gotten run over by a car somewhere or finally taken off like he threatened to do every night he drank.

I didn't have a lot of freedom to think about what I *wanted* to do when what I needed to do was so much more important.

I wanted my mom to miraculously be cancer-free, but I didn't think Anna was looking for impossible wishes. As usual, she wanted something real.

Something to hold onto or manifest.

I smiled. There was something, actually.

"Did I tell you that I love you yet?"

She looked at me, her face angled down so it was hard to read her features. I didn't want to tell her like that but it felt natural. I'd loved her since day one, which sounded insane, but it was true.

It wasn't until recently I'd thought to actually tell her.

Somehow saying it made it more real. After everything with her Dad, I was more certain than ever. I wanted her, and I was ready to do whatever it took to be good enough for her. Between her going to college and me working, we were going to figure it out.

I watched her expression, searching for something to hold on to.

Her mouth, open in that perfect 'o' she always made when she was in shock and didn't know what to say, shrank until it vanished. She pulled her lip between her teeth, biting it lightly like she did when she was stressed about something or deep in thought.

Shit. It was too soon.

"No pressure to say it back or anything. I just wanted you to—"

"I love you, too, Carter."

My skin bristled and a heat like heavy molten metal spread through my gut.

Anna let out a watery giggle, bending to press her lips to mine. I wrapped my arms around her, as if I just held her a little tighter, a little closer, nothing could ever separate us.

I pulled her back, looking into those incredible jade eyes.

"Then make me a promise."

She wiped her nose, still smiling. "Anything."

"Promise you'll always be mine."

Her gaze softened. "I don't think I could ever belong to anyone else."

I shook my head. "No, Anna, I need you to promise me."

It took her a minute, but she nodded. "Okay. I promise."

The molten metal cooled, settling into place, melding us together in this moment and forever.

"And I'll make you a promise in return," I said, pulling her hand to my chest, pressing it flat against the hammering heart beneath my ribcage. "This is yours. I swear to you I will *never* give it to anyone else."

23

ANNA

"Is this a jellyfish?" I asked.

Carter and I lay in bed, both still naked, while I examined his black ink tattoos. I propped up on an elbow to see where the tentacles wrapped around his forearm, dangling down his wrist on the left arm.

"Yes."

"Why a jellyfish?"

"You don't remember?"

I pressed my lips tight. I couldn't believe I actually thought he was going to die if I didn't pee on the sting. The worst part was that he actually let me do it.

When I went home that night and googled it, I was absolutely mortified.

"Don't tell me that's why you got this?"

He shrugged noncommittally. "It reminded me of you."

Oh my god. Of me *peeing on him*.

I gave him a shove, but I was already looking at all the other tattoos, studying each one more closely than I ever had the opportunity to before.

On one arm there was a lion. The jellyfish. Shattered diamonds and a skull. A geometric pattern holding it all together.

On the other was a great ship with powerful sails pushing into a storm at sea. Waves crashed and the moon and stars glittered in between the angry clouds above.

I remembered the lyrics to a song I hadn't allowed myself to listen to in six years.

I remembered telling Carter I wished I was strong enough to smash every diamond my father ever made me wear.

No. No way. He wouldn't get tattoos for all those silly, meaningless things.

I stopped tracing the ink, a weight settling in my gut as I met his intent stare.

He didn't say it, but he didn't have to. The ability we once had to communicate so much without saying a word was already coming back, and I could see the truth there in his eyes.

They're all for you.

I swallowed hard.

You're imagining things, Anna. Snap out of it.

Why would he do that after...

In my post-sex haze, with the phantom feel of him still in my most intimate places, I want to relive that. I pointed to another tattoo on his wrist.

"Brandy? I thought you were more of a whiskey man."

It was a trap. I had a feeling it was a woman's name, and I wanted him to admit it. It would make walking out of this dreamland and back to my cage a hell of a lot easier.

"It was my mother's name," he said quietly, and I felt like an idiot for forgetting. "I got that after she died."

His expression shifted from blissful to a perfect neutral, like he was donning a mask.

I clasped his hand in mine. "When was that, exactly? How long after I...after I left?"

"Right before I turned 22. The treatment really worked for a while. We thought she was better. It looked like she was headed for remission and then...she wasn't."

Carter's eyes were fixed on the ceiling, purposefully staring away from me. I couldn't imagine how huge the loss was for him. I knew his father was a piece of shit, but from what I knew, his mother was the calm in the storm. He used to say he never understood how someone as good natured and pure hearted as his mom could wind up with someone as vile as his father.

"I'm sorry," I said quietly.

He took a long, deep breath. "Tell me something else," he said, changing the subject. "Something about your life while you were gone."

I bit my lip. I knew Carter always doubted my cover story about charity work building houses, but I hadn't come out and told him the truth myself, though I suspected he already knew. I wasn't ashamed of it anymore; it was good, honest work. It was where I met anyone who gave a damn about me in St. Louis.

"I didn't go to Malawi," I said. "I went to St. Louis. I was a cocktail waitress at this member's only club—"

"—The Butterfly Room."

"Of course. You already know everything."

"Not everything. Did you like working there?"

I thought about it. "No. But I liked the girls I worked with, and the tips were really good."

He drew circles on my shoulder, and I remembered how

ANNA

easy it was to just *be* with him in the silence. Now, with the shutters raised, I could hear the ocean clearly through the window and it reminded me how much I missed this.

Ask him.

You need to ask him.

"Can I ask you something?"

Why? It was what I wanted to know, but the one question I still couldn't seem to make myself ask. Why did you break my heart, Carter?

"Shoot."

I opened my mouth, but chickened out at the last second like a total fucking coward. "What did you mean before?" I asked instead. "About it being *good* that I forgot to take my birth control pill?"

"I meant exactly what I said," he replied roughly. "I want to be tied to you in every way humanly possible. Putting a baby in your belly is a step in the right direction."

I was too stunned to speak, let alone meet his intense stare. I fingered the duvet, trying to ignore his eyes on me.

"Carter, you don't even want kids."

"I didn't. For years, I was so sure I never would. But then you came back, and I can't stop thinking about it. I've never been more certain about anything, Anna."

"And what if I don't share this certainty?"

"You will."

My brows rose and I finally looked at him. He seemed so sure. So secure in that sureness.

"Marry me."

I choked, blinking, coughing as saliva went down the wrong hole, and I threw myself up into a seated position, trying to get air back into my lungs.

"I'm sorry, *what?*" I blurted between fits of coughing.

Carter didn't miss a beat. "Marry me."

"Oh my god, you're serious."

He nodded gravely, a knot forming between his brows at my expression. Carter Cole never liked being laughed at and that's exactly what my eyes were doing right now. They were laughing at him.

Soon enough, my mouth followed.

"Anna," he warned.

I held my hand out, waving it in a placating gesture as I struggled to get control of myself. "No, it's just—did you actually just propose?"

"Would you like to see the ring?"

"*You have a ring?*"

"I've had it since the day after I found out you were back."

No lies detected. "That's a little presumptuous, even for you."

"Is it?"

A frustrated sigh fell from my lips. "You're psychotic, you know that?"

His lips pulled up in a half smirk.

For just a second I let myself imagine it. Giving Carter those last firsts.

Marriage.

A child.

I couldn't ignore how right it felt, even as nothing more than a wild imagining.

I let my eyes fall shut.

Carter brushed his thumb across my cheekbone. "Can you accept that? All of me? Even the parts that are a little less *refined* than you thought?"

Less refined? Those parts weren't just less refined, they

were sharp as broken glass.

"I don't know," I admitted. "What if there's more? What else don't I know, Carter?"

He took my hand. "Let me show you."

I let him lead me down the hallway to another room. It was another bedroom, with sage green walls and a huge bed covered in luxurious bedding. Crystal vases holding elegant, dried bouquets sat on every surface.

Yet another room that didn't look *at all* like it'd been designed for Carter.

"I had this prepared when you came back to town."

"And what is this?"

He guided me to a large walk-in closet and lights automatically flicked on. It was overflowing with brand new clothing. In clear drawers, there were heaps of lacy underwear and bras in a rainbow of colors. I checked the tag of the nearest summer dress and gawked at him.

"It's my size."

"It's all your size, Anna. The personal shoppers at Bloomingdale's still had everything on file. When they realized how much money I planned to spend, they were happy to give me the details."

I quickly opened the other drawers. There were soft cotton pajamas and sets of workout clothes waiting. I opened a panel in the wall and there were rows upon rows of shoes, and another wall of purses.

To my surprise, everything wasn't just my size, but looked like it was my taste, too.

I would have picked out any of the sundresses on display.

"You really expected me to wear this?" I gave Carter a pointed look.

"No. I didn't *expect* you to wear any of it. I just wanted you to have the option. Well, *options* to wear whatever you liked best. And in the spirit of being possessive and fucked up, it gives me some kind of...twisted satisfaction...to be the one who clothes you and feeds you. Who gives you what you need."

My chest tightened. The way he talked about it was almost sweet. In a totally weird fucking way.

"Come on," he said, snatching a satin robe from a hanger to help me into it. "There's more."

He brought me to the next room—a home office. I quickly noted the big, sturdy desk and windows with ocean views. But once I noticed the photo leaning against the wall, everything else ceased to exist.

I took that photo of our beach. Years ago, I gave it to Carter. I expected that by now it was in a landfill some-where, not hanging in a place of honor on his wall. I walked close to it, looking at it in wonder. There was something haunting about the moon and clouds in black and white, making the scene both peaceful and eerie. Like something bigger lurked just beyond the frame.

"I had it delivered from my downtown office yesterday. I didn't think I'd be able to make it in for a while, and I can't go long without seeing it."

"You kept it. All this time, you kept it."

"This is as big as I could get it without it getting grainy," he said, taking a couple of steps toward me, looking down at the shot.

"But why did you bother having it developed?"

"Because you gave it to me."

"Thank you," I said quietly, trying to make sense of the feelings swirling inside me. There were too many.

Surprise. Confusion. Pain. Grief. Worst of all...there was hope.

"I didn't think I'd ever see this one again."

"I kept the negative."

I couldn't hide my elation at the admission. This was my favorite shot. The best picture I'd ever taken up until that point. And I loved it so much that I wanted him to have it. I mourned the loss of it as soon as I was finished mourning Carter himself.

"Really?"

He nodded. "I keep it in the safe. It's yours if you want it back."

I did, I realized, but I wouldn't take it. It felt wrong somehow to even ask. It was a gift. It belonged to him.

Carter stroked my shoulder. "What's wrong?"

"No. Just... it doesn't make sense. Why keep it? Why have it developed and blown up and put it somewhere you can see it every day after..."

After you shattered my heart.

I still didn't get it. How could Carter have let me go if he still cared about me? If he was this obsessive, and apparently had a crazy PI who could find anyone, how come he never found me? How much of what he said was even real?

Carter's brow furrowed. He took my face in his hands, gazing down at me.

"Tell me what you're thinking," he demanded. "I need to know."

I swallowed. "I just...did you really love me then, Carter? Or was I just some trophy, to prove that you could have anything that the rich assholes in this town did?"

"I loved you," he said fiercely, never breaking eye contact. "I never stopped."

I didn't see any hint of a lie in his eyes and there it was, dangling there for me. The worm wriggling on the end of a hook that would spear me if I wasn't careful.

I wanted so badly to believe him.

"I haven't let a woman in here since I moved in. I haven't had a girlfriend. Never dated. Never even wanted to. I was waiting for you, Anna. And then you come back and you could barely stand to be in the same room as me. I know I fucked up but I can't fucking fake this."

His arm tightened around me, the swell of his cock even harder. My mouth was too dry to speak. My lips parted but the snappy comeback didn't come.

I grabbed the back of his neck and kissed him. His body surged into life, hooking a hand under my backside and sweeping me up into his body. He placed me on the couch, covering my body with his. His lips were hungry. He claimed my mouth, my tongue, my breath.

"Wait," he said, pulling away. "There's one more thing you need to see."

The last room on his tour of rooms masquerading as hammers meant to break down my walls was downstairs, tucked away behind the kitchen.

I wouldn't have even noticed the door if Carter hadn't brought me to it. He flicked on one of two light switches, bathing the room in a red glow, and I gasped.

It was a darkroom, fully stocked with sinks, enlargers, neatly labeled chemicals. Everything I would need to develop film. I knew, without him telling me, that the room had been built for me alone.

"How long has this been here?" I asked.

"Since I moved in. I had the architect put it into the designs."

"How did you know I'd ever come back to use it? What if I'd given up photography, found something else to do?"

Carter shook his head. "I knew you'd never give it up. You loved photography too much. And if you never came back..." He took a long breath. "Actually, I never really counted that as an option."

My heart pounded in my chest.

"I'm not going to change, Anna. I'm possessive, controlling, fucked up. But I'm also devoted to making you happy." His eyes searched mine. "You just need to decide if that's enough for you."

24

ANNA

W e were quiet on the short drive back to my parents' house. So many unsaid things lingered in the air between us.

When Carter pulled up outside my parents' house, he turned to me with an eerily placid expression.

"I want you to promise me you'll keep your phone on you at all times and you won't set one foot out that door without telling me where you're going first."

"Okay."

"Anna."

"I promise. And you promise me that if you find Josh, you'll tell me. I have...evidence. I can put him in prison."

"I can think of a few better places for him."

"*Carter.*"

He ground his jaw. "I'll tell you if we find him."

I didn't miss how he didn't agree to let me try to put Josh behind bars. The fucked up truth was, I wasn't sure if I would feel safe even if he did go to jail. One day, he'd be let out, and then what?

I shuddered at the thought.

Before I could get out of the car, Carter caught my wrist and pulled me back to him. He gave me one last, bruising kiss. I buried my hands in his hair. My heart pounded in my chest, but my blood felt icy cold. This kiss felt like a goodbye.

Tears stung my eyes when I tore away from him, but I didn't let him see them.

I strode up the walk to the Vaughn estate and I didn't look back. If I saw him waiting for me, I might change my mind, turn around and go running back to him. I owed it to myself to at least think about everything he said without him being so close he clouded all my judgment.

I opened the front door and was greeted with the familiar smell of soap and lavender. Obediently, I slipped my shoes off at the door, intending to walk straight up to my room, but I stopped when an orange light caught my eye.

Since when did anyone light the living room fireplace in the middle of the day? I loved when we lit fires. It made the oversized, empty house feel more homey. Usually, we only lit them for holiday parties.

I dropped my bag by the stairs and padded into the living room to see Dad sitting in front of the fire, staring into the coals beneath the flames.

He looked tense, hunching over with his elbows on his spread knees. Sensing me, he turned, resting his temple against his clenched fists.

"Look at you..." he said in a dangerous whisper, mouth tight with malice. "Right back where you started. Do you enjoy being Carter Cole's little whore?"

I reeled back a step. He might as well have slapped me across the face.

"How did you know I was with him?" My voice sounded feeble, even to me.

Dad scoffed.

Of course he knew. When it came to prying into other people's business, Hudson Vaughn was even worse than Carter, and that was fucking saying something.

At least Carter did what he did to find me. To keep me safe. *Mostly.*

What was my father's excuse?

Straightening my shoulders, I shook it off, refusing to be that sad little girl anymore. I was a grown woman now and he couldn't—*wouldn't*—dictate my life.

"I'll see whoever I want. I'm an adult. You don't get to dictate who my friends are."

"*Friends*? That boy is not your friend. He's trash. He doesn't deserve to breathe the same air as my daughter."

"Then how come he's invited to every society gala in town? Hell, they practically make him the guest of honor. Because all anyone in this town really cares about is money. You're the only one who cares about the fact that he used to be poor. Get over yourself, *Governor*."

"He's not good enough for you!"

I rolled my eyes. "As if you care about what's best for me. You're all about your image, just like always."

"I forbid you from seeing Carter Cole again."

I couldn't stop myself from laughing. "You *forbid* me? Okay. Sure. Well, if you're so bothered, I could always move out."

And I realized I could. I didn't have much money, but I

could stay with Summer. She'd let me crash in her guestroom without a second thought and I could get a normal job. Pay her back for my living expenses. I *could* do it. Maybe I should.

"You'd move in with him?" Dad looked aghast.

"Maybe," I said flippantly, even though I hadn't considered it, not really, anyway. "Or maybe I'll just get my own place. I don't know."

Dad pushed to his feet. Even in his middle age, he was still tall and imposing. "Before you throw your cards in with that man, there's something you should know. I offered him a bribe to stay away from you six years ago. He happily accepted."

My stomach dropped, and I needed to grip the back of the sofa to stay standing.

He...*what*?

"How do you think he got to where he is now, *hmm*? My money, that's how."

No. Wouldn't.

There wasn't any way the Carter I knew would have thrown me away for a payday.

...was there?

Unless there was a reason.

His mom's cancer. The money could've paid for her treatments. My eyes burned and my chest ached as if it was empty, hollowed out to the bone.

Would he have done it to try to save her?

Could I forgive him if he had?

I remembered that pain, feeling it like a fresh cut instead of an old scar.

He'd been so cruel. So punishing.

No. I couldn't forgive him for the things he said to me. The way he left me broken and all alone when he promised he would never do that. But a part of me could understand, even if I couldn't live with it.

"You're just as bad as him," I choked out before clenching my teeth at him. "How could you do that to me? *To him?* He was just a kid. An abused kid on the verge of losing his mom. God. You're not just as bad, *you're worse.*"

"Me? You think I'm the bad guy here?"

"I don't think it, I know it."

"You want to see bad, Anna Grace?" He sneered at me, rushing forward to snatch my wrist and drag me from the room.

"*Ow*, let go."

He didn't release me until we were in his office. I rubbed the sore spot on my wrist as he unlocked a filing cabinet and began tearing through files.

I should have left right then, before his fingers closed on a worn manilla envelope and opened it, drawing out a fist full of images he threw over the desk in front of me.

Because now I couldn't unsee them.

It was a menagerie of pain and gore and horror.

Images of a man so broken I couldn't even tell who he once was. His face was completely smashed in as if it'd been bludgeoned with a sledgehammer. There was hair and blood and bits of bone and teeth. No face. A prone body with no face.

I turned and bent at the middle, spewing the breakfast Carter made me all over my dad's Persian rug.

"What..." I gagged, coughing to get the acid out of my throat. "What is that?"

"That's the work of your beloved street rat, Anna.

He climbed a pile of corpses to get to the top.

No. Those images could be from anything. Carter wasn't even in them. This could be another one of my father's lies.

In my gut, I knew I was in denial, but I couldn't rectify them together—the Carter I knew as a kid on the beach and this man he'd become. Though he'd always had this in him. I'd seen it in glimpses before, he'd just stopped hiding it.

I shook my head. "I don't believe you."

"Go ahead. Ask Carter. He'll tell you that it's true."

I held back a sob.

"You know what, Anna, *go*."

"What?" When I looked up, I found him not staring at me anymore, but rubbing his palm over his mouth, leaning a hand against the wall for support like he was too tired to stand on his own.

"Go. You've been nothing but trouble since you were a teenager. So go ahead, run off and find some ramshackle apartment or move in with Carter, let him be the end of you. I don't care, as long as you keep the family's secrets while you're still breathing."

He might as well have twisted the knife. I always knew he didn't care, but hearing him admit it still stung more than I ever realized it could.

"What family secrets?"

"You know which ones."

The ones I accused him of six years ago. I'd had evidence then, too, of him siphoning money from his fancy charity. I should've done something about it then and saved us all the heartache.

"I've seen your photographs," Dad held up a handful of

film rolls. I knew, with sickening certainty, exactly which rolls they were because I left them at Summer's place. She texted me to say she'd drop them by the house for me, and I hadn't seen the message until it was too late to stop her going. Of course he looked at them. *Of course.*

"Did you really think I wouldn't find out? You've gone around telling people about that disgusting club you worked at. Worse, you showed them the evidence."

"It was a cocktail bar," I said in a low voice. "And I'm not ashamed that I worked there."

"You should be ashamed! We gave you everything. You could have gone to Yale, and really made something of yourself. Instead, you were an ungrateful brat. You spat on all the sacrifices we made for you. You would rather be a whore than act like you give a shit about this family."

I felt like all the blood had drained from my veins. All the worst things I ever thought about myself, Hudson Vaught just gave them voice. The worst part was that he wasn't just trying to hurt me. That was what he really thought.

I stared at the floor. My brain repeated all the insults people threw at me in a shitty refrain. I'd never felt more pathetic. More breakable.

Dad put a heavy hand on my shoulder, squeezing hard enough to bruise. "Well, I won't let you ruin our family name," he muttered. "I let you have your little hobby, but photographing weddings and sunsets is one thing. Showing off how you lived like a degenerate for six years? I won't let you destroy us like that."

He left the room and it took me three precious seconds too long to realize he was still holding my film.

I gasped, rushing after him, slingshotting myself into the sitting room where he was already standing by the fire.

With a flick of his wrist, he tossed my negatives into the flames.

"I had my tech team erase the versions you saved to your laptop's hard drive as well. If you have any other copies, you better hope I don't find them."

He turned swiftly on his heel to storm out the other archway and back out to the hall.

For a moment, I froze, watching the film light. Then I was there on my knees, reaching into the embers. Trying like hell to save even one frame.

Because I didn't have any others save for the few small prints in my bag.

Before my skin could fully burn, slender arms grabbed me and pulled me back. I fought them, but I didn't have the strength. My muscles felt broken and unusable as my vision went and my body wracked with chest aching sobs.

The film quickly flaked into cinders, and I collapsed against my mom. She stroked my hair as I cried.

"I'm so sorry, darling," she whispered into my hair after a few minutes. "So, so, sorry."

"They were...they were...the only good thing I've done since I left."

"You've done so much that I'm proud of," Mom said gently. "You'll take other pictures. He can't take away your talent."

I wished I could just believe her. Just wipe this away and forget all about it. But I couldn't.

"I have to get out of here."

I sniffed, disentangling myself from her. "I'm leaving."

"I know. It's okay. Let me give you my credit c—"

"I don't want his money," I snapped, fixing her with a stare I hoped conveyed just how serious I was. "I'm never coming back here, Mom. As long as he lives in this house, I'll never step foot through that door again."

I felt Mom nod, her fingers gently rubbing my back as her blue eyes welled with tears.

"I understand, darling. Do what you have to do."

25

CARTER

Six Years Ago

Governor Vaughn was a punctual man. When he said the money was mine as soon as I took the deal, he meant immediately. He set up an anonymous fund that covered the full cost of my mother's current treatment at the hospital and any other treatments she could ever possibly need. The other funds were dropped into my meager checking account, prompting a slew of calls from my bank asking me what I intended to do with my new 'inheritance.'

That was three days ago. Now Ma was getting her treatment, I wasn't under arrest, my father had been scrubbed from existence, and I was left to plan my revenge.

I was scared every morning that when I woke up, it would all be a scam.

Just an elaborate plot to get me in jail on worse charges and eventually a convicted murderer on a lifelong sentence. I was barely sleeping, scared that any footsteps I heard through the flimsy door were the cops coming to get me. Or Hudson Vaughn's men.

It hadn't happened yet.

"Do you want something to eat? How are you feeling?" I asked Ma hollowly, bending forward in the chair next to her bed.

"How are *you* feeling?"

"Me?"

"About your father," she said.

I flinched. She didn't know the truth. Hudson's people had it all cleaned up as though it never happened by the time she was ready to come back from the hospital. The official story was that he died in a hit and run. Some kind of big rig truck must've rolled right over his head.

I swallowed back bile. "Can't say I miss him. I mean, can you?"

It'd been three days but she had known the guy longer than I'd been alive. Maybe they were...I don't know, *bonded* or something, if not in love.

"I've missed him for a long time," she said wistfully. "I miss the man I married. The one who I fell in love with."

"I well... I guess I never met that one."

She sighed and crossed her arms, running her hands up and down her biceps like she was cold. I pulled her blanket up for her.

"Anyway, he was still your father, I just thought..."

My jaw clenched as I worked to stuff down the memories of that night. They were still so fresh. So raw.

I could still smell his blood as if it were stuck in my nostrils. I could feel the grip of the hammer in my hands as if I were still holding it. What I did to him was...*barbaric*... but when he said in a drunken stupor that maybe it was better if Ma were to die—that he could make it look like an accident and then the hospital bills would stop, I just...I saw red.

I couldn't even remember picking up the hammer. Not really. By the time I was lucid again, I was hovering over the beaten pulp of his head and Hudson Vaughn's men were already breaking through the front door.

They held me down while they took photos. While they waited for Hudson himself to arrive. They'd been waiting weeks for something like this. Something he could use against me to force me to stay away from Anna, and I handed it right to him.

What kind of man did that make me?

The sort of man who could be bought.

A killer.

The kind of man that shouldn't be anywhere near a girl like Anna Vaughn.

"I just can't believe he's gone," Ma said in a rough voice.

"It's just you and me now, Ma. You and me against the world. I'll go see what we have for food."

I hadn't had time to grocery shop and while it was easy to explain away a charitable donation for her treatments, I wouldn't be able to explain my sudden ability to afford takeout for every meal.

I closed her door and went to the kitchen to see what we had. First chance I got, I was going to fill this thing to the tits with all her favorites. Shit, my favorites, too.

Our rent was already pre-paid out for the next three months. After that, I intended to move us somewhere better. Closer to the hospital so she wouldn't have to travel back and forth so much.

Anna's face filled my mind and I screwed my eyes shut, slamming the fridge closed.

All this freedom for what?

What was it worth when I couldn't share it with her?

My thoughts were loud but empty like an echo. The weird, empty feeling in my chest hadn't gone away since I'd taken the deal.

It had to eventually, right?

It wasn't like I'd live the rest of my life like this.

I checked the time. It would be dark soon. Any other night, I'd already be chomping at the bit as I waited for 11:30 so I could sneak out the front door and head for the beach.

Someone knocked at the door.

I jumped, stared at it like it might swing open itself. The light was on so it was obvious we were home. A terrifying montage of my arrest and sentencing in court for murder played in my head. I took a few shaky steps toward the door. They knocked again. I didn't want my mother to hear it. She was well enough right now that she'd come out here and answer it herself if I didn't.

My stomach turned as I opened it.

"You're home," she said.

Ice spread through my core. I looked over my shoulder and quickly stepped out onto the cement stoop, shutting the door firmly behind me.

"What are you doing here?" I whispered angrily. Even in a loose hoodie and jeans, she stuck out around here. Her skin was too flawless. Hair too shiny. Sneakers too obviously brand name. And she was alone by the look of the empty streets devoid of black sedans in either direction.

Fucking hell, did she take the bus? A cab?

"Why haven't you been answering my texts?" she asked, her round eyes pleading.

"How did you find my address?" I asked, ignoring her, still angry as fuck that she'd come here alone.

"Your work. They gave it to me. I went there last night when you didn't show up."

"It's not safe here after dark," I snapped.

"Then just tell me why you've been ignoring my calls and I'll go home."

I scoffed, pinching the bridge of my nose when a throbbing started behind my eyes. This was it. I'd been avoiding it for days but I couldn't anymore. She was forcing my hand before I was ready.

"Because I didn't want to talk to you," I shoved the words from my throat.

Anna's face flattened, the answer stopping her in her tracks.

"Why? Did I do something? Did something happen?"

No, she didn't do anything. Besides being born to an evil, sociopathic megalomaniac, no. She was perfect. I loved her. I couldn't believe how lucky I was to have her. Shame burned in my chest knowing what I had to do.

"There's no nice way to do this so I'm just going to get it over with. I'm done."

Her face screwed up into a scowl and her gaze narrowed. "Done with what?"

I sneered, irrationally angry at her for not figuring it out on her own. For making me say it.

"*This*. Summer's over. You're going to Yale. I'm not. It's just not going to work anymore," I said. She was silent for a few seconds.

"Is that it? We talked about this already. I'm not—"

"It's over, Anna. We're done," I repeated, louder, like she was hard of hearing, stupid or both. She was neither, but she needed to get it through that stubborn head.

Don't make me hurt you, Anna.

Please. Just go.

"Are you fucking kidding me?"

I looked away because if I held her stare for another second, I'd buckle under it and ruin everything.

"Would you at least fucking look at me?"

She put her hands on my chest, and I recoiled away, sucking air in through my teeth as my entire body sang with her touch as if shocked by an electric current.

Anna shoved me until my back hit the door. "No. We're not doing this. Talk to me, Carter. Tell me what's really going on. I know you wouldn't—"

"Stop!"

I'd never shouted at her, and I could feel her shock without needing to see it on her face.

"Just...*stop*. You need to go home, Anna."

"You told me you loved me."

I could hear the tears in her words and it was ripping me apart.

She wouldn't let this go. I should have known that. It was one of the reasons I loved her so much.

I bit down on my lip hard enough to taste blood. If he knew that she was here, I was fucking finished. He'd pull his money, he'd pull the deal completely. We'd have to stop treatment, *again*. I'd end up in prison. No one would be there to take care of Mom while she withered away to nothing.

Chills ran through me, but I was sweating. She needed

to go and I had to make sure she never came back. I blinked hard, grimacing.

"You're not very smart, are you?"

"What?"

I forced myself to look at her, picturing her father and all the horrible, vile, wicked things I'd like to say to him. Projecting that hatred on her instead.

"You're an idiot. You think your dad setting you up with connections and opportunities is him forcing you to do things you don't want. Do you know how many people would kill to be in your position?"

Her head shook slowly side to side.

"My dad used to fucking skewer me with a hot chimney poker. What's the worst thing yours ever did? Get you into law school?" I asked.

"Used to?"

The memory of the gore I made of my father had my stomach roiling. Hudson was right, I was deranged. A psychopath. Not for the likes of her.

Anna's brows lowered. "Wait, Carter... I never said—I didn't even—"

"Did you really think anything was going to happen after this summer?"

"But we—Carter, you said you—"

I laughed, harsh and loud enough to make her look around, self-conscious that someone had heard.

"Haven't you ever lied a little during an interview before?"

The soul slowly drained from her eyes and my momentum stalled. "Oh wait, no, of course you haven't, because you've never worked a goddamned day in your pathetic life."

"Why are you being so cruel?"

"You don't get it. You're a clueless, entitled little princess. That's why you think that when a person stops talking to you, it means *come to my house* instead of *leave me the fuck alone.*"

I was so glad the door was closed. She never made me feel bad about where I came from but I'd seen the other houses on the beach where she lived. This shack would fit in one of those place's kitchens.

But she didn't care. It bothered me more than it ever bothered her. Even if I wasn't doing this, I knew it would have bothered me when we went out into the world together and the differences between us became even more obvious in the light of the day. It wasn't a problem but it would've become one. Eventually.

Hudson Vaughn was right.

"You really...want me to...go?" she gasped every few words, starting to hyperventilate.

God. Fuck. Shit.

This needed to end.

"Yes, Anna. I want you to go."

If I slapped her she couldn't have looked more hurt. I restrained myself from going to her, wrapping her in my arms and telling her I didn't mean it. Dropping to my fucking knees and begging her not to believe it. Any of it because it was a lie. Even as I tried to make myself believe it all to be true.

"But you promised."

Her chin quivered and tears streamed down her face in a river that I was powerless to stop. I couldn't speak.

"And I believed you and oh my god, I gave you my..."

"I didn't ask for your virginity, babe, you practically threw it at me."

She crumbled, hugging herself around her stomach.

"I wish I never met you." She sneered at me, finding that fire through the rain and like it always did, her rage mirrored itself within me.

"That makes two of us."

She staggered back. Her hand went to her mouth, choking on a sob.

"Did you ever mean it when you said you loved me?"

Every fucking time, with everything I had in me.

"No," I said instead, the word tasing foul in my mouth.

That was it, she turned and bolted, her footsteps quickening to a full out sprint as she tore down the street toward the beach.

The instant she was out of sight, I couldn't hold it in anymore. I slumped against the door, my legs completely giving out beneath me. My heart clenched so painfully I thought I might be having a heart attack. Hot tears streamed down my face and I couldn't. Fucking. Breathe.

I swiped the tears away angrily and made myself get back to my feet.

Anna Vaughn wasn't the kind of girl that a guy like me got to have. I got to be her mistake.

26

ANNA

"Can I get you anything?" Summer asked in a low voice.

All morning, she'd been knocking at the guest room door, then lingering in the doorframe, waiting for me to spring up and be happy again.

As if that was ever happening.

My photos were gone, and it felt like my career burned up in the fire along with them.

I'd severed my relationship with Dad, and along with it, any connection to my home.

I desperately wanted to talk to Carter. He would hold me tight and stroke my hair. Then, he'd probably spank me, choke me, or fuck me until I forgot everything and turned into a wiggling pile of want. At least I wouldn't feel like this.

But I still didn't know if he'd really let my dad bribe him into staying away. And with all our history, I didn't even know if I could be with him the way he wanted.

Basically, the only thing I had going for me was how

comfy Summer's guest bed was. So I wasn't getting out of it anytime soon.

"I don't need anything. I'm fine," I told her.

Summer sighed. "Well, I hope you don't just sit there and mope all day. Maybe take my advice and start shopping that portfolio around to galleries. You could be out of my guest room in a blink if you sold a couple of those photos. Oh! God. Not that I want you gone. I didn't mean—"

"Summer, it's fine. *I'm* fine. Just go. You're going to be late meeting up with James."

I couldn't bring myself to tell her what Dad did to my negatives. She still had so much hope that I'd be showing them in a gallery in no time when in reality, I'd never have more than a few small prints to show for all that time. All she knew was what I told her; that I couldn't stay there anymore. She didn't pry, but I knew she'd want at least some answers eventually.

"Okay, well, you should at least take a walk. It's nice today."

"We're in California," I pointed out. "It's always nice."

...and I didn't feel like being followed around by Carter's men.

She rolled her eyes. "Ugh, you know what I mean. At least take a shower, will you? Eau du sad bitch is not your scent, babe."

I wanted to snap at her and say I didn't feel like doing anything except lying in bed and staring at the ceiling. But Summer didn't deserve that. When I told her that I needed a place to stay, she invited me to take her spare room, no questions asked. The least I could do was act a little grateful.

"I will."

"Good."

Satisfied with her work, she closed the door behind her, blowing me a kiss on her way out. I sniffed my pits and my nose wrinkled.

Fuck, she was right. It'd been days since that bath at Carter's villa and eau de sad bitch was *not* in fact my scent.

I really meant to get up right away, but before I knew it, my eyes were heavy and I could barely keep them open. It wasn't like I had anywhere to go.

I'd run away. Again. *That was what I did.* That was what I was good at.

I flipped over in the bed, facing away from the window so maybe I could get back to sleep. I slipped in and out of consciousness, the sounds of vehicles and the ocean outside merging with the images and sounds of my dreams.

Vicious images of my father and fire and Carter and blood and Josh and pain and the ocean and drowning, drowning, *drowning*—

I gasped, sitting bolt upright in my bed, sobs fighting their way out of my chest. I looked around the room wildly. Right. Summer's guest room. I was alone.

You're alone.

You're okay.

Except I wasn't.

If Carter just wanted to know what it would be like to fuck the rich girl and then break her heart, that would've gone down easier than him taking money to abandon me.

All those years ago, I thought he was different and I loved him for it. I didn't care how wide the divide was between us. We were the same in the ways that mattered. Coming back to town, I didn't want to admit it but I still had hope.

At least my dad was upfront about it. Carter lied.

I wrenched myself out of the bed, not ready to think about it anymore. Not yet.

I'd promised Summer that I'd shower, and frankly, it was the least I could do. I went to the bathroom and splashed water on my face.

Patting it off with a towel, I stared down my reflection in the mirror. I looked like hell. My eyes were bloodshot and puffy, the skin beneath them dark and sallow.

It was a face I recognized.

That was months ago, stepping foot in my childhood bedroom for the first time in years. I looked in the mirror over my vanity and saw the reflection of a beaten, bruised, sunken-faced version of myself looking back at me. I didn't look quite as bad as I had then, but this was a close second.

Tossing my pajamas on the floor, I started the hot water. Steam quickly filled the bathroom, and I sighed when I stepped under the stream. Summer's jasmine-scented soap was nice, but it made me miss my Dior body wash.

Fuck, *Rosie*.

Thinking about Rosie made my heart clench. I said I'd never step foot in that house again. Would I ever see her? If I asked her to meet for coffee, would she even come if my dad asked her not to?

I stayed in the shower until my fingers turned to prunes. Finally, I forced myself to turn the water off. I'd have to reenter the world at some point.

I pushed aside the shower curtain, only to meet a pair of crazed hollow blue eyes. Eyes I hoped I'd only see again in my nightmares. My blood felt like ice water in my veins.

After everything I'd done to stay out of the spotlight, he'd still found me.

My ex-boyfriend, Josh, stood mere feet from me.

Instinctively, I wrapped my arms around my wet, naked body. All the fear and vulnerability he made me feel came flooding back. All the bruises and black eyes, every mark he left on me. My stomach twisted painfully as I moved to snatch the towel from the hook next to the shower, covering myself.

Run.

Run, Anna.

I froze. I couldn't think, couldn't figure out what to do next. He just stood there, staring. His eyes looked hollow. His skin pale. Lips almost purple.

He was using again.

Fuck.

Fuck.

Fuck.

He shifted forward and I blurted out the first thing that came into my head, trying to buy time.

Stall him. I needed to stall him.

"How did you get in here?"

Where was my phone? I scanned the bathroom counter. The floor.

Shit, it was still plugged in in the bedroom. Was Carter listening right now? If I screamed, would he hear me? I swallowed hard, watching Josh warily as his lips turned up in a devious smirk, like he'd been very clever.

"Actually, I got in much more easily than I anticipated. Did you know your girlfriend's downstairs neighbor is into ketamine? Has a nice Prius, too. The trunk isn't very big, but it'll work."

I was going to be sick.

He stepped forward, and I shrank back against the wet tile of the shower to try to keep distance between us.

He cocked his head.

"I've been looking for you, you know," he said in a low tone, reaching out to run a finger down my arm, making me want to gag. "Since you left, actually. You should've told me who you were, *Annie*. Things could've been so different for us."

"They could still be different," I lied. "You don't have to do this."

His eyes narrowed and I noticed how blown his pupils were. Not good. This was not good.

"It's already done."

"Y-you need to leave. Summer and her boyfriend are going to be back any second."

"You think I'm just going to *leave*? After all the trouble I went through to find you? Your friends in high places might've stopped my collection team, but not before they told me exactly where I might find you. Exactly *how* I might get to you. They were smart guys, Annie. You would've liked them."

His expression darkened and like it always did, Josh's mood shifted as quickly as the flick of a light switch. I readied my lungs to scream, but the sound was choked off as his hand wrapped around my throat and he pressed me hard against the tile.

I clawed at his hands, the towel dropping as dark spots danced in my vision and I struggled for air. "Josh," I wheezed. "Josh, stop. *Stop*. I can't...I can't breathe."

The words were nothing but barely audible wheezes but just as the world started to darken, he released me. I slumped to the wet shower floor, gasping for air, my head spinning.

He threw his head back and laughed, a deep, spine-tingling laugh.

Cruel fingers twisted into my hair, wrenching me up and out of the shower to land on my hands and knees, coughing and spluttering as I continued my fight for air.

Muscle memory kicked in and I crumpled. I survived Josh's fury before, plenty of times. I knew how. If I folded into a ball, protecting my face and stomach, the pain wouldn't be so bad. I could go somewhere else in my head —think about Carter, think about our beach—and deal with the pain later.

This won't be like the other times.

A voice that sounded a lot like Carter's floated into my head. I already knew Josh was escalating. He'd hired men to find me. To *capture* me. He wouldn't settle on just leaving me battered and bruised this time. This was different.

I couldn't afford to cower.

I had to fight back.

You have to fight back.

Gathering my strength, I shoved to my feet and took a swing at him, putting my whole weight behind my fist. I caught him in the mouth and he let out an animal cry, swaying on his feet as blood bloomed from the side of his mouth.

My knuckles and wrist ached from the impact and a strangled sound came out of me.

Carter. Carter! I had to get to the phone. I needed to scream.

"*Cart—*"

"You fucking bitch!" Josh roared. He tackled me,

bashing my head against the tile and knocking the lights out in my mind. Blindly, with half-dead arms, I pushed at his vicious hands, scratching and kicking.

But Josh was so much bigger than me. I couldn't move his weight, and my muscles burned with the effort. This close, his unwashed stench overwhelmed me and I gagged on it.

I wasn't going to be able to force him off me.

"Help!" I shrieked desperately.

Josh swore and covered my mouth with his filthy hand. I screamed against his grimy palm and he shifted his grip, covering both my mouth and my nose, making it practically impossible to breathe.

"Shut the fuck up, bitch!"

I panicked, thrashing against his grip as he hooked his other arm around my arms and his legs pinned me against the floor.

Without oxygen, my strength dwindled fast. My kicks got slower and weaker. Keeping my eyelids open felt impossible. The edges of my vision grew dark and hazy, and all I could see were Josh's horrible, horrible eyes. Eyes that I once loved.

This can't be how it ends.

My vision blackened and my lungs ached with a burn so deep it felt like they were on fire.

No.

Not yet.

I gave one last thrash and felt my limbs go uselessly limp.

But...I just...got him back...

It was Carter's face that filled my mind as the world went black.

SOMEBODY WAS POUNDING AT THE BACK OF MY HEAD. LIKE A little man had crawled in my skull and was banging on the bone, trying to force his way out. I shifted, rubbing my eyes. When I opened them, I saw the heavy metal shackles around my wrists.

What the hell?

I was sitting on the floor of a strange room, propped up against a wall with my hands cuffed in front of me. My mouth was bone dry, and every one of my muscles ached. The light was dim, but it still hurt my sensitive eyes.

Slowly, it all came back. How Josh appeared outside my shower, then suffocated me until I passed out. He slammed my head against the bathroom floor during the struggle—that explained the headache.

You're still alive.

That meant there was a chance I could still get out of... wherever I was.

The room was dimly lit, all the light filtering in around the tobacco-stained curtains hanging in the windows. The carpet underneath me was rough and synthetic. It looked like there had been a print on it once, but now, it was muddied into obscurity.

I searched for anything that would tell me where I was, piecing together that I was in a cheap motel room. Discarded fast food cups and bags littered the floor and overflowing ashtrays covered every other surface.

Through the open bathroom door, I could see used syringes scattered on the floor.

And on the couch...

My breath caught. For all his faults, Josh had always been good-looking. He had meticulously styled hair, clear skin, and a well-filled out physique. Now, he was barely recognizable. He looked like he'd lost thirty pounds. His cheeks were hollow, his skin pockmarked and pale. He hadn't shaved in at least a week, and there was hair missing from the underside of his chin as if he'd burned himself.

He looked sick and wretched, like he'd given up on being human the moment I left. Or maybe, the moment he found out who I was.

His unfocused eyes were trained on the TV. He couldn't really be registering the infomercials playing there. He just stared ahead, like he had no idea I was there.

Trying not to make any noise, I looked down at my own body. I was wearing an oversized t-shirt, probably Josh's, and a pair of someone else's panties. I shuddered, imagining who they might have belonged to, trying not to throw up.

I took stock of my body, feeling for more than the aching muscles and the pounding in my head. I didn't think he hurt me or touched me while I was passed out. Whatever he had planned for me, it would happen later.

I shifted, testing the bounds of my constraints. Apart from having my wrists handcuffed in front of me, they were also connected to the radiator by a long chain and padlock. The manacles didn't feel super tight. Maybe, just maybe, I could squeeze my hands out of them.

Pressing my thumb in as tight as possible against my palm, I tried to force my hand free. For a few minutes, it felt like I was making progress, even if I was taking off a layer of skin. The right manacle was almost to the knuckle of my thumb. I pulled harder, and the metal chain rattled with movement.

Time seemed to stand still as Josh turned to look at me, and I pulled my arms in tight to my body, not letting him see the loose manacle as my heartbeat skittered behind my ribcage.

"Hello, Annie." His voice sounded eerie and wrong. Not like himself at all. Or had I just forgotten? "You're awake."

"Let me go, Josh."

I tried to put as much authority into my voice as I could, but he just laughed in my face.

He tilted his head to the side, the angle looking unnatural.

"Now why would I do that?"

Shoving to his feet, he shuffled over to me. I noticed again how huge his pupils were and gulped.

"Little *Annie Taylor*," he crooned. "You didn't tell me you had a big fancy family. You should have said. I have one, too."

Of course. Josh was always bragging about how wealthy his family was. Maybe I could appeal to that.

"I know," I said, my voice taking on a tone I recognized and hoped I'd never have to use again. A placating tone meant to diffuse him. "Your parents are probably so worried about you. Have you called them since you came after me?"

He blinked, confusion crossing his face. "What?"

I pushed ahead. "I know, it's been a hard time for you. I —I shouldn't have left like I did. I know that if we told them —I know they'd pay for rehab, probably somewhere exclusive. Like that place they sent you before that you told me about. The place with the horses. We could call them together."

I could practically see his mind working as he opened his mouth and closed it, eyes turning down, brows drawing in.

"I—I haven't..."

Then, the storm cloud crossed his face and I knew I lost him. The switch flicked.

His hands tightened into threatening fists. "You're so full of shit, Annie."

"No," I said, shaking my head. "Josh, look at me. I want what's best for you. It's like you said. We're toxic together. Remember?"

My words were starting to tumble together in a rush and I licked my dry lips, trying to swallow past the razor-blades in my throat.

"You said if it weren't for me you wouldn't even have started using again. Maybe if you let me go, you can get yourself better."

In a flash, he crossed the room, his hand shooting forward, fisting the hair in the back of my head to jerk my face close to his. I sobbed as he hit the tender spot where I hit my head against Summer's tile floor.

Summer! She would've noticed I was gone by now, right?

Would she have called Carter? The police?

Maybe they were coming. They had to be coming.

"*Shut up!*" Josh spat in my face, flecks of saliva scattering over my cheeks. "I know what you're doing, you stupid whore. You ran away from me, and now you want to escape your punishment. And I'm gonna ruin you, like the dirty slut you are. You *chose* to be Annie Taylor. You're the reason I had to treat you like that. I would have treated you better if I knew that you were a Vaughn."

Tears welled in my eyes. The only value I had was my last name. If people cared about me at all, it was because they wanted my father, not me. Because when I was Annie Taylor, I was just another faceless girl in a sea of others no one would ever miss. A girl without family or many real friends. The perfect girl to isolate and hurt until he got tired of me.

If I disappeared from this hotel room, would anyone really care? Even my photos, the only thing I'd ever done that really mattered, were gone, turned to ash. As far as the world was concerned, I was just the vapid, unworthy heir to what Hudson Vaughn had built.

Carter's face swam before my eyes. His sharp blue eyes looking right through me, telling me I was his.

He would care.

And he knew the real me, stripped down, with all my flaws and insecurities laid bare.

And if Carter saw me cowering in front of Josh and acting like what he did was okay...

His voice drifted through my mind, a memory from the beach when we were kids and he was talking about the first tyrant in my life; *you have to fight back, Anna. Don't let him control you.*

It was possible no one would ever find me in this motel. I had to fight for myself like Carter would fight for me or I'd never forgive myself.

I squared my shoulders and gave Josh a superior, icy glare that would make Carter proud and then I screamed.

If this was a motel, that had to mean there were other guests, other guests who would hear me.

I braced, my pulse racing as I anticipated being hit or choked or suffocated, but Josh just watched me scream.

He released his hold on my hair, and I stared at him with so much unconcealed hatred as I screamed again. And again. Until my lungs started to hurt and the sounds came raw and broken and I needed to stop to catch my breath.

"Are you finished?"

It hurt to swallow. I struggled to listen over the drone of the TV. The whir of the bathroom fan. The sound of my own breathing as loud as my heartbeat in my ears.

I couldn't hear anyone, I realized. No one was coming.

"There isn't anything around here for miles, Annie."

"My name is Anna."

"I bought the place last week with my money from my father's shell company." He spread his arms wide with a mean smile. "We're the only guests."

"Fuck you, Josh," I spoke over the ball in my throat, refusing to cry again. "You don't even deserve to breathe the same air as me after what you did back in St. Louis."

He smiled, showing newly yellowed teeth. My mouth went dry. Josh had completely broken from reality. He told me how he was before we met. How he had it under control now. That the drinking wouldn't lead him back to using, no matter what his sponsor said.

In this state, I didn't know what he was capable of, but I didn't want him to see how scared I was. That usually only made it worse.

"If you're hoping to collect ransom from my dad, I've got bad news," I told him. "He's done with me. He won't give you a cent."

Josh's crazed eyes widened. "Why would I ransom you

when I worked so hard to get you? Do you know how expensive it was just to *find* you?"

"Any idiot with half a brain and an internet connection could've found me, Josh."

Grabbing my collar, he ripped the grungy t-shirt I wore down the middle, making me jerk forward. The sleeves caught on my handcuffs, keeping me partially covered. Josh growled in annoyance, spinning to prowl over to the bed. He rummaged through a pile of stuff on the bedside table. I shivered when he held it up to the light.

A dull blade.

Josh sauntered back, getting off on the fear in my eyes that I was working so hard to hide.

He sank to a crouch and brought the knife to my wrists, tutting when he saw my one hand a third of the way free. He heaved the manacle back down, taking a layer of skin with it until it was back around my wrist and my throat burned with tears I wouldn't let myself cry.

His hands were shaky as he tried to cut away the t-shirt fabric. The tip of the knife flicked against my skin, making me wince, but it wasn't sharp enough to break the surface.

But Josh paused at the sound, a slow grin widening over his face.

"*Josh—*"

He pressed harder. I screamed when he sawed the blade against the sensitive flesh of my forearm.

Fuck.

Fuck. Fuck. Fuck.

It stung like hell. Blood bloomed on my pale skin and Josh's eyes lit with grim satisfaction. He made quick work after that, slicing through the fabric until my chest was bared to him.

"Just as pretty as I remembered," he whispered. He pressed two dirty fingers hard against the fresh wound in my forearm. Bitter tears flooded from my eyes, and I gritted my teeth, willing myself to be silent.

Maybe if I could get the joined manacles around his neck, I could—

He traced his bloody fingers up my stomach and all thoughts ceased to exist in my panicked mind.

Josh circled my breasts, outlining them in red as I tried to cave in on myself, trying to absorb myself into the wall at my back, anything to put space back between us.

"Josh, please..."

He pinched my nipple, watching with satisfaction as my body responded. It didn't matter that it was cold and fear that made my skin prickle and my nipples tighten. I could see Josh's cock hardening under his dirty sweatpants, and my stomach roiled.

He dragged two skeletal fingers along the side of my face.

I jerked away from his touch and he frowned.

When his hand cupped my pussy through the borrowed panties covering it, I let out a gasping sob.

He wouldn't, I told myself, needing the lie. Josh had done a lot of things to me, but he'd never raped me. He wouldn't.

He couldn't.

"We're going to have so much fun, Annie."

CARTER

I normally wouldn't pick up a call from a number I didn't recognize. But anything was better than sitting at my desk, just staring at Anna's photo and obsessing over everything I could have done differently.

She'd asked me for space but I hadn't expected this. It'd been days since I heard from her.

A week ago, I would've come for her, no matter how much she pleaded for me to leave her alone. But after my last night with her, everything changed.

Now, I understood that if I wanted Anna, I had to let her take control. She'd had enough with Josh manipulating her, living in her father's cage, and it was my job to prove that I was different. That her freedom was important to me.

So I was stuck waiting, and all too happy to pick up the phone.

"Hello?"

"Carter?" said a familiar female voice. Summer.

About the last person I ever expected to call me, but I knew Anna was staying with her. Maybe she was going to ream me out on behalf of her friend. I'd take anything she wanted to sling at me and then some if she'd put in a good word. Make Anna return my calls.

"Is Anna with you?"

I sat up straight, tapping the speakerphone button as I flipped through to the app to track Anna's phone. I'd just looked at the damn thing fifteen minutes before.

"No. Why are you asking?"

I ignored the stab of fear in my stomach as I opened the map, zooming in on the little red dot that blinked with her location.

"Well, she's not here, but she left her phone. I told her she should go for a walk earlier, but I thought she'd be back by now. It's almost nine and I'm getting worried. If she's not with you, then where would she be?"

The dot hadn't moved. It was still firmly over Summer's townhouse.

"I'll be there in ten minutes."

I sped over to Summer's place as quickly as I could, calling Paulson for an update from his men along the way.

"Where is Anna?" I asked as soon as he picked up.

"Uh, just one sec." I heard him tapping a few keys and speaking into a radio and every second felt like an eternity. "Yep, still at the best friend's house. She hasn't left in days."

Someone was going to die for this.

Maybe a lot of someones.

"She's not there," I seethed down the line.

Paulson floundered. "That's not possible. We have seven men around the perimeter. No one went in or out without us seeing it. Not a fucking chance."

"I'm on my way there now, and if I don't find Anna safe in her fucking bed, someone's head is going to roll."

I hung up just as I reached the foot of Summer's driveway. She was already there waiting for me, anxiously shifting her weight back and forth in the doorway.

I took the stairs two at a time and shoved past her. "Show me where she was staying."

"Do you think something happened? Hey! *Carter*."

I cleared the hall in three strides and stalked through an all-white kitchen to a power pink living room, searching for the bedrooms with Summer right on my heels.

"Should I call the police?"

"You should call the fucking undertaker," I growled, throwing open the door to the first bedroom and then the second, my hands shaking as something hot and uncomfortable slithered up my back.

"This is about her ex, isn't it? She said she was worried he'd find her, but I didn't think—I mean, she didn't say that he was—"

"Dangerous?" I filled in, whirling on her with enough lethal rage that she shrank back from me with a yelp.

I spied Anna's phone on the nightstand of the next room and stalked inside, tearing it off the nightstand and the charger from the wall.

The blankets were all messed up and it smelled like her in here.

I scanned the room, looking for signs of a struggle, and finding none.

"What's through there?"

I was already halfway over to the only door in the room when Summer answered in a squeak. "The en suite."

I broke the door handle trying to open it and shouldered through to a dim en suite bathroom with a stand up shower and ring lighting around the mirror.

It smelled different here. Like...cigarettes.

Anna didn't smoke.

She almost bit my head off when I brought a pack to the beach once, making me swear I'd never touch one again.

"What is that?"

I followed Summer's gaze to the towel sopping wet in the base of the shower. Was that...blood on the corner of it?

Icy rage consumed me. Someone must have come for Anna.

I *never* should've let her leave my villa.

Idiot.

Fucking idiot.

Tile cracked under my fist, biting into the thin skin over my knuckles and raiding down over the floor.

A vision of Anna's emerald eyes closing forever filled my head and I tore at my hair to get rid of it, as if I could pull it out by the root, hot air sawing out through my teeth.

If I believed that, it would break me—and I couldn't afford to imagine it. Not when she needed me to find her.

I focused on the bathroom, looking for clues. The struggle was contained here. There wasn't any other blood that I could see, and nobody had bothered to clean up. How the hell did they get in?

Paulson picked up on the first ring.

"She's gone."

"We're already searching. My guys are trying to sort out what went wrong."

"I don't *care* what went wrong. I need you to *find. Her.*" Two more punches to the tile to sate the fire in my blood.

"I know and we will. Give me time, Mr. Cole."

Anna might not have time.

"Do you have a location for Josh Porter?" I demanded,

already moving back through the townhouse, ignoring Summer following several paces behind me.

Out the front windows, blue and red lights flashed over the neighborhood.

"Not exactly," Paulson said. I heard him typing on his keyboard. "He's been moving between motels like we said, but he did come closer to the city. Last known location was Prescott."

That was *way* too close.

"But we don't have a lead on his current whereabouts. The guy's not a total idiot. He knows someone's following him, and—"

"Find him. Or it's your head. And Paulson?"

"Yeah boss?"

"Which of our men was responsible for watching all movement coming in and out of the house?"

He paused, sighing. "Chris Waterstone."

Chris Waterstone was a dead man walking.

I turned on Summer as I peered from the window to the two police vehicles parked at the end of the driveway. "Did you call the fucking cops?"

She shook her head, eyes wide. "No. No I didn't."

"Wait, I have something coming in," Paulson said and I held my breath.

"The cops aren't there for you," he said. "They were called by Summer's neighbor. Something about a stolen vehicle."

"What vehicle?"

"A silver Prius. We're trying to get the plates. Hold on."

I pulled the phone from my mouth. "Your neighbors drive a Prius?"

She nodded. "Yeah. It belongs to my neighbor's son, Alec. I let him park it in my garage when he comes to town."

That's it.

That was how the fuckers got in. How they got her out.

"Paulson, do we have the plates?"

"Got it. Texting to you now."

"Start searching every motel in a hundred mile radius."

"That will take—"

"I don't care how long it takes, just fucking do it. Start with the most likely suspects and work your way north. I'll start to the south."

"On it now."

I hung up, rushing back outside to my car. Summer followed me out.

"Where are you going?" she asked.

"To find Anna. If they have her, then they're bringing her to him."

"To her ex?"

The panic in Summer's voice was not fucking helping me right now.

"He's been staying in motels outside the city. That's where he'll have her."

She gasped. "Oh my god."

Summer chased me all the way to my car, like a stubborn puppy.

"How do you know which motel he'll be in?"

"I don't. Until my PI has a better answer, I'll go to them all."

"Then I'm coming with you," she said fiercely.

"No." There was no time to waste arguing. Summer would be a liability, just slowing me down. Summer's heels clattered insistently behind me on the pavement. I opened my driver's side door, and saw a flash of baby blue underneath me.

Summer had dived into my seat. She glared stubbornly up at me.

"You're not the only one who cares about Anna. Maybe I can help."

"Get the fuck out of my car."

"I can help you search the motels. We can check twice as many rooms in half the time."

Logical.

"Fine," I barked. "But I won't slow down for you, and you might see some shit you wish you could unsee. I don't have time for hysterics."

Summer nodded and scrambled into the passenger seat. "I promise, no hysterics. I watch true crime documentaries to relax. I *won't* slow you down."

I wondered how long it would be until she broke that promise.

Neither of us spoke while I drove to the first location in a long list Paulson had sent via text—the most likely suspects based on the parameters of every last motel Josh had stayed at leading up to today.

The first was a shitty motel in the part of town where I grew up. Back in the day, my dad used to meet his loan shark here. I doubted it'd gotten much classier since the last time I'd walked by it.

I was quickly proven right. Multiple rooms had their windows boarded up, but the neon OPEN sign still blinked from the lobby door. I parked my car right outside the front entrance and stormed in, Summer scurrying behind me.

The front desk was manned by a skinny, redheaded guy in his early 20s. If he wasn't selling weed, he was definitely using it by the reek permeating the entire room. He looked up at me with glassy eyes.

"Hey man, checking in?"

"I'm looking for a tall man, brown eyes, brown hair," I said, not wasting time. "He'll have a young woman, pretty, long dark hair with blonde highlights and green eyes. Are they here?"

The redhead blinked. "I can't tell you who's staying here, man."

Reaching into my wallet, I pulled out three hundred dollar bills and put them on the counter. "Yes, you can."

"Sorry, I'm really not supposed to," he said, scratching his chest.

I grabbed the collar of his polo and pulled him forward. "The woman is in danger. Talk."

He shook his head. "Man, privacy. I can't."

I slammed his head down hard against the desk. The guy cried out, while Summer shrieked behind me. So much for no hysterics.

"Have you seen a silver Prius?"

"I...I..."

I punched him in the jaw. His bones felt damn good under my fist. When he didn't answer I grabbed his hair, pulled him out from behind the desk, and kneed him in the stomach. Each cry of pain soothed the rage building inside me.

Anna's gone. She might be dead. Every minute this asshole wastes is the minute I might have needed to save her.

"Carter Cole!" Summer screeched. I looked up to see her standing beside the desk, holding up a ring of keys. "Enough wasting time. We can check the rooms ourselves."

The front desk clerk was huddled on the floor, a bruised

and bloody mess. I had no idea how long I'd been punishing him. Wordlessly, I took the keys from her, pulling the first half from the ring and pushing them back into her hand.

"Go, you get the ones on that end."

She nodded and took off.

I unlocked each door, then made a quick look around the room. Most of them were empty, with no traces that anyone had been staying there. Three rooms had guests; none of them were Josh or Anna. I could hear Summer squeaking apologies to the motel guests the closer we got to meeting in the middle.

The motel was small; it only took ten minutes to thoroughly search the entire place.

Summer didn't say anything when we got back in the car. I texted an update to Paulson then plugged the next hotel into the GPS. After fifteen minutes on the road, she finally opened her mouth.

"I really hope she's okay..."

She trailed off, holding back tears with a sniff.

"What will you do to her ex if you find him?"

"*When,*" I corrected her. "When I find him, I'll kill him."

FOR TWO STRAIGHT NIGHTS, I HADN'T SLEPT.

My men and I tore through every motel, trailer park, and camping site in northern California. Paulson managed the entire thing with the sort of organized precision that might save his life when this was through *if* it led to my Anna back where she belonged.

I declined his insistent offers to have a small team accompany me on my end. Truthfully, at this point, I'd end up throttling my backup soldiers the minute they breathed wrong or did anything to piss me off.

Last night at midnight, Summer called me for an update. She sighed when I reported back that I still had nothing.

"I figured out how he got in the building, if it helps," she said. "Apparently, Josh sold Alec some pills. They met at a park and after the drug deal or whatever, Josh knocked him out and stole the keys to his car. He drove right into the parking garage and used my spare key to get in. Your guards couldn't have known it was him."

I rubbed my brow, annoyed. Paulson and I circulated photos of Josh to all Anna's bodyguards. Even through tinted windows, they should have recognized him. As soon as I found Anna, I'd have them all fired and their careers torched. They'd never work in security again.

"Have the cops found the vehicle?"

"Not yet. I asked Ms. Bailey to let me know as soon as they do. Where are you now?"

I checked my GPS with bleary eyes. "Super 8 by the San Jose airport."

"Get a room. Seriously, Carter," she said bossily. "You need at least a few hours of sleep, or you're going to lose your edge and fuck up when Anna needs you. I can bring you supplies. James and I want to help."

"I already told you—"

"Yeah, yeah, stay here in case she comes back. But *both* of us don't need to be here."

"Just stay there. Keep your phone on you and keep me posted on that Prius."

I hung up on whatever she'd been about to say next.

Blinking awake, I cursed to myself, not realizing I'd fucking fell asleep. I pinched the sleep from my eyes and blinked to look at the time.

Fuck.

Sitting in the passenger seat was a pink and white duffel bag with Summer's initials embroidered on it. She'd left a note in pristine cursive right on top. *I told you to get a room.*

I unzipped the bag and found energy bars, water bottles, and a set of clean clothes. The clothes must have belonged to her boyfriend. The hoodie and workout pants weren't my size or style, but they would fit well enough. The clothes I was wearing reeked by now. I stripped and changed quickly right in the parking lot, not caring if anyone saw me.

I was downing a bottle of water when Paulson's name appeared on my phone. I picked it up immediately. "What?"

"I think I have a lead," he said. "A motel just outside San Jose. It was listed as sold last week. Looks like it was purchased by a subsidiary of Porter Holdings."

Josh's father's company.

I was already driving.

"Keep looking, see if you can get security footage or anything useful. I'm on my way there. Send backup and a medic."

I hung up, putting the location in my GPS.

The Castle Inn was every bit the piece of shit I expected it would be. There were two levels of rooms, each with their own outside entrance. The exterior hadn't been painted with anything but graffiti in decades, and the parking lot was full of potholes. Several rooms had broken windows covered in cardboard and duct tape.

It looked completely empty. Abandoned. Not a single car in the lot.

Nothing for a mile in either direction.

The perfect place to make someone disappear.

I pulled the pistol from my glovebox before carefully making my way to the first door.

I pressed my ear against it and listened, my skin tingling with anticipation. Nothing. I walked quickly but quietly, not wanting to give anyone who might be inside any heads up that I was coming.

The next three rooms were just as dead silent as the first.

Just before I moved to the final room on this floor, a cold sweat broke out over my back. It was like my intuition was telling me, this was the one. Gripping my pistol, I set my jaw and leaned my ear against the rough wooden pane.

Was that...

A woman sobbed softly, distantly, in the room.

Anna.

My vision went black at the edges as I kicked in the door.

Anna lay in the corner, slumped against the radiator in just a pair of panties. Her breasts were streaked with dried blood. Her hair was a tangled, ratty mess.

Crouched next to her was the man I meant to crush with my bare hands.

His grubby hands were on her legs. He'd pay for every tiny bruise and cut on her thighs.

I aimed the gun right at his face. "Step the fuck back."

Josh looked over at me with genuine surprise. The asshole was high as a kite, his eyes unfocused and movements strange and jerky. He raised his hands and stumbled to his feet.

"Whoa, whoa, whoa, chill, man," he said.

I didn't bother saying another word. There wasn't a real, rational person behind those eyes. Just some pathetic fuck-up pumped full of drugs.

"Sorry. Y'know I was lookin' fr Annie. But turns out, thas not Annie."

He was slurring, not making any fucking sense.

Josh pointed over his shoulder at Anna. She was coming to groggily, swallowing slow, blinking those big beautiful eyes open.

"Carter?"

Christ, she sounded so weak.

"*On your knees,*" I bellowed to Josh when he turned to look at her. I didn't want his eyes on her another second.

Josh looked confused. Instead, he stumbled a few steps closer to me.

"I said, on your fucking knees!" I shouted.

Josh rushed me without warning, and I fired the gun. With his wild movements, the shot missed the kill zone, cutting through the flesh at the side of his skull.

He kept coming, too high to feel the pain, his fists flying.

I got him with a knee to his gut but as he went down he got hold of my arm and sank his teeth into the meaty flesh at the base of my thumb, biting down to the bone. The gun fell from my grip, misfiring into the ceiling.

Anna shrieked and distracted by her, it took me a second to register that he was making a grab for it.

Fucker.

I threw out a knee to catch him in the side of the head and he staggered to the right.

I searched the floor for the gun.

"Carter!"

Something hard slammed into the side of my head, making my right ear ring and my vision go spotty. Double.

A wet laugh, and I blinked, finding two of Josh with pipes in their hands. Which one was the double?

Fuck.

My vision swam and I felt rough carpet under my palms.

"Carter! Carter, get up!"

I tried to stand, but the floor tipped up and I went down. I willed my eyes to fucking focus, and they did—a moment too late.

"Nice gun," Josh slurred, and I blinked, finding the double image of Josh holding my Beretta, twisting it this way and that before turning it to aim at me.

He leaned back, staggering a step, fighting for balance. He couldn't seem to keep his arm from swaying in messy lopsided circles.

"Josh, *please*," Anna begged, her voice breaking. "You don't have to do this."

He grunted in frustration and found his balance, steadying the weapon, his finger on the trigger.

"Sorry, man, you really shouldn't have come here."

Anna screamed.

Anna.

She was behind Josh, throwing her chains around his neck.

I was up, moving, falling, up again, moving.

Josh gasped for air and spun wildly, but she clung to his back like a fucking koala. His face turned purple as he struggled to breathe and the double image merged back to one.

He threw himself back, slammed her into the wall, hard enough that she lost her grip and gasped, slumping to the floor.

I bent to scoop the rusted pipe from the floor, advancing on him with an animal sound in my throat. His skull made a crunching sound as it caved in under the metal.

He went down, the gun clattered away.

And then I was on him, seeing red, seeing black.

Seeing nothing but the violent rise of the pipe over and over again in my hands as I smashed his fucking brains all over the floor.

I came back to myself with the feel of his blood on my face and an icy cold climbing down my spine like a winter frost.

The soft sound of Anna crying reached me through the ringing in my ears.

Anna.

I rushed over to her, dropping the pipe, holding her face in my hands. Her cheeks were wet with tears. Her eyes wide with horror.

Her still manacled hands clung to my jacket sleeves as she shook like a fucking leaf in my arms. "I'm sorry," I said, not recognizing my own voice, the wobble in it as something burned in my eyes. "Anna, I'm so sorry."

I pulled her into my chest, wrapping myself around her, shielding her. "It's my fault. It's all my fault. I should've been there."

My little siren's body wracked with the force of her tears as she cried into me.

Pulling her back enough to look into her eyes, I scanned her face, her neck, the dried blood on her chest. "Are you hurt?"

"My wrist," she sniffed. "I think it's broken."

"Did he..."

She swallowed hard and her face broke. "He..."

Oh god.

My hands shook.

There was a burning in my chest.

"He t-tried," she managed between hiccupping gasps. "I—s-s-stopped him."

"What do you mean, he tried?"

"I d-don't want to think about it," she said in a rush and I wished I could smash his fucking head in all over again.

He might not have raped her but the fucking bastard had still scared her, kidnapped her, put his filthy fucking hands on her body.

Anna let her head fall heavy against my arm and let out a shuddering sigh.

"It's okay. It doesn't matter. You found me."

I sucked in a trembling breath and dropped a long kiss on the top of her head. "I found you," I echoed. "And I'm never letting you go again."

28

CARTER

Anna and I must have looked like we survived the fucking apocalypse, me in nothing but my boots and boxers with my bloody fists and face. Her in the sweats and sweater Summer gave me. I carried her from the motel room to my car, setting her down in the passenger seat like she was made of glass and could shatter at any second.

"Can I take you back to my villa?"

"Anywhere but here."

Once I pulled out of the motel, she grabbed my hand and didn't let go. I hated getting Josh's filthy blood on her pristine skin, but I'd wash it off her later. I'd wash as much of him away from her as I possibly could. I'd spend forever doing it if I needed to.

When we made it back to my place, we both stripped our clothes off and left them at the door. Anna said nothing as she went up to the shower and made the water scalding hot. She didn't protest when I followed her into the over-sized glass stall and used my body wash to scrub every part of her, until her skin was rubbed clean. Only then did I wash myself, cleaning away every last trace of her ex.

I couldn't take the silence any longer after I got her dressed and into the bed, propping the pillows around her like a fortress or a throne.

"Talk to me, baby."

She picked at the skin around her thumb and I placed my hand gently over hers, stopping her.

Her throat bobbed. "I don't know what to say. I don't— I don't know how I'm supposed to feel."

"Stop thinking about how you're supposed to feel. Tell me how you *do* feel. It doesn't have to be right, Anna. Not when everything is wrong."

"How did you find me?"

"His father's company bought that motel, but before that I searched every seedy fucking dump in this state looking for you. I'm just...I'm sorry it took me so long."

There was an odd smile on her lips. It grew and she giggled madly, letting out the pent up feelings of it all, covering her mouth. Until the laughter started to turn back to crying and her throat thickened as she tried to hold it in.

"Shouldn't we be calling the police?"

It was my turn to smile. Paulson's guys were already cleaning up the mess. They'd make Josh vanish, but his corpse wouldn't even touch the ocean. Knowing any part of him was somewhere under the water when I looked out over our beach would ruin the view.

No.

Better to burn him. I had a pal with a line to an incinerator at a mortuary. He'd take Josh off our hands. Fucker owed me a favor or two anyway.

"Come on," I said, ignoring her question. She might not

like the answer. "Let's sit on the balcony, get some air, yeah?"

She nodded, letting me help her into the swinging macrame seat overlooking the beach.

"Carter?" she asked, her gaze never straying from the beach as she spoke.

"Hmm?"

A single tear fell onto her cheek and my insides twisted up.

"Six years ago..." She trailed off.

I waited.

"Did you take a bribe from my dad?"

"I did," I said and felt her break all over again, even if she kept an even expression.

"I did something," I started to explain. "You remember how my dad was gone for a while? Well, he came back."

The memory was so fresh, I could still remember the feel of that fucking hammer. I clenched my fists, the ground feeling like it was starting to move under me.

"What happened?"

I wrenched my eyes open to look at her. She was looking at me now, that adorable knot between her brows.

"I killed him."

Her lips parted, betraying her surprise.

"That's when he showed up, and it wasn't the first time. I should've told you your father came by when it first happened. He tried to pay me off to break up with you. I said no. Of course, I said no. But after that...he was having our house watched, waiting for just the right moment and I handed it to him on a silver fucking platter."

I wasn't looking at her. I didn't want to see the moment

where she stopped just hating me and started fearing me too. I wouldn't be able to take that.

"I was screwed. They barged in and I was—I was crouched over him with the fucking hammer in my hands and his—his fucking head was all..."

"The photos," she muttered to herself and my jaw ached from clenching so hard. He fucking showed her.

I licked my dry lips, needing to explain. *Make her* understand.

"If I went to prison, there would've been no one to help my Ma. She would have died alone and in pain and probably starving. After the shit she'd already been through..."

"Oh my god."

"I regret it," I told her. "But it bought my Ma one more good year before the cancer came back and took her."

"He blackmailed you."

"Pretty slick, honestly. I can tell why he's been so successful in his political career."

She didn't say anything for a few moments.

"Your mother's treatment," she said finally. Smart girl.

"That was the original offer. As much money as I needed for my mother's treatment at the best hospital in the city, no matter how long it took. All I had to do was give you up. The second offer came with an extra payoff that meant I could give her comfort and stability, too."

She went quiet again. I wanted her to say something, but I wasn't sure that I really wanted her feedback, now that she knew. She stood up, pacing.

That wave from six years ago hit me again. It was smaller, didn't knock the air out of my chest like last time, but it was still the same. The feeling that I had made the biggest mistake of my life and that the only person I cared about besides my mother was gone.

"I tried to figure out where you went. Each year you didn't come back, I was searching. You took something from me when you went."

She stopped pacing. "And you took nothing from me?"

"That's not what I—"

"When I left, I did a double take at every tall, brown-haired guy I saw because I thought they were you. I tried so fucking hard to get away from it, to forget you but never did. So, yeah, sorry if I don't feel bad that you were hurting."

I scoffed, looking down. I deserved that.

"You shouldn't. It's on me. All of it."

...but if you let me, I'll spend the rest of my life making it up to you.

She sighed loudly, looking down at the ground.

"I always knew my dad was a bastard, but I didn't know this was his fault too. Whenever I think he can't cross the line again, he jumps right over it."

She pinched the bridge of her nose. "But he offered to save your mother's life. I can't be upset that you chose the way you did."

I stood, walking over to her.

"Are you still here?"

Her eyebrows went up.

"With me? I'm in love with you, Anna. It's been six years and I'm not going to stop. I need to know that you—" I flagged, my throat getting tight. I rubbed my hands over her arms. "I need to know that I didn't lose you."

Her lips were pressed together, but she didn't look scared, or angry or disgusted. She looked calm. Hurt. Tired.

"What happens now?"

"Now," I sighed. "You know everything. If you want, you can go to the cops, the press, whoever you want and ruin my life."

Her pupils shook.

"Or..."

"Or what?"

"Or you could stay here with me."

"Carter, I—"

"Stay," I begged, kissing her cheek, close to her ear, her neck. "*Stay.*"

29

ANNA

Six Weeks Later

Holy shit. Did you see the headlines??

I rubbed my eyes as I reread Summer's text. It made sense that she would text me at 5 a.m., considering she was one of those freaks who ran five miles before everyone else even woke up. For one terrifying second, I wondered if we'd been caught. If they found Josh's corpse, wherever Carter's men had stuffed it, and we were all completely and totally fucked.

I clicked the link she sent and couldn't suppress my gasp.

Michelle and Hudson Vaughn Divorce After 28 Year Marriage.

Of course, that was only the headline for respectable news organizations. As I tapped to the main news screen, the gossip rags had much more salacious takes.

Michelle Vaughn Blindsides Hudson with Divorce Papers.

Michelle Vaughn Spills the Tea about Governor's Charity Theft.

"He Made So Many Dirty Deals": Michelle Vaughn on Governor Ex.

No matter how much I scrolled, they just kept going. Apparently, Mom served Dad divorce papers last night, which were quickly leaked to the public, along with quotes from her "friends" revealing all his dirty laundry.

I'd spent enough time in the spotlight to know that this was a targeted attack. Mom had worked with a publicist to bring Dad down and get all the headlines on her side. She made sure the papers knew everything, all his scandals and sins written out in black and white. It probably took her years to be ready for a move like this.

Maybe six?

A twang in my chest had me clutching at it. I didn't even realize.

When my phone rang a moment later, it took me a second to find the voice to answer.

"Summer?"

"Can you believe it? It's so insane. Did you have any idea she was planning to leave him?"

"No, I didn't."

"Seriously? She really screwed the bastard. Must've taken her a long time to get all that in place. God, what a badass, she totally dropped a bomb on him and then said, '*you like that, Governor?*'"

Yeah. She really did.

I was so proud of her.

"It's crazy. I can't believe she didn't say anything. Feels like everyone is always keeping secrets from me."

I laughed hollowly.

There was an odd pause on the other end from Summer before she cleared her throat.

"Summer?" I prodded. "Not you, too? Did you get engaged?"

"Okay, so, don't be mad," she said. "But I have been sort of keeping a secret from you. I was actually going to tell you over lunch next week but maybe now is better since they keep calling."

"Since who keeps calling?"

"The galleries. Hold on, let me start at the beginning. So, you know how you left those negatives at James' place when Carter came in all Batman sans cape?"

"Uh, yeah. Don't remind me."

"Well, I may have done something a little naughty."

It felt like I was sitting on pins and needles. "Summer, what did you do?"

"You know how I'm on all those charity boards? You know, for the Cancer Research Center and the Historical Renovation Program?"

"Yes. You're a very busy do-gooder, get to the point."

"Anyway, I'm on the board for the Modern Art Museum," she went on. "I actually have a lot of contacts in the art world. And I knew you'd never submit them yourself so..."

"Oh god, Summer, what did you do?"

"Well, before I returned the negatives, I kind of, sort of had them digitized..." I could practically hear her bracing for a bite back.

I was too stunned to say a word.

She blew out a breath.

"Don't hate me."

My eyes burned.

"You have the images?"

"Well, yeah. I still have the whole digitized file."

I choked on a sob, covering my mouth with my hand to hold it in.

"Anna? Anna are you there?"

When Dad threw my film in the fire, I thought my best work was gone forever. I'd kept taking photographs, but my heart wasn't in it. Now, I felt a new spark of hope.

"Fuck. You're angry."

"No," I blurted, unable to keep a tremble out of the word. "No, I'm not. I—I thought I lost them. My dad —*Hudson*," I corrected myself. "He threw the negatives in the fireplace and erased the digitized versions off my laptop."

Summer inhaled sharply on the other end of the call. "That bastard!"

I laughed. "Yeah. I didn't think I'd ever see them again."

"Well, don't thank me yet," Summer warned. "I'm not done. Because I didn't just make copies. But don't worry, I went through all, like, two thousand freaking images and did my best to find the ones you showed us. Actually, you remember our old art teacher? I went to her for help and she said you showed her the photos, too, and..." She was rambling now. "So she sort of helped me re-put together your portfolio and then I just sent it to, like, all the galleries on this side of the country under the guise of being your agent."

"WHAT?" I squawked, and heard Carter's footsteps pounding down the stairs.

"Hang on, let me finish. Ten of them said, *thanks but no thanks*. Eight of them said they didn't have a place, but asked you to send future work. But seven of them offered you an exhibition! I knew you were a star. Everyone wants to be in the Anna Vaughn business!"

Carter came around the corner, taking in my teary eyes and no doubt shook expression with a darkness in his eyes. I waved him off, mouthing *it's okay*. He looked doubtful, but went to the kitchen, busying himself with putting on a pot of coffee even though I knew he just didn't want to leave the room.

"That's really amazing, Summer, but I couldn't accept," I said, the words sounding hollow.

Everyone wants to be in the Anna Vaughn *business.*

"Those museums only wanted me because of my name and the publicity."

Oh god. And now? They'd love the opportunity to feature the work of Hudson Vaughn's daughter. It would be a total media circus.

Summer shook her head. "You don't get it, Anna. They didn't have your name. All they knew was that you were an up-and-coming photographer and that I was your agent. And they all wanted to show your work. Of course, the Anna Vaughn name might get some extra promotion, but you got in for your talent, girl, *not* your name."

My chest swelled and the burn was back in my throat.

"Summer, I could kiss you."

"Please don't. Carter is jealous enough as it is," she said jokingly. "Ope, I got to go, but you can be properly angry at me over lunch next week while we discuss which galleries you want to exhibit it, deal?"

I snorted. "Yeah. *Deal.*"

I turned to see Carter twirling a spoon in a mug of black coffee. "Care to explain?"

Even in the dim light, he looked unfairly good with bedhead. I clicked back to the articles about my mom and the divorce and passed him the phone silently as he slid into the seat beside me.

"Good for her," he said after a few moments of careful reading. "Couldn't have done it better myself, though I'd have loved to take a stab at him."

Probably literally, I thought, and tried not to overanalyze how the thought didn't bother me.

"How do you feel?"

"I feel...free," I said with a laugh. "Mom and I are both free now. And there's more."

He raised his brows.

"Summer made copies of all my negatives from The Butterfly Room. She has the entire shoot."

"And why do you look so nervous?"

I stopped biting my lip.

"Because she sent the portfolio to half the art galleries in the country."

His gaze darkened. "And?"

"And at least seven of them want me to exhibit."

He softened, and I realized he was probably readying himself to systematically dismantle half the art galleries in the country if they'd all said no.

"Of course, they did. You're brilliant, my little siren. It was only a matter of time before the whole world saw it."

I chuckled as he pressed a hot kiss to my temple.

"Just one problem," he added, nuzzling me with a little growl. "I don't like sharing."

Anna came into the home office with a smile on her face. She'd never looked like that after a visit with her family.

"I assume it went well?"

"Better than that."

She came around to my side of the desk and perched on the edge. "Mom got sober while I was gone. Apparently, she's been plotting to divorce Dad and ruin his life for years. Since shortly after I left home, actually."

"Smart woman. Can't say I saw that one coming."

After Anna left, I'd reached out to my political contacts to find out how badly Hudson Vaughn was screwed. They reassured me that if he didn't resign, he would definitely face impeachment. His party had already disowned him, and I doubted he would ever be elected to a political office again. He would retire in indignity, while Michelle enjoyed the majority of his fortune.

I really couldn't have fucked him over better myself. As much as I wanted to hurt him, I was glad it was her. If I ever did to Anna what he did to Michelle, I hoped she would have the strength to do worse to me.

I pulled her onto my lap in the chair and she chuckled, looking over my face as if trying to decide something. It was the same look I'd been getting from her for weeks.

This was as far as we went. Close but not close enough.

I was dying to touch her. To taste her.

But beneath that, I was just so fucking relieved she decided to stay.

"What is it?" I asked quietly. "What are you looking for?"

She thought for a moment. "I'm not sure. Maybe the other part of you."

I held her stare. "What part?"

"The dark part. The one that...hurts people."

"Have you found it?"

"I'm not sure I'd recognize it if I did."

I let out a long breath. "Well, it's there. There is a darkness in me, Anna. You've seen it for yourself. I'm not going to pretend it doesn't exist."

She chewed on the inside of her cheek.

"But let me ask you this; have you ever been afraid of me? Afraid that I might do anything to hurt you?"

I didn't breathe while I waited for her response, not knowing how I would accept it if she said yes.

"No. Never. Even when you're doing crazy shit like throwing me in your trunk and locking me in your house." She scoffed. "It's actually ridiculous that I'm not afraid of you."

I grinned. "That's because you know me. You know this."

I put her hand over my heart, just like I did that night on the beach all those years ago. "That this belongs to you."

She pressed her lips tight against an emotion I couldn't name.

I stood and set her down on the chair, kneeling before her. I kissed her right knee, then her left, watching her face heat and her fingers twist in the hem of her skirt.

"I remember," she said on a breath.

"You remember your promise to me?"

"To be yours." She gasped as I set my hands on her calves, running them up to the bends in her knees, higher along her thighs.

"That's right."

"Will you be able to keep that promise, Anna?"

Her green gaze searched mine, making one last search for something inside of me she couldn't find. She wouldn't, because that monster would never turn its sights on her.

Her lips quirked up on one edge and something in her eyes softened.

"I think I might."

I gripped the edge of her tight t-shirt and pulled upward. Obediently, she raised her arms so I could tug it off and see her pink lace bra. *The one I bought her.*

"You wore the clothes I picked out for you," I said with satisfaction.

"You picked these out yourself?" Her eyes widened. "I assumed you got a personal shopper or something."

I shook my head. "You're mine. I wouldn't let anyone else decide what touches your body. That's my job."

I kneaded her breasts through the delicate lace. Her nipples stiffened under my hands and her back arched, then she was leaning into my touch. She was so perfectly responsive. I lowered my head to suck on a nipple through the fabric, and she moaned sweetly.

"These are mine."

"Yes, Carter." Anna's eyes fell closed and she threw her head back in pleasure.

I lowered my hands to her knees and crawled them slowly under the hem of her skirt. Anna fell back into the chair with a moan. I took my time teasing her inner thighs, then groaned when I touched her wet cunt. I set my mouth against her chest.

"Bad girl," I said against her skin. "Not wearing panties. What if you weren't thinking, and you bent over? Anyone could have seen your bare little cunt."

I pressed harder against her pussy and felt warm wetness drip down my fingertips as her thighs started to clench.

"Fuck, I can't wait to get inside you."

I shoved my fingers fully inside her and felt her walls spasm around me.

"Wait," She said abruptly. "I never refilled my birth control. I...I didn't even think about it with everything—"

All the blood in my body went right to my cock and she seemed to catch on to exactly where my thoughts went, her breath hitching.

"Does that mean I could get you pregnant?"

"If we don't use protection."

As if I would ever put a fucking rubber between myself and that pussy.

"Fuck," I groaned. The idea of my seed implanting in her that night had me harder than I'd ever been. My cock ached to be inside her tight velvet cunt. She'd look like a goddess when she was really pregnant.

I shoved her green skirt up around her waist so I could see her bare pussy, heat flushing up my back.

"Tell me no," I ground out. "Tell me no, Anna, because I'm about three fucking seconds from burying myself in your pussy bare and fucking my baby into you."

Her mouth fell open.

"Carter, no one gets pregnant on the first try. You can't just put a baby in me because you decided."

"Not going to stop me from trying."

I kicked off my shoes and tripped out of my pants, watching Anna's expression go from anxious to almost delirious with need by the time I got finished kicking my boxers off.

Grabbing her around the middle, I lifted her from the chair, knocking the laptop and files off my desk to place her atop it.

She hitched up her skirt for me like a good girl, and I lined my cock up with her entrance, watching my swollen head brush against her. A drop of my precum dripped down onto her, and my balls tightened.

"This is insane," Anna breathed against my lips.

"This is perfect."

I slipped my tip inside her, until the flared edge disappeared.

She looked down at our joined bodies, eyes slitted with desire.

"Are you ever going to tell me what that symbol means?" Her words ended in a high pitched moan as I slid further inside of her, but not enough so that the symbol inked into the base of my cock could be swallowed up.

"It's a word," I told her, grinning. "A name actually. I'll give you a hint—four letters."

She gasped, lifting herself up onto her elbow to get a better look at the simple monogrammatic symbol. I could see the exact moment she recognized the shapes of the letters. A N N A.

"You didn't."

"I did. Six years ago. I told you Anna. You are mine, and I am yours. You might've left, but that never changed. Not for me."

Her chin quivered.

I ran my hand down her chest to our joined bodies. "Now, I'm going to bury this cock inside you. And when I'm done and you're filled with my cum, you're going to hold it there for me until I say."

She nodded.

I wanted better than that. I tweaked her nipple between my fingers.

"*Yes.*"

"Good girl."

I could feel her walls squeezing my head tight.

"That turns you on, doesn't it? Knowing you could end up pregnant."

She nodded eagerly, clutching at my shoulders. The fact that she was turned on by it too just got me even fucking harder. But I held myself back, not letting her get my full length. I wanted to tease her a little longer.

I'd waited weeks for her to be ready. I wasn't rushing through this.

I tore off her bra, palming her bare breasts. "Fuck, I can't wait to see these when you're pregnant. They're going to be so gorgeous."

Anna's breathing turned ragged with want. Her nipples went diamond hard. I palmed her stomach next, grinning.

"You'll be so sexy when this grows, too. I'm not going to be able to keep my hands off you."

She shivered as I ran my fingertips down her sides. Her eyes were glued to where my cock disappeared inside her. "Please, Carter," she begged. "I need more."

I spit on my fingers and circled her clit with them. "Like that, little siren?"

She shook her head. "Feels so good, but I want your cock. All of it."

I'd never get tired of hearing her beg. So I gave her what she wanted, burying my length inside her in one smooth stroke. Anna whimpered as she stretched to accommodate me. The tight squeeze was so delicious, I could barely stop myself from releasing.

"Yes," she gasped. "More, *more*."

I eased her back to lie on my desk, her legs still wrapped around my waist while I stood. I held down her hips as I pushed forcefully inside her. She reached back to clutch the edge of the desk for support while I fucked her hard. With every stroke of my cock, I watched it emerge even more wet with her desire.

"Fuck," I muttered. "I love watching your pussy swallow my cock. You're so beautiful, Anna."

She moaned incomprehensibly. Good—I was fucking her senseless, like she deserved. Her tits bounced beautifully as I pounded into her. Anna's body was stunning now. Picturing her in the same position with a pregnant belly made my balls tighten painfully. I couldn't hold on for much longer.

I brought one thumb back to her clit. She keened at the sensation, her pussy tightening even more around me. I watched her gorgeous face contort as she struggled to hold on in the face of the overwhelming pleasure.

"Let go," I said gently. "You're mine. I've got you. Now... come for me."

She cried out and her pussy tightened around me as her orgasm took her. I bent down and kissed her before I followed her over the edge. My cock emptied inside her while her eager inner muscles milked me in. Nothing made me more satisfied than my cum filling my girl.

Careful not to dislodge my cock, I let myself fall over her, resting my head against her chest.

As long as I kept her full, I could keep my seed inside her.

Over the curve of her hip, I could see her photo hanging on the wall. The clouds parting to show the full moon, lingering like a promise. The moon and the black sea were meant to be together, just like Anna and me.

Her emerald eyes flickered open and she smiled down at me. "I never thanked you."

"For what?"

She didn't need to thank me. Not for anything. Ever.

"For never giving up on us."

I smirked, kissing the space between her breasts. "Does that mean you'll marry me, then?"

"Maybe," she teased.

"Better decide quick."

I made my cock jump inside her, punctuating the fact that I was keeping her full of my seed.

She swatted my arm. "I guess I could look at the ring. If you wanted to show it to me."

I almost pulled out and went to get it right then, but decided better of it. Just a few more minutes like this, first.

Chapter 30

Giving her a wicked grin, I decided, "Not until you say yes."

She pursed her lips.

"Too bad since it's a really nice ring."

Her mouth opened on a mock scoff.

"Fine. I can wait," she teased, a challenge in her eyes.

"So can I, little siren. So can I."

Let's see who would break first.

EPILOGUE

ANNA

THE ANNA COLE EXHIBIT

"Do you want me to take you home?"

I shook my head vigorously, but I was tempted. I was sweating, and if I'd eaten anything today, I would've thrown it up already.

"I can't go home. This is my first show."

Carter and I lingered in the museum's back office, waiting for the official reception to start. I finally stopped pacing and sat down in an armchair. He came behind me to rub my tense shoulders. His firm fingers worked the knots that had situated themselves there over the last several weeks planning the exhibition.

I sighed, relaxing into the sensation.

"Artists don't have to be present at their shows. That's what the curator is for." He pressed a kiss to one of my temples.

Yeah, and I would leave, eventually, but I'd been waiting for this day for months. Technically, I'd been waiting for this day for years.

When I first decided I wanted to be a photographer, this was what I envisioned. An exhibit where I could use my images to tell a story and watch as the people slowly made their way through, finding that story one photograph at a time.

"Do you know how many people are outside?"

"I didn't count them. Maybe a hundred?" Carter offered with a shrug. I turned around, frowning at him. He cupped my face and kissed me.

"Maybe?" I snapped, more annoyed than I needed to be. We weren't all used to being right in the middle of the spotlight, though I should've been more used to it by now, after all the insanity of my father's trial and the press that came with it.

For the first month, I could barely leave the beach house without putting the paparazzi in danger of being offed by my fiancé for coming too close.

"You got this, okay? You do it all the time. Milling around a crowd and making small talk? You're a pro."

If he was referring to the stuffy formal events I used to go to with my family, and now with him, yeah, I was. That didn't mean I enjoyed them.

This was different.

Here, I was showing people my photographs. Putting a piece of myself on display. Somehow I couldn't have felt more exposed even if I walked out there stark naked.

"If we go out there and you decide you'd rather hear the praise later in the paper and from the curator than right from the public's mouth, we'll say our goodbyes and leave right then."

I closed my eyes, comforted by his tight grasp. But I knew there was another reason he was so eager to get me out of here. Why he didn't really want me presenting in person at all.

And that reason just kicked, making me wrap a protective arm over my swollen belly.

"Okay," I allowed.

"You know what beats stress?" Carter's dark brow raised deviously. "Orgasms. Lots and lots of orgasms."

I pushed him away as he laughed.

"I am not having sex in the museum's office," I snapped, unable to keep the smile off my face. Carter was so many things at once, it was hard to keep up. Living with a boyfriend wasn't new to me, but living with him was. I was still uncovering new sides and shades of him every day. Some familiar, some not.

But each day I stayed with him, he seemed to relax into us just a little more and little by little, that boy on the beach was coming back to life.

"Nobody's going to walk in. Besides, the door locks," he said dubiously. "I checked."

Of course he did.

I shook my head again, getting up to walk past him, feeling the weight of my round belly more heavily than usual.

He wasn't totally wrong—normally, sex with him made me relax. He could get me out of my head and back into my body with a few well-spaced orgasms.

But I didn't want to relax this time. I wanted to feel all of this, anxiety and nerves and all.

"It's time," I breathed, placing my hands over my belly. "Let's go."

Carter's expression tightened a fraction, but he swept open the door despite his own unadmitted anxiety.

Heading out into the exhibition space, I took a couple of deep breaths to occupy myself with something other than my racing thoughts. I wiped my sweaty hands on my deep olive-toned dress, searching for one of the waiters.

One passed with a tray of champagne and what I wouldn't give to take the edge off with one of those shimmering flutes...

"Could you bring my wife a glass of water," Carter asked the waiter, stopping him with a grip on the elbow.

"Right away."

"You have to stop that," I chastised as the waiter scurried off to fetch me a non-alcoholic drink.

"Making sure you're hydrated?"

"Calling me your wife."

His sea blue eyes glimmered with amusement as he lifted my left hand and pressed a kiss to the diamond on my ring finger. "This is *my* ring on your finger, is it not, little siren?"

I tugged it from him with a coy smile. "Maybe."

"And this." He rubbed his palm over my belly, earning himself a little kick from the growing babe within. "This is mine, too?"

"Ours," I corrected him.

"Ours," he conceded. "And remind me again the name of this exhibit. Was it...the Anna *Cole* Exhibit?"

I swatted him. "That's because I didn't want the press using the Vaughn name."

"Well, Anna, darling, I've considered you my wife since the moment you said yes. And you know what I think?"

"What?"

He leaned down to flick my nose with his, whispering over my lips. "I think you like it."

When he kissed me, my body hummed with feeling, making my belly tighten and a tingle shoot all the way to my toes.

I mourned the loss of him with a sad moan as he pulled away with victory in his stare.

"Come on, *Mrs. Cole*. We better get you out there before I change my mind and drag you back into that office."

The crowd in the gallery looked about as big as he had estimated. People walked around the space, viewing my work in the way I intended, directed by the curator and her assistants.

I agonized for months over how to display it. The museum's curator was a huge help, and I had Olivia and Summer to give me second opinions. A few group shots were blown up to the full wall-size. Immediately, viewers could feel like they were walking right into the Butterfly Room. They were a little more spaced out as you walked deeper into the room, so you could spend time examining each one in finer detail before moving on to the next.

The day before, I'd shown the gallery off to the harshest critics of all. My friends from the Butterfly Room had agreed that they didn't want to come to the official opening. They didn't want to have to answer questions about their lives from strangers. But each of them was thrilled to be featured and couldn't wait to see how much each image would earn.

It was surreal—seeing them again. Carter flew them

out from Chicago a day early and put them each up in a luxury suite. I brought the women into the museum yesterday, fully prepared for them to tell me they hated it. Instead, every single one of them told me they loved it. We laughed together, remembering the time Vanessa got food poisoning from eating expired chocolate cake, or when a patron tipped me 200% for convincing the DJ to play nothing but Shania Twain music for an hour.

They left me with long bear hugs in exchange for a promise that I'd visit them soon. I left the preview feeling like I was floating on air.

Now, I felt like I was nothing but a tiny spec in a sea of giants.

It was one thing for your trusted friends to tell you they liked your work. It was another to face the criticism of a hundred upper class art collectors, ready to tell you exactly how derivative you were.

I watched as patrons filtered in from the outside. Clutching their champagne, they examined each photo with expressions I couldn't read.

Photographers snapped pictures of them in all their finery. Some frowned as they examined my photos, and a few laughed. I wished I could know they were having a real emotional reaction to the shots, or if they were laughing at me.

My stomach tumbled.

"Satisfied?" Carter asked. "Can I take you home?"

He brushed his arm against mine, a wolfish smirk on his face. That face made a shiver run down my spine.

I kissed him, knowing there were people with cameras around and not giving a single fuck. Seeing my name next to his on a tabloid site had been surreal the first time it happened. I always knew he was considered the city's most eligible bachelor but I wasn't ready for the attention, negative and positive, that the woman who managed to lock down a man like that ended up getting.

I received hate mail and congratulations at an almost 1:1 ratio. I couldn't blame them. I was lucky. Possibly the luckiest girl alive.

"Am I interrupting something?"

I pulled away, seeing my mother standing there with a small smile on her face. My lips parted in shock as I self-consciously slid out of Carter's arms.

"Mom, so glad you made it." I swallowed, hands unconsciously going to my belly. She hugged me, pausing to say hi to the baby, and went to shake Carter's hand.

He ignored it and pulled her into a bracing hug. She looked at me with wide eyes over his shoulder, and I suppressed an awkward laugh.

"I'm happy to be here, darling. I'm so proud of you," she said, flattening out the creases in her blouse as Carter let her go.

I'd never seen in her a shade of lipstick so bold and red, and with the spider brooch on her blazer jacket she looked every bit the Spider-Woman the tabloids had named her. Over lunch all those months ago she told me she secretly loved the name and planned to embrace it. It seemed she had.

"Have you thought of names yet?"

I had, but Carter and I hadn't discussed it so I shook my head. "I have an idea, but nothing official yet. You'll know as soon as we do."

Carter gave me a curious look before turning his attention back to my mom. "Have you had a chance to walk through the exhibit?" he asked.

His hand on my waist felt protective, and I put my hand over his, sliding closer to him as my pulse began to slow and calm.

"Not yet. I wanted to say hello first, I haven't seen you since you were barely showing. But look at you now. You're glowing."

My cheeks flushed. At least she hadn't seen me in the first trimester. I'd been a wreck, all too happy to let Carter barricade us into the villa to avoid seeing a soul while I was perpetually green with nausea and he had doctors coming to take my vitals daily.

"Thanks, Mom."

"Well, I don't want to keep you. I'll take a walk around. Maybe we can do lunch this week?"

I nodded. Things would never be perfect between us, but they improved the longer we were without my father's cage.

He turned to me when she walked away. "You've thought of names?"

Nervous energy raced through me, raising goosebumps along my arms. "If it's a girl I was thinking maybe Brandy."

Carter's face went absolutely still with momentary shock before his eyes began to soften and I watched his Adams apple bob.

"Brandy Michelle," I added. "It has a nice ring to it and honors two of the strongest women I know."

His lips pulled up at one edge and he bent to plant a kiss atop my head. "It's absolutely perfect."

I closed my eyes, just breathing him in for a few heartbeats before I had to go back to being a nervous wreck in a room full of people who wanted my attention.

"She saw it by the way," Carter said, distracting me. "The ring."

"No way, I totally hid my hand," I said, my thumb feeling for the platinum band on my finger at the mention of it. It was the first time I'd worn the obnoxious ring in public and to be totally honest, it was kind of hard *not* to notice it.

Carter looked pleased with himself, as if now that my mother had seen the ring it made it more real. In his mind, there were no take backs now.

I rolled my eyes. Carter had proposed at least ten times before I cracked. It wasn't that I didn't want to marry him. I think a part of me always knew I would. I just wanted to do it on my terms.

"Now that she knows, we have to get hitched," he said, the mirth in his eyes and seriousness of his voice contradicting each other.

"Is that so?"

"We can do it however you want. Big and lavish. A quiet ceremony. I'd settle for going to the courthouse if you prefer. I just want—"

"To be tied to me in every way possible," I finished for him and he gave me that rare soft smile.

"Exactly."

"Fine."

"Fine?"

"After the baby is born we can set a date. And I want it small, just our closest friends and family."

He looked down at me like I'd just given him the world

on a string. "I can't wait to get you out of here. How much longer are you going to make me wait?"

"I'll let you know when I'm finished," I said coyly.

He groaned, reaching out to give me a squeeze before I pulled away to mingle, feeling just a smidge more confident than I had five minutes ago.

I shook a few hands and gave a few smiles, all with Carter hovering next to me like my own personal shadow monster, intimidating most people away before they could get too close.

"Carter," a voice came from the front entrance, and we turned to see some of Carter's friends enter with their wives.

"You bastards actually made it," Carter said, shaking the hand of the man on the left. I'd met him once before, when he stopped by for a drink with Carter as he was passing through. His name was Ruarc Monroe, and he was probably the most terrifying human being I'd ever laid eyes on, but he was polite enough, and had a great laugh.

"Wouldn't miss it. You remember my wife, Emily?"

She was a vision in black silk. A real life Morticia Adams but with a heart shaped face and big, soft eyes.

"Nice to finally meet you," Emily said, making a point of shaking my hand before Carter's.

"Okay, move along," Carter's other friend, Enzo Zanetti said, shoving Ruarc out of the way as if he hadn't just affronted the devil. "He pulled Carter in for a manly hug, thumping him on the back. Even though Enzo was nearly twice my age, he didn't really seem it. Especially when he was with his wife, Nina. Probably because she was *also* half his age. She was such a bright light with her long golden hair and perpetual smiles.

"And look at this," Enzo said as Carter pulled away, reaching for my belly.

Carter stepped in his path, putting his hands on Enzo's shoulders as he leaned in to whisper something into his ear that had Enzo straightening with an amused, if a little concerned, expression.

"Right," Enzo said, straightening his jacket. "We're here to see some photos. Where do we start."

I explained how they should view the Exhibit and their wives dragged them away to start the show.

"What did you say to him?" I asked Carter when they were out of earshot and he fake coughed into his fist, looking innocent as he asked me to repeat myself.

"What did you say?"

"Do you really want to know?"

I thought about it. "Yes."

He pursed his lips. "I told him if he touched your belly I'd break his hands."

I felt my lips part in surprise. If that was how he reacted to a friend, how would he react to a stranger trying to cop a feel of the belly?

"Are you angry?" he asked, his jaw tight.

But...no. I wasn't. Not really.

"I know who I agreed to marry," I answered instead, feeling a smile pull at my lips that was mirrored on his.

He dipped his head to my cheek, whispering against my neck. "Please tell me you've had enough because I can't stand not being inside of you for another second."

His words went straight to my core, setting me on fire, but I needed to at least let the curator know we were leaving.

"Give me a minute?"

"I'll give you forever."

THE END

Thank you for reading *Cruel Dominion!* This one really took me for a ride. If you loved Anna and Carter's story, please consider leaving a review 🖤

Sign-up for the Petal & Thorn Newsletter and never miss a release from Poppy St. John!

ALSO BY POPPY ST. JOHN

TWISTED DEVOTION

- DARK Romance
- Stalker/Obsession
- Billionaire Crime Lord
- Captor/Captive
- Elite Sex Club
- Smut for Dayyyys

SINFUL TEMPTATION

- Age Gap
- Arranged Marriage
- Mafia
- Forced Proximity
- Forbidden Romance
- All. The. Taboo. Smut

ABOUT THE AUTHOR

Poppy writes steamy contemporary romance with a focus on all things forbidden, dark, and taboo. She likes her main men morally grey and has always had a thing for bad boys who will do anything to win the hearts of the women they love. All her stories end with a hard-won HEA ♡

Get Signed Paperbacks:
    https://www.poppystjohn.com